PREPPY

The Life & Death of Samuel Clearwater, Part One

King Series, Book 5

T.M. FRAZIER

Samuel Clearwater, A.K.A Preppy, likes pancakes, bow ties, suspenders, good friends, good times, good drugs, and a good f*ck. He's worked his way out from beneath a hellish childhood and is living the life he's always imagined for himself. When he meets a girl, a junkie on the verge of ending it all, he's torn between his feelings for her and the fear that she could be the one to end the life he loves.

Andrea 'Dre' Capulet is strung out and tired. Tired of living for her next fix. Tired of doing things that makes her stomach turn. Tired of looking in the mirror at the reflection of the person she's become. Just when she decides to end it all, she meets a man who will change the course of both their lives forever.

And their deaths.

For most people, death is the end of their story.

For Preppy and Dre, it was only the beginning…

Acknowledgements

These things are always hard for me because there are so many people I need to thank. First and foremost, I'd like to thank the readers. Without you guys I would have stopped at book one. It's because of you and your love for the characters that I keep writing more and more. I love all of you.

Thank you to Ellie McLove, Manda Lee, and Kim G. for making my words pretty. I know it's a rough job but you ladies get it done and make the editing and proofing process a less frazzled affair.

Thank you to model Travis DesLaurier and photographer Corey Pollack for helping make this cover my favorite yet.

Thank you to Kimberly Brower, my agent who has believed in me since the very beginning. Thanks for going on this wild ride with me. I'm looking forward to much more craziness to come.

Thank you to Julie, Clarissa, Kimmi, Jen, Rochelle, Sunny, Jennifer, and on this one I have to give a big special thank you to Jessica Viteri. You are a crazy violent motherfucker and frankly your suggestions make me afraid to be your friend, but also makes me think that you could be my hetero life-mate.

Thank you to everyone in Frazierland. The best group of readers in the entire world.

Thank you to my husband. My partner in life. My TRUE best friend. Logan, without you, none of this would mean a damn thing. Thank you for being you and thank you for allowing me to be me.

Thank you to my daughter. Mommy loves you baby girl. To the moon and back…

Dedication

For Mr. Frazier

From the Author

Dear Readers,

Thank you so much for loving Preppy. He was just a voice in my head at first. He wasn't even meant to be a character in King until finally the voice grew so loud it could no longer be ignored.

But that's Preppy for you.

Please note that in order to best enjoy Preppy's books, I recommend reading the other four main books in the KING series first. King, Tyrant, Lawless and Soulless. Thank you so much for reading and for your continued support. I couldn't do any of this without you.

LOVE,
T.M.

PROLOGUE

PREPPY

PRESENT

TINY FLASHES OF dim light spark in the darkened corners of my mind. Slowly, it turns from dusk to dawn, awakening my thoughts as the inner light grows brighter and brighter.

I hear a sound, a faucet running, and I realize it's the blood rushing through my ears. When it reaches my heart I choke as it comes back to life like a bass drum. Boom. BaBOOM it beats, on and on, until it falls into a quick yet steady rhythm. The new life inside me grows louder, stronger, until death fades away and I awake on a gasp.

My eyes spring open. I try to take in air, but nothing happens. I try again and my lungs burn as they finally decide to cooperate. I can breathe, but it hurts like a son of a bitch.

I'm fucking alive.

My first thoughts shock the shit out of me. They're of a girl. A sad looking girl with shiny black hair and huge dark eyes sitting on the edge of the water tower.

My heart falls out of rhythm, beating faster and faster until it's thrumming against my chest like the vibration of a jackhammer.

Her.

Although my vision is blurry as shit, my thoughts of her are clearer than they'd ever been, and for the first time in my adult life, I'm fucking scared.

I don't even need to see the big motherfucker standing over me with a baseball bat to know I am completely and totally fucked.

CHAPTER ONE

PREPPY

THREE YEARS EARLIER

*F*UCK *THAT'S SOME good shit.*
    I wiped the excess powder from under my nose and rubbed it on my gums. "Grade A blow. Thanks, man. This shit day sucks just a little bit less," I said. We'd just pulled up to Grace's house after dropping King off to start serving his sentence. We'd see him again, but not for 2-4 years.

"Fuck," Bear said, echoing my thoughts about the coke as he snorted a line off my dashboard. He pinched the bridge of his nose and shook his head from side to side, his long, blond hair flapped around his face like a wet sheepdog shaking itself dry as the rush from the blow slammed into his brain.

I knew the feeling.

I knew it well.

I fucking loved it.

Bear wiped any residual evidence of our pity party off the dashboard with his hand. He got out of the car, but I hesitated with my hands on the wheel. I glanced up at Grace's little cottage and sighed. "You coming?" Bear asked, leaning down in the open window. He lit two cigarettes and leaned up against the car, obscuring my view with his jean covered ass.

Reluctantly, I got out and as I rounded the car, I smoothed down my khakis, straightened my bow tie, and took a deep breath. I joined Bear against the car as we both stood in silence, staring up at Grace's front porch. He handed me one of the lit cigarettes and I took it, taking a long deep drag.

"You pissed he told us not to visit?" I asked. Bear hooked a thumb into his pocket, kicking a loose shell with the toe of his boot.

I took another drag and exhaled slowly. Bear shrugged. "Some of my brothers, when they get locked up, they say the same thing. No visits, no calls. When they're on the inside they have to concentrate on life on the inside. Can't imagine it helps to have visitors reminding them all the time of the freedoms they don't fucking have."

"I wasn't talking about your Beach Bitches, Care Bear. I was talking about King," I said, stubbing out my cigarette under my shoe.

Bear rolled his eyes and flicked his cigarette into the road, blowing the smoke out of his nostrils. "Come on, let's get this over with."

"Bear?" I asked, feeling suddenly uneasy as we made our way up the front walkway, tapping my fingers on the front of my pants. I straightened my bow tie again.

"Yeah, Prep?"

I followed him onto the porch and lowered my voice to a whisper, "I think weed would have been a much better idea than blow."

Bear turned around, his pupils the size of pancakes. He pointed to my eyes. "Yeah man," he agreed as we both broke out into a fit of laughter. "I think you might be fucking right."

"THE WAY I see it, there is only one fucking solution to this problem of ours," I announced, glancing between Grace and Bear, and the depressing-as-all-fuck looks on their faces. They both stared down at the table as if it were going to magically offer up the answer we were all looking for. Grace's eyebrows were knitted tightly into a downward point, causing more wrinkles to form on her already heavily lined face, as she circled the rim of her glass with her spoon over and over again. It killed me that I couldn't fix this for her. For us.

"Samuel," Grace said, covering my hand with hers and offering me a small reassuring smile that was anything but reassuring. "You don't have to fix this right now. You don't have to make it better. We will think of something." Her tone sounded like she was trying to convince herself as much as she was trying to convince me.

We were talking about Max. King's baby girl who'd been tossed into the system the second he was put in cuffs. The three of us had been trying everything we could think of to get her out and home with one of us, but the state is fickle as shit. Apparently, they didn't want to give an infant over to a biker, a degenerate, or a sickly elderly woman.

Damn the man.

Bear's knuckles were white as he flipped a napkin ring from one hand to another, snapping the plastic with a growl. He flung it across the table, shooting Grace an apologetic look before dropping his face into his hands.

I slammed my hand down on the table, rattling the pitcher

of Grace's famous mojitos, finally drawing their attentions out of their own asses and up to me. "All right. It's been decided." I reached out and squeezed Bear's hand like Grace had squeezed mine, and he retracted it like I'd given him a severe case of the cooties. "We are just gonna have to get gay-married."

"Shut the fuck up, Prep," Bear grumbled, stubbing out his cigarette in the ashtray and trying to swipe me across the side of the head, but I was too quick, dodging him before he had a chance to make contact.

"Boys," Grace warned, although my words seem to have the affect I was looking for because the corners of her mouth turned upward, her frown straightening into a line. A tiny bit of the light in her eyes returning as she naturally fell into her roll in our crazy lives.

Her roll as our mom.

"Bear, at least pretend you care about this shit," I said, watching Grace out of the corner of my eye as her shoulders relaxed and she settled back into her chair with her drink. "I mean, look at you, motherfucker! For Christ's sake, they aren't going to give us King's baby if my man-husband won't even put on a god damned shirt!" I pointed to Bear, who hadn't worn a shirt under his cut since the day he turned prospect for the Beach Bastards. Seriously, you'd think the guy was allergic or something.

"What are you talking about? I'm totally covered," Bear said, looking down and adjusting his cut to cover his left nipple, exposing the right one in the process.

I rolled my eyes. "Tattoos don't fucking count," I said, and that's when I heard Grace's small laugh and inwardly, my own shoulders fell.

"Sure they do," Bear said, patting the ink on his abs with both hands as if it somehow proved his point.

"Samuel," Grace said, sounding a little tired. "As much as I appreciate your enthusiasm, we live in the south, dear, they haven't quite embraced the idea of gay marriage here just yet."

I stood from the table and paced up and down the three steps leading from the deck to the yard and back again. Of course I knew that gay marriage wasn't legal in the south, and I knew that the idea was fucking ridiculous, but I was willing to spew just about anything to come up with a solution. Not to mention, that someone needed to thin out the thick cloud of dread looming over our little family.

"Samuel, we will think of something. It will just take time," Grace reassured me. I looked down at her and took hold of her outstretched hand, bending down I pulled her into a hug and she wrapped her tiny arms around my waist. She smelled like peppermint and the potpourri she always kept out on the table in the living room that I might have mistaken for trail mix once or twice.

Or six times.

"We've got this, Grace," Bear said, echoing my thoughts. Although, he didn't sound as convinced as I was.

I squatted down next to Grace "We will just have to be a little more...creative."

Grace patted my cheek. "You're a good boy, Samuel," she said, and if I was a dog my tail would be wagging so fast it would've fallen right off. "Oh, and before I forget, don't forget to check in on Mirna like I asked. She's been more off than usual lately and I want to make sure she's looked after while I'm away."

"You got it," I said, planting one last kiss on her forehead and standing up, straightening the crease in my pants. Mirna's house was one of the first Granny Growhouses in our operation. Plus, she made these amazing chocolate chip cookies that were so fucking good, I've seriously thought about rubbing them all over my nuts. "I'm going today, actually," I assured her.

"When will you be back?" Bear asked.

"A few weeks or so. Not too long," Grace answered, with a little too much enthusiasm. Bear and I exchanged a knowing glance above Grace's head. She was heading out of town to some facility she'd talked up to sound like a resort and spa for a few weeks, but Bear and I had our suspicions so we'd called the place after she'd first spoke about it and sure enough, it was a medical treatment facility for patients with advanced stages of cancer. Grace rarely said the C word when we were around and vowed that she was going to live forever.

"You need a ride up there?" I asked.

Grace waved us off. "Boys, stop worrying about me. They are sending transportation for me in the morning. Now go! Go! I'll see you two in a few weeks."

I was the kind of man who packed a gun at all times, but even I wasn't stupid enough to try and argue with Grace when she had her mind set on something, and if she said she was going to live forever then it was best to believe her and leave it at that.

Bear rounded the table and said his good-bye's, and I followed him through the yard around the side of the house. "You still got the number of that place?"

"Yeah, I called to make sure she's got a private room," I said.

"Good, one of the brothers has a stepsister who works there. She's going to keep an eye on her," Bear said.

There wasn't much Bear and I agreed on, but taking care of Grace, even if it was behind her back, was one of those rare things that didn't require an argument or a flip of a middle finger.

"Drop me at the club," Bear said. "I don't get my bike back from Dunn's until the morning, right before we ride out."

I nodded. While Grace was gone Bear was going to be out on a ride with the Bastards, something about something and them going somewhere. I didn't really know the details because I really never listened to what he said, and right then there was something still nagging me about our earlier conversation. "I mean, you really wouldn't get gay-married with me to help King's kid? That's kind of bullshit." I knew it was odd to be offended because my very heterosexual friend wouldn't marry his other very heterosexual friend in a gay-wedding to save the kid of their other very heterosexual friend, but there wasn't a fucking thing I wouldn't do to make shit right again. It wasn't the fucking marriage part, it was the thought that Bear might not be in this as much as I was that was making me all twitchy.

Some fucking people.

With one hand on the front gate of the fence lining Grace's yard, Bear stopped and turned around. "The truth? Ain't nothing I wouldn't do to get King's kid back for him. And stop being such a dick, Preppy, because you fucking know that. Believe it or not, this shit isn't all about you."

I felt better knowing we were on the same page. "That might be true, but what's also true is that all this sucks major fucking asshole."

"That it does, my friend," Bear agreed, pushing open the gate.

"Hey Bear, you want to know what they call gay marriage in states where it's legal?" I asked as we reached the car.

"No, but I have a feeling you're going to tell me anyway," he said with a laugh, struggling to maintain his semi-permanent state of looking annoyed.

"Marriage, you fucking idiot," I said, flicking him on the back of his head as I jogged over to my car. He shot me a tattooed middle finger.

"I CAME IN like a wrecking baaaallll." I belted out the open window at a bunch of teenagers walking across the causeway. The group of mostly girls scrunched up their noses in confusion as if they'd never been the victims of a drive-by-singing before.

"Fucking teenagers," I muttered, propping my elbow up on the door and waving my hand through the wind to the beat of the music, continuing my radio duet at a volume not fully appreciated by most, and especially not appreciated by the party-pooper next to me who had a pained look on his face as if my singing was causing his dick to tie itself in a knot.

"We're all feeling shitty about King and Max, Bear, but do you have to look so constipated?" I asked, punching him in the shoulder.

Bear was silent for a moment. He blew out a breath and scratched the back of his neck. "It's not just King. It's my old man too. He's been all over me lately, even more than usual." I parked outside of the gate. Bear looked up to the darkened clubhouse, staring at it like he could see something more than windows and walls.

"Fuck your old man," I said. "That motherfucker best never

step to me or I'll show him the Preppy special."

"What exactly is the Preppy special?" Bear asked, one bushy blond eyebrow quirked up.

I made the shape of a gun with my thumb and index finger and pointed it up to the clubhouse. "A bullet with a side of bow tie." I shot my finger gun and made my best exploding gun noise with my mouth.

Bear laughed, not that fake-laugh shit he'd been trying to pass off as the real deal these last few weeks, but a real, live, genuine laugh, which was a relief to hear, considering the cloud of doom he's been walking around in. Motherfucker could be so serious sometimes, it made my dick hurt.

Bear got out with a good-bye salute and disappeared behind the gate.

I headed to Mirna's, feeling more determined then ever to get Max back for King, and protect the people I called family.

There was nothing I wouldn't do.

No one I wouldn't kill.

If only it were that fucking easy.

CHAPTER TWO

DRE

I *HAVE CUM in my hair.*

Blood caked underneath my fingernails.

Bruises between my legs.

I was so over being me that I needed a new word for over. I needed a new fucking life. I patted my bra over my shirt, feeling for my bus ticket for the hundredth time. I breathed a sigh of relief when the paper crinkled against my skin, my reminder that a fresh start was only a bus ride away.

I righted my shirt and took in my surroundings. The small house was once very familiar to me, in what seemed like another lifetime, but in reality was only a few years ago. I used to feel at home there.

Oh, how things have changed.

I nervously crossed and uncrossed my legs, as Mirna shuffled around the kitchen. I felt everything and anything *but* at home. This had nothing to do with Mirna (I'd always called her by her first name) and everything to do with me.

I pulled down on the hem of my shorts as if I could somehow make them longer, suddenly all too aware of the hole in the pocket exposing the skin on my upper thigh. After uselessly yanking at the worn denim, I switched to my sleeves, stretching the fabric over the palms of my hands and folding my fingers over it to keep it in place. Sunlight beamed through the large window of the living room. The last light of the day rendered the thin material of my shirt completely see through, and I hoped with everything I had that Mirna wouldn't see my arms.

My stomach twisted. The H I'd had over the past week wasn't nearly enough to get me high, only enough to keep me from plowing head first into major withdrawals. My head throbbed and my body ached like I had the flu. The major hangover that never really went away.

My stomach could have also been twisting because the second I'd entered my grandmother's house, I'd officially become the worst fucking human being on the planet.

Unofficially, I'd already held that title for quite some time.

I rocked forward to quell the nausea, but there was little that could help me that didn't come in the form of a syringe, or a less used and abused body.

I wondered what was taking Mirna so long because I was't sure how much longer I could sit there without vomiting into the planter next to the front door. Another wave of nausea washed over me and without thinking I bit down hard on my bottom lip to keep the contents of my stomach down. I licked the blood from my lip, the taste of copper adding to the already disgusting taste of bile on my tongue.

Mirna came back into the living room with a big smile on her face. She set down a silver tray on the coffee table, the one she only used when company came around.

My grandmother, seemingly unaware of my discomfort, poured tea into two mismatched cups. One was light blue with a chip on the rim, and I recognized it immediately. The chip had been a result of me running my big wheel into her coffee table as a kid. I'd sent her entire tea set, a wedding gift from my late grandfather, crashing to the floor. Mirna had sat with me on her lap on the kitchen floor, stroking my hair and comforting me for hours, even though it was me who ruined her entire tea set beyond repair. All had been lost, except for one cup.

The one cup I now took from Mirna as she passed it across the coffee table.

My hands shook, rattling the teacup against the saucer. I smiled as politely as I could, setting it carefully back on the table without so much as taking a sip. My grandmother returned my smile and watched me curiously over the rim of her teacup, and just like when I'd first knocked on her front door several minutes earlier, I waited.

Nothing.

The last time I visited, Mirna was having trouble remembering things. Where she'd put the keys. What time her friend Hilda was picking her up for Bingo.

It seemed things weren't only different for me, but Mirna as well, because I never expected the woman I spent every summer with during my childhood since I was four years old to not recognize her one and only grandchild.

When had things gotten so bad?

"Do you know who I am?" I asked softly, in one last attempt to stir up some kind of recognition. I stared unblinking at her and tried to will the recognition into her eyes. Eyes that matched mine. Eyes that used to hold so much life but were now dulled like they'd been frosted over.

Maybe, there wasn't anything wrong at all. Maybe, she was totally with it and just didn't recognize me. After all, last time she saw me I was all glossy black hair and tanned skin, and now I wasn't even a shadow of my former self. Gaunt, with sharp collarbones and pointed elbows. Deep dark yellowy circles under my eyes. Pale grayish skin.

I didn't need to look in a mirror to know I wouldn't be able to recognize myself.

"I'm Andrea," I said. Nothing still. "Dre?" I asked, switching to my nickname, just in case it could ignite a spark.

"Oh!" Mirna exclaimed, holding up her index finger. I sat on the edge of the cushion, leaning over the table, waiting for her to confirm that I'd broken through. "You're from the church, right? They keep sending people by to keep me company while Rick's overseas, but I'm just fine. My nurse training keeps me busy, and in my free time I'm learning how to be a better cook, although, I need to work on perfecting Mama's meatloaf or she'll never come over for Sunday dinner."

My heart dropped into my stomach when Mirna referred to my grandfather as if he was still alive and overseas fighting in the war.

Guilt, sickening guilt, twisting guilt, washed over me and clung to my rotten insides. In the grand scheme of things, it was probably better she didn't know who I was.

Or why I was there.

I was reminded of that reason when a crash sounded from the back of the house. I cringed while Mirna seemed unaffected by the commotion. She was sipping tea with a polite pinky raised in the air like the proper southern debutante she once was.

Just as I told myself that she hadn't heard the noise, she tilted her head and pointed down the hallway. "How much longer do you think they'll be, dear?" she asked, as I'd been wondering the same exact thing.

My pulse spiked. "Uh, I don't know what you're...um...who?" I again pulled down on my sleeves.

She smiled and leaned forward, crooking her index finger for me to do the same, so I did. "There are two men in the back room," she whispered. "They broke my window and they are stealing from me." She slapped her knee and a burst of laughter shot through her mouth as if she'd just told me the punchline to a joke. "Can you believe it? Isn't it all so very exciting?"

"I'll...I'll just go tell them to leave for you," I announced, keeping my voice as steady as possible and ignoring the head rush I got when I stood abruptly from the couch. Then, as calmly as I could, I made my way down the hallway.

"Thank you so much, dear," Mirna called out. "But you don't have to do that, someone is already on the way. He'll be here shortly."

"Who?" I asked, turning around.

"Samuel," she offered, like it was a name I should know. She picked up her cup and crossed her legs, settling back into the sofa and turning to stare out the front window into the yard.

Pinkie back in the air.

I turned and raced down the hall, pushing open the back bedroom door. I almost fell over at the sight before me. What used to be a guest bedroom and doubled as Mirna's scrapbooking room, was now filled with rows of green plants. And not just any plants.

Weed.

Mirna was growing weed out of her guest bedroom.

Green leaves jutted out in every direction over a complicated web of clear tubes and glass planters hanging from the ceiling, and the walls creating several aisles of stacked plants.

Stumbling around the room, shoving as much of it into garbage bags, and sending the glass planters and tubing crashing to the floor as they went, were the two men the bus ticket in my bra was going to get me far, far away from.

"What the fuck is all this?" I asked, my mouth gaping as I took it all in. "And why is it here?" Eric and Conner both looked as if they'd won the weed lottery, yellow toothed grins plastered on their gaunt faces. Eric's ripped t-shirt hung like an old potato sack off of his thin frame. His cheeks were sunken in. His sneakers were mismatched, both in color, one black and one white, and in condition, one had a hole with his toes poking out the top and the other had the sole coming loose on the side. Conner didn't look any better, although his shoes were the same color. "Tell me what the fuck is going on?" I demanded, wishing that sober didn't feel so god damned awful.

"You're a dumb bitch, you know that?" Eric snapped. "This…" he said, holding up one of the plants, shaking it in the air, "…is exactly the reason why we came here. Did you really think we came all the way down to this shit town to lift shitty cheap jewelry from your Granny?" He shook his head in disbelief and continued to fill his bag. "Dumb, fucking bitch," he muttered.

Conner chimed in. "When we heard what was here we thought it was just a rumor, but we hit the mother load. You know how much this shit is worth on the street?" He crossed the room and shoved a bag into my hand. Just him being near me made me more disgusted than any withdrawal ever could. "Help load this up. That shit you like to shoot up with isn't fucking free, you know."

I know, because I've paid the price.

No more.

"You knew all this was here?" I asked, dropping the bag and taking a step back.

"Fuck yeah, we did," Eric said, holding up his hand for Conner to high-five him. Conner shot him the bird instead and continued his destruction of the room, knocking over equipment and pulling tubes from the wall. Water from those tubes sprayed around the room like a sprinkler, soaking everything within, including Conner and Eric, who either didn't notice or didn't care. "We were watching when your Granny opened the door. That bitch has no clue who you fucking are, does she?" Eric asked. "Maybe I should go see if she can take a pounding as good as her granddaughter can," he said, grabbing the crotch of his sagging sweatpants.

Conner, someone who used to be the first to come to my defense, was now laughing at my humiliation. At the sick joke Eric had made about something not even remotely fucking funny.

"Who knew that an old lady could do all this?" Conner said, kicking over some sort of machine by the window, splitting it open to reveal it's red and blue wirey guts.

Which was when it hit me.

Conner was actually right. Mirna couldn't have done all this. Not even at her best. Mirna was the kind of person who refused to take aspirin when she had a headache so drugs of any kind weren't exactly on her radar. And as far as botanical skills went, hers didn't go any further than the small flower box under the front window.

"Look around you, you fucking idiots!" My words came

slower than my mouth could move, and with my head throbbing like I'd been clubbed, it was a wonder I could speak at all. "This is high-tech shit. Whoever you're really stealing from, it's not my grandmother, and I'm pretty sure that you've seen enough movies to know that stealing drugs from someone who deals it never ends well, so chances are that they aren't going to forget this. They'll be coming for you."

Conner laughed and pointed between the three of us. "Yeah, when he finds out what WE did. The three of us. As much as you like to think you're better than us you're not. This is as much you as it is us."

"He? So you know whose stuff this is?"

Conner rolled his eyes at me. Eyes that used to contain kindness and sympathy had grown to hold nothing but hatred and contempt. "Stop asking so many fucking questions and help us carry this shit out." His smirk twisted into a sick, knowing smile. "Or don't. But then I can't promise that we're going to be as gentle with you tonight as we were last night."

I'd never liked guns. Even my dad's hunting gun that he kept on display in his office made me uncomfortable.

But then Conner said something that reminded me that if I had a gun, I could never pull the trigger. "Or maybe I'll call Mellie and she can ride my cock for a while," Conner said, stepping up into my space, glaring down at me with all the hatred in his soul. "Oh, that's right. I can't. Because she's dead."

The familiar guilt bubbled in my gut and exploded in my heart. The heavy, never ending, too much for one soul to bare, guilt. It was what the bars of my imaginary cell were made out of, the one Conner built around me with his words, the one he'd just pushed me back inside and slammed the door shut.

"I don't mean to interrupt," Mirna sang, coming to stand beside me at the door. Her hand on my shoulder. Conner backed down and went back to work, stuffing his bag. "But would any of you like some cookies?" she asked, holding up a plate of her famous double chocolate chip cookies. Eric and Conner ignored her, continuing to loot the room of its plants and damage and destroy everything else.

"I'm so sorry," I said, turning around to Mirna. Without caring if she remembered me or not I wrapped my arms around her, selfishly needing the comfort of my grandma. The same way I'd needed it when I'd broken her tea set.

She gently patted me on the back, "It's all right, dear," she said, pulling back and holding up the plate again. "Don't be upset. Whatever's bothering you will be okay, there's always tomorrow and that's another day." She took a bite of a cookie and spoke with her mouth full. "My Rick always says that when I'm having a bad day. Here, have a cookie. I just made them. They're Samuel's favorite."

There was that name again.

"Who's Samuel?" I asked, expecting to hear about someone from her past, or someone long dead, but then out of the corner of my eye I noticed that both Conner and Eric had froze. My guess was that they knew who Samuel was, and if I had any money at all, I'd bet that this was his shit.

"Where is he now?" Eric asked, the cocky smile nowhere to be seen.

Mirna took another a bite of her cookie, slowly chewing. A car door slammed. She waited until she was done swallowing to say, "He's here."

Conner and Eric darted through the back door faster than

I'd ever seen them move. My first instinct wasn't to run. I didn't want to leave Mirna in her state, and on top of that I hadn't done any of the actual stealing. Chances were that this Samuel guy wouldn't see it that way. I hesitated only long enough to wrap Mirna in another hug. "Again, I'm so sorry," I said, placing a kiss on her forehead before running through the living room and out the back door.

"Come on!" Conner called out, waving to me from the field behind the house that lead to the train tracks. But then I stopped.

It could be my only chance, and if I wanted to be on that bus tomorrow I didn't have a choice. I had to take it.

With one last glance at Conner I shook off the voice of the guilt, the voice that told me I owed him for what I'd done, and I took off in the complete opposite direction, crossing the yard into the woods. I heard him calling my name over and over again as I ran deeper into the trees, down the overgrown foot path.

The bark of a nearby tree suddenly exploded, sharp pieces of bark lodged into my thighs, warm blood trickled down my calves. My heart pumped faster and faster. My body, who wanted nothing more than to give up on me, warred with my mind which was fueled only by adrenaline, keeping me moving, one foot in front of the other.

A whistling sounded past my ear. Another tree exploded. This time, right in front of me. I stopped and turned around, catching a brief glimpse of the man standing in Mirna's back yard. I started right back again in the other direction. I hadn't been able to see much of the man, but I knew right then what I had seen would be burned into my brain and haunt me forever.

A wicked smile, a bow tie…and a gun.

CHAPTER THREE

DRE

W HAT THE FUCK *have I done?*
It was the thought racing through my head, over and over again, as I watched the world go on without me from my perch high up on the water tower. Over the tops of the bending pines, just beyond the leaves, was the small town of Logan's Beach, a place I'd once loved.

Despite the way I was circling the drain, and much to my surprise, there were signs of life everywhere. Cars drove up and down the two lane road below. Lights flickered on and off. The faint smell of BBQ wafted through the air. Echoing bass from music playing somewhere in the distance vibrated off the cold metal platform, thudding softly underneath me in rhythmic succession. The ground below appeared flattened, much like I imagined the earth would look from space.

It was all so far, far away.

Somewhere down there, eating the food and dancing to that music, were people. Happy people. I remembered the last day I was happy. A slow running silent movie, except in vivid technicolor. I could recall every single smile, every laugh, every exaggerated hand gesture as stories and jokes were exchanged.

It was how it ended that haunted me. A scene that never

drifted far from the screen playing it on a loop over and over again in my nightmares.

With the back of a shaky hand I wiped the tears from my cheek, smudging my heavy black eye-makeup across my face.

My stomach suddenly wretched. However, no amount of purging could expel the kind of decaying impurities keeping me trapped in a life I hated. I breathed in and out slowly, in an attempt to gather my thoughts and quell the nausea, but despite my efforts to hold my shit together, the world spun. A violent pain slashed behind my eyes like someone was trying to hack their way out of my skull.

Despite everything, I still wanted it. Craving the high that had nothing to do with being up on the water tower.

Heroin.

I don't remember who got it or when we first decided to try it. I only remember the wave of euphoria that took over that very first time.

I was lost and somewhere along the way heroin took notice and moved in and took my place. It decided my every move. It was the reason behind my every terrible decision. It didn't just take over my life. It was my life. The more the heroin did the thinking for me, the less I had to do for myself. Heroin allowed me a retreat that sobriety couldn't.

An oblivion.

I'd chosen that oblivion over my friends, my family, college.

I scooted to the end of the platform, dangling my feet over the ledge. One of my shoes, cheap flip-flops from a gas station, slipped off my foot. I leaned over the railing to watch as it flitted down to the ground, gaining enough momentum to send a small poof of dirt billowing into the air when it smacked against the

23

earth.

A crazed laugh that sounded nothing like me burst from my mouth, echoing across the tops of the pines lining the dirt road beside the tower. I kicked off my other shoe and watched in wonderment as it followed the path of its mate, landing only inches away in another poof of dirt and dust.

I wondered what it felt like. To fly. To be a bird above it all. Maybe it would end just like my shoes…poof.

I stood up too quickly, falling back down onto my boney ass. My knees wobbled and gave out. I tried again, this time much slower. Holding on to the railing, I focused my gaze down on my shoes as I lifted one bare foot onto the bottom rung of the rail. The sharp metal cut into the flesh in the crease of my toes. My entire body began to shake more violently than before, almost as if I was having a seizure. It wasn't just because I was needing a fix. It was my entire being recognizing and realizing what I was about to do.

This was it.

Bending at the waist, I raised my other foot and was met with the same cut of flesh. I shifted my hands to the top rung and slowly straightened my knees until I was standing upright, the only thing keeping me from falling over the side was the thin guard bar pressed against the middle of my thighs which bent against my weight.

With my hands at my sides, I used my fingers to slowly pull up the hem of my t-shirt until I had enough of the material in my hands to lift it up over my head. Raising it into the night sky I released my clenched fist and watched as the breeze picked it up and carried it into the pines, and I was glad to see it go. I gave a quick press of my lips to the silver cross Mirna had given me for my first communion and let it fall back between my breasts. I carefully removed my shorts and underwear, lifting one foot at a time until I was standing bared to the world.

Clean.

It was the beginning of the end.

A baptism into death.

I stretched my arms out wide, embracing the night.

I was ready to fly.

On the count of three.

One.

Two.

Three.

I DON'T WANT to do this.

But it was too late. It wasn't as if I could jump back and change my mind. I was already falling.

Until I wasn't.

I was ripped back from the very edge of death by strong arms and for a naive second, I thought it might have been God himself who'd heard my last second change of heart and saved my life. A life I'd so stupidly chose to throw away in a moment of delusion and weakness.

What the fuck is wrong with me? What am I doing here? I thought, coming back to my senses as my body was thrown sideways, elbows, shoulders, and knees crashed against metal, railing, wall, and finally flesh. My spine arched off the platform like a fallen cat as my tailbone landed unceremoniously with a sickening crunch that made my eyes water.

I was pushed onto my back. Powerful thighs straddled me,

and again I was stupid enough to think that maybe I was being protected. That thought was short lived when my wrists were jerked above my head and held at an awkward angle that made my arms throb. After a few excruciating moments, the pain in the base of my spine dulled to an ache and I was able to open my eyes to the blurry world around me.

I blinked rapidly. When my vision cleared I found myself staring up into the dark amber-colored eyes of a man who most certainly wasn't God.

He was older than me, but only by a few years at most. I'd never seen anyone like him. One side of his neck was covered in colorful and intricate tattoos that disappeared into the collar of his yellow button-down shirt. When he adjusted my wrists, his sleeves rode up his forearms, revealing very little unmarked skin there as well. His sandy-blond hair was shaved short on the sides, longer and slicked back on top. His beard was neat, short, and several shades darker than the hair on his head.

For a brief moment I was relieved that whoever the man was, at least he wasn't Conner or Eric.

However, that relief soon gave way to unadulterated panic.

I didn't recognize him. Not at first, anyway. Not until he smiled and my gaze traveled from his full lips and straight white teeth, down to his pink and yellow polka-dotted bow tie. Then the recognition slammed into me like a freight train.

Oh fuck.

This man was my savior.

He was also anything but.

"I see you remember me. Well, at least now it all makes a fuck of a lot more sense," he said, his voice a deep rumble that I felt in my chest as he leaned down over me, his lips a breath away from mine. I tried to struggle, to free myself of his grip, but he only chuckled and held me tighter. He was right by laughing because my fighting back was exactly that. Laughable. I was weak.

Too weak.

"What exactly makes sense now?" I managed to bite out, blowing out a breath of frustration at my lack of ability to fight him off.

"It's a common knowledge around here that anyone who steals from me or my partner has got to be either dumb-as-fuck or suicidal," he said, leaning back onto his knees. Still holding my wrists with one hand, he gestured with the other to the ledge I'd stood on seconds earlier. "The truth is that when I followed you up here I had my money on dumb-as-fuck, but hey, you surprised me by trying to take the final leap over there, I didn't expect that. Almost didn't catch you in time." He then leaned back down and had the audacity to pinch my cheek, the way a crazy aunt would.

"So what? You only saved me from killing myself so you could have the honor?"

"Maybe," he admitted, adding, "You should be proud of yourself, kid, 'cause nothing much surprises me these days. In a way," he paused and looked around into the night sky, taking a deep breath through his nose, releasing it with an audible sigh out of his mouth, like he was sitting in an open field, relaxing and literally smelling the flowers. "It's kind of refreshing. I hope those other two stupid fucks surprise me like you have, but I doubt it." He looked back down at me and winked. "My money is staying on dumb-as-fuck when it comes to those two."

"What did you do to Mirna?" I asked, my words as shaky as

the rest of my body.

"Is that a new thing? Is that what the kids are all doing these days? Ripping people off, then pretending like they give two fucks what happens to them?"

"Please. Tell me. Is she okay?"

He chuckled, like the panic in my voice was amusing to him. He leaned down, his cheek firmly against mine. "I'm. Not. Telling. You. Shit," he said, squeezing my body hard between his thighs, as if to prove to me that it was all it would take to crush me.

That's when I saw it.

That thing I'd never forget that made the hair on my arms stand on end and my mouth open with a gasp.

Whenever I thought of someone who was "scary," I thought of men from movies or books. The overly muscled type with no necks, wearing black clothes with scowls on their faces. Someone like a security guard or bouncer or biker who could warn people away with their large statures and brooding silence. Someone you wouldn't want to cross in a dark alley, never mind a lit street.

The man on top of me could never be described that way. He was far from a brute with his lean build. And his clothes consisted of pastels and suspenders, not exactly big scary-man attire. In essence, he looked as if he'd stepped out of a page from *The Notebook*.

Upon first glance, the guy was about as scary as the Easter Bunny.

Until I saw IT.

It was a spark. Just a glint of depravity lurking behind his amber eyes. I saw it in the way he smiled as he held me down. I heard it in the way he told me I was dumb-as-fuck and adorable in the same breath. And when he spoke about his plans for revenge, I felt it in my soul.

It was then I knew he was capable of things I couldn't even fathom.

Where Conner and Eric were bad guys in an obvious way, they didn't instill in me the same kind of fear this man did.

I'd thought I'd known true fear when I'd stood on the ledge and decided to recklessly end it all, but I hadn't. I hadn't even known it when Conner and Eric had beat me, brutalized me, and then took turns forcing themselves on me.

Into me.

No.

I never knew true fear until I met pure evil.

He wore a smile and a bow tie.

CHAPTER FOUR

PREPPY

T HE NIGHT HAD taken a turn for the worse when I showed up to Mirna's house on the tail end of being robbed of my fucking plants.

However, I was now straddling a naked chick on top of the water tower, which was one of my favorite places in Logan's Beach.

Shit was looking up.

Although, when I followed her up to the tower I hadn't known she was planning to defile my sacred space by tossing her boney body off of it.

There was something about her, something almost familiar, although I knew I hadn't met her before. I watched as she stood stark naked, with her face tilted toward the sky, and her arms out, like she was king of the world on the front of the mother-fucking Titanic. She was fascinating.

The bitch was in rough shape. Bruises and dried blood patched all over her skin made her look like a puzzle missing some pieces. I'd stood there in the shadows, taking in the sight before me for such a long time that I almost missed the slight tilt of her body in a forward motion. If I was a nanosecond later in making a run for her I'd be calling for a clean up instead of sitting on top of her, caging her in with my thighs. Fuck, if she hadn't been such a tiny waif of a thing, she probably would've pulled me over with her.

"Why did you save me?" she suddenly asked, pausing her adorable struggling which was getting her nowhere fast.

"Awe, thats cute," I said, peering down into her doll-like eyes that were so dark, they were almost black.

She huffed, her small perky tits heaved up and down as she tried to catch her breath. So did her rib cage, which was outlined under her purple and yellowed skin. Her collarbone was sharp and so were her elbows. She reminded me of one of those starving dog commercials with the sad music playing in the background. "What's cute?" she asked on a strained exhale.

"That you think you've been saved."

"Well, I'm not dead," she argued.

"Yet," I shrugged. "It's hard to get answers from a flattened corpse. Trust me. I've tried."

She growled and tried to free her arms from my grasp, and that's when I got a better look at the inside of her arms. Suddenly, it sunk in that this chick wasn't just covered in bruises, these were pock marks. She wasn't just some skinny bitch.

She was a junkie.

Bruised. Broken.

Vulnerable.

She was shaking like a fucking leaf, and with every tremble my dick grew harder until it was begging to be free of its khaki confines.

She gasped, when she felt me hard against her leg, "What...why?"

I raised my eyebrows. "Really? Why? My cock only knows that I'm on top of a naked chick. It's simple biology. Don't feel too flattered, I once got a chubby when the lady who runs the deli tried to wipe a mustard stain off the front of my pants." If she really knew that I was thinking about how her bruises and dried blood looked like art under the moonlight, and how I'd like to paint a line or two on her skin myself, she'd probably scream.

Loud.

I grew even harder.

"What's your name?" I asked, easing up on my grip, slightly.

"Why?" she asked, warily, her voice now a whisper.

I rolled my eyes. "So I can know what to doodle on the cover of my notebook," I said, sarcastically. "Okay, so here is how this is gonna go. I'm going to let go of you and let you sit up. Then I'm going to introduce myself, and then you're going to introduce yourself. Got it?"

She tipped her chin in agreement and never took her eyes off me, even when I let her go. She tried to sit up but was struggling, her muscles visibly shaking from the strain. At the rate she was going I'd be next to throw myself off the tower from the pure boredom of waiting. She swatted at my chest when I picked her up by her hips and pulled her up to a sitting position, pressing her back against the wall. I grabbed her hands in mine. "No hitting," I said, shaking my index finger at her like I was scolding a toddler.

I released her again and plopped down next to her. This chick was exhausting, but shit I was kind of having fun.

Junkies. Who knew?

"I'm Samuel Clearwater," I said, extending my hand. I didn't wait for her to take it, instead I picked up her hand off her thigh and shook it hard, as if to show her how introductions were done. My gaze dropped to the tiny patch of light colored curls between her legs. My mouth watered.

Huh.

Dark hair on her head.

Light body hair.

Interesting little druggie.

"But everyone calls me Preppy." I gave her delicate hand a hard squeeze. "And you are…"

"Andrea, but most people just call me Dre."

"Like Dr. Dre?" I asked, excited by her unique name. "That's fucking awesome. Please tell me you have a sibling named Snoop. For the love of all that is holy, please tell me that. Shit, never mind, don't tell me, I'm just gonna pretend that you do." Her eyebrows squished together like she was trying to figure me out.

Good-fucking-luck to her. She wouldn't be the first one.

"So Dr. Dre, you strung out?" I asked, already knowing the answer.

"Fuck off!" she spat, turning her head. I grabbed her chin and forced her to face me.

"I can fix that for yooooouuuu," I sang. Her lips parted. "I can get you what you need to turn this little frown upside down." I released her chin.

"You just pointed out that I'm strung out, but you're offering me a fix?" Her pupils dilated, like the junkie part of her already knew the answer to my question.

"Listen, I could take you to a twelve step meeting or I could offer you an all expense paid trip to rehab, but if you haven't noticed, I'm not your parents, or Dr.-Fucking-Phil, so that's not gonna happen. A life changing solution, I ain't got. But H? H I can get you with one little phone call." She turned her head to the side. "So. What'll it be, Doc?"

"What do you want??" she asked, and that's when I knew she was considering my offer. Although, there was more to it than that. MUCH, MUCH MORE.

"Your buddies."

"What…what are you going to do to them?"

"Does it fucking matter?" I asked. "Let's just say that they aren't going to be offered an all expense paid trip to rehab either."

"Tell me," she begged, perking up and sitting straighter. She grabbed my arm and squeezed. "Please, just tell me the fucking truth."

If anything, I've always been "overly honest" so the truth wasn't a problem for me. It poured easily from my lips and Dre listened intently as I told her, "I'm going to slit their throats, take my motherfucking plants back, call for someone to clean up the bodies so I don't get my khakis dirty, and probably come back up here and smoke a joint afterward. Maybe snort some blow if I feel like a party. Haven't really decided yet, depends on my mood."

Dre didn't respond right away. She seemed lost in thought, staring over the railing as she mindlessly reached up to her neck, pushing back her hair and exposing a fresh bruise/welt combo in the shape of a large hand print. She ran her fingertips over it and her eyes welled up with tears.

I'd only followed her from Mirna's because she was a lot slower than those other two cunt-buckets, and I'd thought she'd eventually lead me back to them.

What I hadn't realized was that she wasn't just running from me.

She was running from them, too.

"I don't want the H," she said, shocking the ever-loving-shit out of me.

"You're not a very good junkie," I pointed out.

"I'm not a junkie. I'm a junkie at the end of her rope, which until this very moment, I didn't know were two different things, but they are a lot different."

"Yeah, I kind of noticed that while you were circling the drain up there," I said, again pointing to the ledge. She didn't look, instead she closed her eyes tightly and wrapped her arms around her stomach, like she couldn't stand to relive what she'd almost done.

"And it's not that I don't want it because I DO WANT it. I want it so bad I can taste it, literally, because when you shoot up it leaves a taste in your mouth and I just…" she said, reaching up to touch her lips. "But…"

"But?"

"But what's crazy is that I DON'T want it even more," she exhaled a shaky breath. "I'll deal with my shit, but I was being honest when I said I wanted something else from you. Two things, actually."

"You're not exactly in a position to be making demands," I reminded her, although both me and my curious cock were very intrigued by what this tiny little person could possibly want from me.

"No, I'm not," she said, her voice filled with something that sounded a lot like new found determination. She looked up, and when her eyes locked on mine I swear it was like I could see her balls growing bigger with every word out of her mouth. "But I'll take my chances because life isn't always sunshine and whiskey."

"Nope, more like dark storms and moonshine," I offered, laughing at my own joke. "But if you're going to ask me to toss you off the tower, the answer is no, and not because I'm morally against it. I'm not actually morally against anything but having morals, I just don't want you haunting one of my most favorite places. However, I hear the Causeway is excellent. Has mostly five stars on **Yelp** for best places in Logan's Beach to end it all. Tell me what you want little junkie."

She looked up at me, obviously not as amused by my hilarity as I was. "Just need you to tell me where the fuck Tweedle Dee and Tweedle Dum went and anything within reason is yours," I pushed.

"And you're going to kill them." It wasn't a question.

"Yes. I'm gonna make 'em Tweedle-Dead."

★ ★ ★

DRE

"DAD?" I ASKED in a whisper. Surprisingly, when I told Preppy I wanted to use his phone, he'd handed it over without hesitation. His only stipulation was that I make the call on speakerphone so he could make sure I wasn't calling Conner or Eric to warn them off. It was impossible even if I wanted to do it, considering neither of them had cell phones.

"Andrea? Is that you? What time is it?" my dad asked, clearing his throat. I didn't answer, and not just because it didn't matter but because I had no idea. All I knew was that it was really late.

I just hoped it wasn't TOO late.

"Daddy, I'm coming home."

"Andrea," he said, followed by a sigh of frustration. "Do you still have the ticket I sent you?"

"Shit," I said as panic washed over me. My ticket was in my bra, which was now somewhere below the water tower. "I don't..." I started, when my dad interrupted.

"I'm not sending you another one, Andrea. This is your last chance. I love you, but you need help and I can get you help, but you have to be on that bus."

I'd find that ticket if it was the last fucking thing I'd ever do. "I will be. I promise. I'm coming home. For real this time."

"No more lies."

"No more lies," I choked out.

"Andrea, one more thing," he warned. "If I go to the bus station to pick you up and you're not there, then this is done. Over. No more excuses. I'm too tired for any more excuses. No more calls. No more chances. If you're not on that bus, then this isn't your home anymore, and I'm not your family." The threat was a well deserved one. The result of a classic case of the-girl-who-cried-heroin, one too many times.

"I promise. I'll be there," I agreed. I looked over at Preppy, who held his hand out for the phone, an unreadable expression on his face. "I gotta go. I love you. I'll see you soon."

"So, that was one request. What's next?" Preppy asked, taking the phone, shoving it into his pocket. He flashed me a smile that told me he was up to something. It was all too easy. One minute, he wanted to kill me and the next, he wanted to help me? Maybe he had no intentions of letting me go.

It didn't matter. I meant what I'd told my dad. I was going to be on that bus this time. No matter what.

Even if it meant I had to kill the man who'd saved my life.

CHAPTER FIVE

PREPPY

D RE'S DEMANDS WERE not at all what I'd thought they'd be. She didn't even ask for money, and I was so sure she would that I'd have bet my left nut on it. First, she wanted to use my phone to call her dad, which I handed her without hesitation, as a sign of trust.

"I need you to keep one of them alive. Conner," she said, looking to her hands and fidgeting with her fingers.

"Why?" I asked, irritated by her request. "He your boyfriend or something."

"No," was all she said.

"Well, he had to do something to earn that kind of loyalty."

"He didn't. But I did. I owe him," she said.

I didn't push her for more because it didn't matter. I helped her down from the tower, found her clothes, shoes, and retrieved her bus ticket from a tree. I even gave her a ride to the bus station to boot because I'm a chivalrous motherfucker.

Even if it was all bullshit.

The only place I was planning on letting her go to, was to lead me back to the other two douchebags. Asking for me to spare Conners life showed me that she had some sort of loyalty toward him, so when she said that they were probably heading to

Coral Pines to meet with their dealer, it wasn't exactly like I was going to take her word for it. She could've been sending me right into a trap.

The second we pulled up to the station, Dre opened the door before it was even in park. "Hey!" I said, thinking she was about to jump out and make a run for it, when she leaned over and puked onto the pavement.

H withdrawals are no joke.

When she was done heaving she sat up slowly, wiping her mouth with the back of her hand. She got out, and I leaned over the seats to shut the door behind her. She turned around to me and flashed me a sad smile as she stood there clutching her only possession, her bus ticket, to her chest like it was a precious newborn baby.

"Is your dad a good guy?" I suddenly asked, surprising even myself. "A good dad? Like does he spend time with you and take you places? He put food on the table and send you to school?"

She nodded. "Yeah."

"There are a lot of people out there whose dad's don't do any of that, or wouldn't give a shit about getting their junkie daughter home, so when you get there, try and go easy on the guy," I said, as if I really believed she was going home and not heading back to the male drugged-out-version of the Olsen Twins.

Maybe I did believe it. There was only one way to find out.

She smoothed her hair out of her eyes. "Maybe you're Dr. Phil after all," she said, before disappearing under the shadows of the awning, heading toward the empty bus benches.

If she felt as bad as she looked, and she really was getting on that bus, then it was going to be one fuck-of-a-long bus ride to wherever it was she was going.

"Not fucking likely," I muttered as I pulled back onto the road, and as soon as I cleared the next block, I turned down the dirt road that used to act as the service entrance to the old motel. I parked in the back of the bus station which wasn't really a station at all, just a small brick building with a flat roof and a ticket window facing the street with a few scattered benches. The light overhead where Dre was sitting was flickering on and off, casting the grassy area in spastic shadows.

Shit, maybe she really was getting on that bus. And for a second, I was happy that the kid was going to be reunited with her father. I wasn't messing around when I told her that most people didn't have dad's that cared enough to give her an ultimatum like he did. I was about to pull back out when I saw the headlights of a bus pulling into the station. I'd just decided that I was going to wait for her to get on the bus before I headed to Coral Pines, when suddenly her feet stopped tapping and retracted back into the shadows.

Not like she stood up, not like she pulled them back.

Like she was being dragged.

I pulled my gun from my boot and got out of the car, shuffling to the side of the building, my eyes adjusting to focus in the dark, until I spotted Dre across the lot.

She was being dragged all right. By her hair, through the parking lot, toward the old motel where the neon sign was blinking between VACANCY and NO VACANCY. The man dragging her was almost as thin as she was, but you didn't have to be big to overpower someone as small as Dre. One of the motion lights clicked on and gave me a better view of Dre, whose black eyes were open, but glazed over and unfocused, she was foaming out of the side of her mouth.

"You shouldn't have left," the man muttered, pulling Dre up and over a parking curb, her legs scraping against the ground as he huffed and grunted through his exertion. "You think you can just leave me? You owe me Dre. Remember that. You can't just go home," he said, to a semi-conscious Dre who looked a million miles away. "If I can't go home, then you can't go home. I'm sorry, I…I'm sorry I did that to you," he said more quietly. "But I just gave you some of my new stash, so you should forgive me. It's good shit, the best, and I saved it just for you."

I crouched and ran through the shadows from the back of the bus station to the overhang of the motel. As much as I wanted to blow the motherfucker away just for dragging her, I had to wait, each second was like a decade with my hand already twitching against the trigger.

"I'm here, Dre. Conner is going to take good care of you like this from now on. I promise. You'll see. You just can't try and leave again because we are having such a great time and you'll ruin everything!" he yelled. "But that's what you do! You ruin things!"

This was Conner? The one she'd wanted me to keep alive?

He took a deep breath, fixing the awkward smile back onto his face. He wiped his forehead with the back of his ratty sleeve before hauling Dre up from underneath her arms, his hands against her tits so he could lift her awkwardly up over the curb. He opened the door of one of the rooms. "I mean, I'm so sorry, Dre." Conner sniffled. "I mean, I think even though you were mad, that you really did like what we did to you. I think they were good screams. When Eric get's back…" Conner's voice faded abruptly as he kicked the door shut. The *9* marking the room number fell off one of its nails, becoming a swaying *6* before clambering to the sidewalk.

Maybe it was his words. Maybe it was the way he treated her, like he owned her. Maybe it was that this was the guy she'd wanted me to save, but all I knew was that I was going in.

Fake promises be damned.

What happened next played out like a violent video game, a halo of blur around the edges of my vision as I advanced on the motel room. The gun in my outstretched hands in front of me as I kicked open the door. Conner was crouched low on the floor over Dre, who was lying on her stomach, face down on the faded blue shag carpet. Her shorts down over her naked ass while the dirtbag fisted his little pecker in his hand. The slam of the door against the wall had Conner looking up with surprise, his reaction delayed by whatever shit was running through his veins. "Who the fuck are you? Get the fuck out…" he said, before zoning in on my gun. "What are you gonna…?" Conner started to ask, his face paling and his bloodshot eyes widening. "Wait, I know who you are…"

"Good, introductions can be so boring and all," I said. "You know," I scratched my head with the barrel of my gun, "junkies like you give drugs a bad name. You're the very reason some of my favorite party enhancers will never be available and marked down at a discount on the shelves of my local neighborhood Wal-Mart at good-ole-American, made-in-China prices." I aimed my gun at his chest. "Move away from her or I will end you right fucking here." Conner stood up with his shoulders hunched forward, his softening little pecker hanging out of his zipper as he raised his hands and did as I commanded, stepping back from Dre. I spotted the open bathroom door. "Back, through there. Stand in the shower."

"Please. Please don't shoot me," he begged as he shuffled backward. I spared a glance at Dre, kneeling down I made sure she was breathing. She was. I flipped her onto her back and turned her head to the side so she wouldn't choke on her own vomit if she started puking again. I followed Conner into the tiny bathroom where he tripped over the rim of the tub, landing on his ass in the shower, pulling down the beige plastic curtain over the top of him. "I'll do anything. Anything," he said, glancing at my crotch.

"Dude, have some fucking self respect," I said. "Unless that's your thing. You a gay man, Conner?"

He shook his head, his lower lip trembled.

"Listen, I respect anyone's choice to fuck the way they want to fuck and fuck who they want to fuck, but since you're telling me that you're a straight dude, then you've seriously just sank to the very last rung on the junkie ladder my friend, which in case you haven't guessed it, is offering to suck another dudes cock."

"I've just…I've got a problem," he said, his feet dangling over the edge of the tub.

"Yeah, you fucking do." Noticing a fingerprint on my gun, I huffed some air onto it and buffed it off on the rolled up cuff of my shirt.

"I just need help. I promise, I'm really not a bad guy…" he stammered.

I rolled my eyes. "Conner, stop your babbling. I believe you, buddy," I said, using my most reassuring voice. I crouched down so our eyes were level. Instant relief filled Conners eyes.

"You…you do? You believe me?" His hope at getting out of that bathroom alive was downright fucking tangible.

I nodded. "Absolutely, I do." I leaned over and pinched his cheek hard. He flinched but smiled awkwardly. "I think you're just a confused kid who made some big BIG mistakes." I turned my gun so it wasn't facing him. Conner's eyes nervously followed my every move. I stood up and leaned my hip against the sink, crossing my legs at the ankles. I turned the faucet on and let it run for a second or two before turning it off again. Wiping the grunge off the mirror with my closed fist, I gave my reflection a once over and straightened my bow tie.

"Thank you! Thank you!" Conner stammered, attempting to sit up in the tub. "I'm really a good person. This junk's got me all fucked up. Makes me do stupid shit. Man, I'm so glad you're not gonna shoot me in the fucking head."

"Don't be silly, Conner. I don't shoot people in the head. You know how much blood and gunk gets sprayed around when you go all gangsta willy-nilly and start shooting people in the head? Let me ask you something, Conner, you ever see a watermelon explode?"

"Uh, what I meant was. I mean. Just thank you for not killing me."

"When did I say I wasn't going to kill you?" I straightened my posture, turned back to Conner, and raised my gun, aiming it straight at his chest. I watched the confusion pass through his eyes, followed by realization, and then fear.

"W...wa...wait!" Conner studdered. The sound of water bouncing off plastic caught my attention as he pissed himself on the fallen shower curtain.

"I really fucking hate it when that happens," I muttered, the scent of urine immediately unbearably strong in the tiny room and made my eyes water.

"No, please no!" he cried, holding out his hands in front of his face, even after I told him I wasn't going to shoot him in the head. It was almost like the fucker didn't trust me. "You said… you believed me. That…that you didn't think I was a bad guy!"

I let out a long breathy sigh, which turned into a yawn. Not because I was tired, but because Conner and the whole will-I-or-won't-I-kill-him situation was growing boring as fuck. "I don't think you're a bad guy at all." I cocked my gun. "But, unfortunately for you…" I squeezed the trigger three times, sending pops of bright red splattering across the dull beige shower tile. "I am."

CHAPTER SIX

PREPPY

SOMETIMES, WE AS HUMANS set out to do things with purpose and clarity. Other times, we carry the unconscious heroin addicted thief back to the very house where she'd helped steal your weed plants from, because the woman who lives there is a nurse.

Humans. Weird fucking animals we are.

I carried Dre in through the back door as quietly as I could. I'd wake Mirna shortly, but Dre wasn't showing any signs of overdose so there wasn't any rush. I carefully shifted the girl in my arms through the door of the guest bedroom, and that's when I noticed the scar on the side of her face, right in front of her ear. It was a faded pink color so it wasn't super old, and I wondered what could have happened to this girl to cause a scar like that.

I shuffled her into the bathroom and set her on the floor. I turned on the shower and propped her against the side of the tub.

The deja vu feeling that I knew the girl was overwhelming.

Maybe she was in porn?

No, because then I'd probably know her name. And bra size. And what her specialty was.

I lifted her shirt and the bruises I'd seen on the tower looked ten times worse under the harsh bathroom lighting. I knew first hand that addicts had a tendency to be bruised up. Either from the marks, from the needles, getting into fights, or just stumbling around. But these weren't those kinds of bruises. They weren't from a fight.

They were from a beating.

My eyes drifted down to the bruised and bloodied space between her legs that both thrilled and sickened me.

They were from a rape.

I swallowed hard and willed my cock to stand down. I tucked her panties into my back pocket for safe keeping and lifted her into the tub, turning the shower head on spray mode so I could wash the dirt and blood from her body.

I never gave a shit what twisted thing turned me on. Some people got off on the vulnerable, it was a thing, I googled it, but I never before in my life wished those oddities away before that very moment in that very bathroom.

And I had no fucking clue why.

I tried to concentrate on washing her, pausing the cloth occasionally to wipe the sweat from my forehead or palm my cock through my pants, but managed to finish washing her and carry her to the bed without coming in my pants.

I pulled the blanket over her and she stirred. Her legs fell open, revealing everything to me, and I groaned at the sight.

My cock pulsed. I licked my bottom lip at the thought of what she tasted like.

I needed to know.

Just one little lick and I'd go.

I crawled onto the mattress fully dressed, but slightly damp. I hovered over her and leaned down between her thighs. I inhaled deeply. She had the sweetest smelling pussy. My cock throbbed and my balls ached. I wanted to bottle that shit up and wear it.

Pussy perfume.

I pressed a closed mouth kiss over her small buttony clit before flattening my tongue and dragging it over her pussy opening. It was just supposed to be one little lick, but it had turned into a deep kiss. My tongue darted just beyond her pussy lips. A little more and a little more I took, pushing the tip of my tongue inside her tightness, holding in a groan when I could fully taste her on my tongue. Holy fucking shit. Good wasn't a word for how she tasted. Epic. Her pussy tasted EPIC.

I shamelessly dry humped the bed, my cock finding little of the friction I needed against the mattress.

I pulled back a little, feeling a bite of anger toward whichever of those fuckers had hurt her magical pussy, and hoped it was the one who was no longer breathing and being sent out to the swamp by Smoke and his clean up crew.

I gave her one last long kiss with my tongue, as if I could heal her with my mouth. I sat up on my knees and released my cock from my khakis, groaning at the sensation of it hot and heavy in my hand. I stared down at her spread thighs, her pussy glistening from where my mouth had just been, her taste still fresh on my tongue.

I imagined pounding into her with every inch of my cock. As I stroked from root to tip and back again, I wondered if she could take all of me or if I'd have to ease up on her and give her little by little.

Then I imagined what she would look like with my hands wrapped around her throat. What she'd sound like gagging on my cock.

I pumped harder, faster. I teased the tip of my cock and just as I felt like I was about to explode, another thought hit me. It was what sent me spiraling over the edge, my balls drawing up tighter than they ever have, and my spine damn near breaking when I came so fucking hard I thought I was going to fall off the fucking bed.

I'd imagined how she'd looked up on the water tower, right before she jumped. Battered and broken, yet free. There was something so sexual about the way she'd accepted death that turned me on something fierce.

I wanted to see her sad. Taste her tears. I wanted to know what she sounded like when she cried. In pain, in pleasure, in both. The thought of me being the one to make her cry was my undoing.

I sprayed long hot streams all over her stomach and thighs, the last spurt landing right over her spread pussy. I tried to catch my breath but when I opened my eyes, I grew instantly hard again when I found myself looking down at the most perfect fucking picture I'd just painted on her body with my cum.

Quicker than I'd gotten on the bed, I jumped the fuck off off. I quickly, yet reluctantly, wiped my cum from her stomach with a wash cloth, then I left the room in such a rush that I tripped over Mirna's pet pig in the hallway. Oscar grunted and oinked, and even in the darkness I saw the disapproving glare in his piggy eyes. "Fuck you, Oscar, don't be all judgey," I whispered. More grunting. "One more look like that and I'll tell Mirna how you like to dry hump her teddy bear collection during her afternoon nap." The oinking stopped and he backed away into the bathroom, where I'd set up the giant dog bed he slept on. I flashed him a smug winning look and flipped him off.

I headed out to the backyard where I could smoke some weed and get a grip on the weirdest fucking night of my life. I saved that girl twice in one night. I was exhausted. But hey, glass half full and all, I DID get to kill someone.

As I sat on the back step and packed my bow tie one-hitter, a thought entered my brain and started running on the days playback reel. I didn't know why the fuck it was there because it was telling me something I already knew. Answering a question I wasn't even fucking asking.

I can't keep you.

CHAPTER SEVEN

DRE

NIGHTMARES. AT LEAST, I thought they were nightmares. Night after night, day after day, they took hold on both my body and mind, delivering an endless kind of agony I never knew was possible. I was sure I'd died because the place I was existing in was pure fucking hell, reliving the very worst moments of my life over and over, never growing numb to the pain.

The sounds haunted me first. Twisting metal. Breaking glass. Screaming.

The smells came next. Cedar trees and burning plastic.

Then it was like watching a slow motion video of myself. I'm outside of my body, watching myself standing in the pouring rain. Water, streaked with red, ran down my face, my arms, and off the tips of my fingers onto the pavement. I was staring at something, but when I turned around to see what I'm staring at, the scene shifts.

The sounds turned to evil laughter. Grunting. The slap of skin. The tearing pain.

The smell became musty mold, sweat, and uncirculated air. The video was now of Eric and Conner standing over me, blood, that dank motel room. More grunting as they took turns with me. Laughing when I cried. Louder and louder, until I realized I wasn't dead.

The sound was real.

Someone was grunting over me.

A deep nasally rumble that grew louder and louder until the noise was pressed directly up against my ear, and I felt whatever it was vibrating against my cheek. Cold and wet.

Wet?

What the fuck?

Sitting up with a start I looked around, but there was no one there. I automatically winced as I prepared for the onslaught of my withdrawals, but they never came. There was a slight pounding behind my eyes, but nothing like the stomach twisting, near death, morning after experience I was expecting.

Something moved next to the bed and I came face to face with the source of the grunting.

Well, face to snout.

Wedged between the small space between the bed and the wall was a good sized pig, larger than most dogs. His black and white markings resembled a dairy cow. It rested its head on the bed by my leg, and I could swear the fucker was smiling at me. Its snout was wet and glistening as he sniffed around the bed, probably trying to figure out who the fuck I was. I covered my bare thigh with the blanket so he would stop wetting it with his piggy grossness.

"Don't think you're special. Oscar's a flirt. He does this with all the ladies," a familiar voice said, and my gaze snapped from the pig at my side to the man leaning against the doorframe, his arms crossed over his chest, his legs crossed at the ankles casually, comfortably. His cocky smirk sent shivers up my spine and made my heart race.

"How am I here? Why?" I asked, wracking my brain for a reason. The last thing I remembered was waiting for my bus and then...and then I had no idea.

"Simple. I brought you here." Preppy's white shirt was perfectly pressed, the sleeves rolled up just above his elbows. He wore a pink bow tie with some kind of design, although I couldn't make it out, but whatever it was, his suspenders matched. He was a contrast of tattoos and class. Like hipster meets teacher. A combination that worked for him, but had me questioning who the fuck he really was and what he wanted with me.

I pulled the covers over my bare chest and noticed the sSrawberry Shortcake pattern on the sheets. A quick glance around the small room confirmed where I was.

My childhood room, back at Mirna's.

"Mirna!" I shouted, forgetting about the sheet and sitting up on my knees in the bed. "Where is she?" I demanded, "Did you hurt her? This wasn't her fault. She didn't do anything!"

He smiled and ran his thumb over his bottom lip. I followed his gaze down to my naked chest. I needed answers more than I needed to cover up. He outwardly ogled me, and if he thought that I'd cower or grow uncomfortable under his inspection, then he'd thought wrong. Instead of grabbing for the sheet again or crossing my arms over my chest, I defiantly placed my hands on my hips.

"You're welcome for saving you twice in one night by the way."

"I wasn't thanking you," I spat. "And what do you mean twice?"

Just then Mirna's white hair appeared in the doorway. She placed a hand on Preppy's shoulder and he stepped aside. Relief flooded me. She was alive and appeared unhurt. My first instinct was to run to her and throw myself into a hug, but I remembered how she was when I saw her last and didn't want to scare her by tossing my battered naked body into her arms, when she didn't even know who I was.

No longer needing to prove my point to Preppy, I reached for the sheet and wrapped it around my body. "Hi," I said with a small wave, clutching the sheet to my chest. Mirna crossed the room, slowly walking over to the bed with her mouth agape. There was something different about her than the day before. More focused. I cautiously reintroduced myself. "I don't know if you remember me from yesterday, but my name is…"

"Andrea." Mirna said, cutting me off. She scooped me off the bed like I was still an infant, cradling me in her arms and burying her face in my neck. "I know who you are, my sweet girl. Oh, thank Jesus. My Andrea is home," she sobbed, her tears warm on my cheek.

She recognized me.

That's when my own tears started to flow. And for that moment, Conner, Eric, or even the man still standing in the doorway didn't matter. The sheet had fallen back to the bed and I again was naked. Wrapped up in Mirna's loving arms like a newborn, surrounded in her superhero like protection. Safe and sound from a life I never wanted to go back to.

There would be no baptism into death. I wanted to live. And there, in my grandmother's arms, I was reborn.

Preppy cleared his throat and our spell was broken.

"Samuel go get my robe please. It's hanging on the back of

my door." Mirna set me down on the bed and sat down next to me, keeping my hand tightly in hers. Her eyes were wet and puffy, just as I imagined mine were. Preppy left and came back seconds later, chucking the robe at me. I quickly covered up, tying the sash around my waist. Mirna tentatively touched her fingertips to my cheek, as if she still couldn't believe I was real. "Samuel," she said, turning back to Preppy. "This is my granddaughter. This is my Andrea. My girl's finally come home."

I leaned into her hand and we both sighed.

I'd always hated being close to people. Never cared to be touched or to hold hands. But my grandmother had always been different. Maybe it was that she was older. Maybe I liked the way her wrinkled skin felt wise and safe.

"Well isn't this a lucky coincidence?" Preppy barked, running a hand through his hair and stepping fully into the room until he was only a few inches away, towering over us as he looked down, his lips twisted in confusion.

"Yes," Mirna said. "What's wrong, Samuel?"

"What's wrong?" Preppy asked, his eyes locking on to mine. Suddenly, I realized that this reunion with my grandmother was going to be short lived. He was going to tell her about the roll I played in destroying her plants, and any hopes I'd had to reconnect with my grandmother would be left in that room when I was thrown out. Preppy paused and glanced between us. "Nothing's wrong," he said, his mood lightening. "I knew you looked familiar, should have known from the six million pictures of you hanging around here." He turned to Mirna. "But she looks a bit different now, doesn't she?" he asked her, like he was setting up a joke for the punchline.

"Yes, she does," Mirna said, taking in my appearance. "Did I do this?" she asked Preppy, pointing to an IV drip next to the bed that I hadn't even realized was there. I raised my hand where tape residue and a bruise from the needle was still on the back of it.

"That's the reason why you're not in a world of hurt right now," Preppy said to me, before answering Mirna. "Yep, you did this, you fixed her up good, like you always fix everyone up good," Preppy said, his kindness toward Mirna taking me off guard. I didn't know what to make of this person. His every word, his every move was as contradictory as his clothes and tattoos. "When I found her in rough shape last week, I brought her here. Never thought she was your granddaughter though, that's just a happy accident."

"Last week!" I exclaimed. Mirna's gasp mirrored my own. "I've been here for a week?"

"Yeah, Mirna gave you some night-night juice and pumped you full of some vitamin concoction that had you snoring worse than Oscar," Preppy said, bending down to pat the pig I'd forgotten all about. "Kept you from feeling the worst of it."

"You've been here for an entire week and I'm only just seeing you now," Mirna said to me. She turned to Preppy, "A week is the longest I've…" she started to say before stopping and putting on a brave face, straightening her posture and wiping at her eyes. "It's okay, it's fine. You're here now, and that's all that really matters."

"Yes," I agreed, wanting so badly for that to be true.

"I'm going to step into the kitchen and leave you girls alone to catch up for a minute," Preppy announced. He bent over and kissed Mirna on the top of the head, and instinctually I flinched.

Preppy chuckled and left the room.

I really wanted to ask Mirna what her arrangement was with him, the plants, all of it, but not knowing the situation, I didn't want to bring up anything that might accidentally upset her.

"Tell me you're here to stay," Mirna said, eagerly awaiting my answer.

That's when I realized that staying wasn't a choice. I had nowhere else to go. "My dad. He thought I was coming home. He was probably waiting for me at the bus station." My heart hurt, and my body again felt sick when I imagined the look on his face when I didn't get off that bus.

"We will call him, dear. I'm sure we can talk to him and tell him…"

"No," I said, shaking my head. "We can't. That was my last chance. If I wasn't on that bus…" I couldn't finish. I didn't want to say out loud that my dad was no longer my family.

"Let's get you sorted out first, and then we'll worry about everything else later," Mirna said, again reassuring me when it was me who should've been reassuring her. But that was Mirna. "Just tell me you're staying."

Preppy answered for me, popping his head back in and unhooking a pink leash from a small rack on the wall. "If she's smart like you, Mirna, she'll be sticking around for a while." He winked and disappeared again with the cow-colored, dog-sized, pig grunting after him down the hall.

His words were disguised as a polite invitation, but I knew what they really were.

A warning.

When Mirna and I were finally alone I turned back to her, prepared to launch into a million questions when she yawned.

Her eyelids were heavy. "I think you and I have some catching up to do, my dear," she said, rubbing her temples. "The only cost of rent here is your honesty. I expect that you'll tell me everything." She turned my hand over and ran her fingertips up the raised scars on my arm, inspecting my shame. "And I do mean everything."

"Yes, ma'am."

Mirna patted my hand. "It seems things have changed quite a bit for the both of us, haven't they?"

I glanced at the wall that separated us from him, like I could see him through it, and wondered what game he was playing at. "Yes, it seems they have."

CHAPTER EIGHT

PREPPY

D URING THE DAYS that Dre was comatose I poured myself into work, determined to have two more Granny Grow-houses set up by the end of summer, which was going to be hard, considering the amount of work each one took and I had no one around to help me. Work was all I did.

Well, and I watched some porn.

And then there was that wee bit of blow I did.

While watching porn.

And the smidge of weed I smoked.

With that waitress from Presto's who takes it up the ass like it's her fucking job.

I motherfucking digress.

While Dre went through her withdrawals as a vegetable, I checked in on Mirna like usual. She did manage to have a few moments of clarity, but most of the time she was back to thinking she was in her twenties and waiting for her husband to get home from the war.

During one of her clearer times she talked about Dre, and it was obvious that she adored her granddaughter, smiling and laughing while telling me stories of her devilish childhood, where apparently Dre had spent a lot of time breaking shit. There was even love in her voice when Mirna told me that she'd received cancelled checks back from the bank in the mail to the tune of $1,700. All made out to cash. All forged. She'd closed the account, but it wasn't until Dre showed up that she knew who was behind it.

I wasn't exactly in a place to reprimand someone for their life choices, but ripping off her own grandmother made me so pissed, I was surprised that when Dre woke up that I hadn't immediately grabbed her by the throat and pushed her out the door.

Shit, if Mirna hadn't come in and been with it, I just might have.

I made a mental note to look into getting a trustee set up for Mirna's finances so there was no chance of anyone ripping her off while her condition continued to get worse. Fuck, she shouldn't even be living on her own anymore.

"Why didn't I get on that bus?" Dre asked from behind me. I turned to find her standing next to the table, her hands fighting with the sash of the robe that swallowed her small frame in billowing white cotton. Her long black hair was wild around her face. Her deep-brown eyes burned holes into me as she waited for me to answer.

I turned my attention back to the stove where I'd burnt yet another pancake. "Motherfucker." I tossed it into the trash bin and started over again, pouring a ladle of batter onto the hot pan. "Seriously, is this making pancake business some sort of holy magic? Do I need a wand and a Harry Potter spell?" I grumbled. "Maybe there is something wrong with this stove." I adjusted the heat setting and again read the side of the box of mix to make sure I didn't do something to it that somehow made the magical pancakes flammable, almost instantly burning. "Where's Mirna?" I asked, ignoring her question and flipping my newest attempt which landed on the side of the pan, batter splattered on the burner with a hiss.

"She's laying down for a while."

"Excellent!" I exclaimed, pointing at her with my spatula. "It will give us a chance to have a little breakfast, a little chat, and a little bit of threatening. Doesn't that sound nice?" I pulled out a chair from the little dinette table and made a grand sweeping gesture with the spatula for her to take a seat.

Her eyes darted to the chair, but she didn't move.

"Sit down," I repeated. "It's not a suggestion," I warned. She came forward, hesitantly. I pushed in her chair with a little more force than necessary, pushing her legs out from under her, causing her ass to plunk down hard onto the seat. I leaned over her shoulder. "Now was that so hard?" I whispered against her neck. Her shiver gave me a deep satisfaction I felt all the way down to my toes.

I made my way back over to the stove and looked over the sad stack of six, lopsided, half-burnt pancakes that looked more like the sad survivors of the pancake apocalypse than breakfast.

I took off Mirna's "Kiss the cock" apron that used to say "Kiss the cook" but with one little swipe of a permanent marker, I had made it way more my speed. I set the stack of zombie pancakes in the center of the table and took the seat next to Dre. I placed a small stack in front of her and the rest I took for myself, pouring syrup over both plates. "Okay, now we can talk," I announced, taking a bite of what tasted more like baking powder and foot than fluffy delicious pancakes.

"You want to know why you're here? Right? You're here

because one of your buddies decided to dose you full of heroin, drag you across the parking lot into some shit bag motel, and play hide the salami while you drooled all over yourself." I turned my head and opened my mouth to mimic her facial expression.

She winced.

"Truth fucking hurts, Doc." I shoved more of the awful tasting pancakes in my mouth, and I knew exactly what they tasted like. Failure.

"Doc?" She wrinkled her nose.

"Yeah, like Dr. Dre. Remember? Or do we have to start at the beginning again? Okay, lets do this. I'm Samuel Clearwater, my friends call me Preppy."

"I remember," she said, her pancakes remaining untouched.

"Anyway, saw what was happening and went and…retrieved you. Brought you back to Mirna's 'cause she's a nurse. Even when she's a little out of it, she still remembers her training. Didn't know you were her granddaughter," I said, speaking with my mouth full. If I didn't hate wasting food so much I'd have spit it out, but instead I swallowed hard and chugged my orange juice.

"You could have just left me there," she pointed out.

"Yeah, I could of."

"Why didn't you?"

I stabbed my fork into another piece. I held it up and examined the food on my fork. I glanced up at Dre's doll-like eyes that were as black as her hair. "I have no fucking clue."

"Why didn't you take me to a hospital?"

"Hospitals tend to ask a fuck of a lot of questions when you bring in a girl who's doped up on H."

"Why would questions be a bad thing when you're the one who saved me."

"Because, Doc, questions lead to answers, and in this case, answers lead to bodies." She gasped.

"Shit." Her face paled.

"There's that realization I was waiting for. I was wondering when that would happen. Took you long enough. But I'll chalk up your slow reaction time to just waking up from a semi-coma. Remind me not to challenge you to a game of sudoku anytime soon."

"Bodies?" she asked slowly, standing from the chair. I grabbed her by the shoulder and pushed her back down.

"Well, body," I corrected, "Just one, though. But you know, bodies sound better for dramatic effect and all that." I took another gulp of juice. "So let's just say that one of them is no longer available for shooting up in a dark alley, beating you to a pulp, stealing my plants, or long walks on the beach." I set down the glass. "In the words of the oh-so-wise Taylor Swift," I leaned across the table. "'Never ever. Like ever.'"

"Eric? You killed Eric?" she asked, and I knew she was confirming that it wasn't Conner, whatever false sense of loyalty she had toward the motherfucker was really pissing me off. Until I realized that was exactly who I'd killed.

Oops.

"Yep, it was totally Eric," I agreed, shoving more pancakes into my mouth and trying not to gag.

"So he's…"

"Dead? Oh yeah. Very dead."

There was nothing readable about Dre's expression, which was disappointing. I was looking forward to seeing her afraid.

After all, I'd just admitted that I'd made good on my threat and had killed someone she knew, albeit not the person she'd wanted me to kill, but she didn't know that.

To-ma-to, to-mah-to.

She was more out of it than I'd originally thought. "You killed him," she said, slowly. It wasn't a question, it was a statement.

I held up my index finger and my thumb, slowly closing the gap between them, peering over at Dre through the tiny slit that remained. "Little bit."

"I don't think you can kill someone a little bit."

"Oh, well then, a lot a bit. I killed him a lot of bit."

CHAPTER NINE

DRE

"**S**O ARE YOU going to tell me now why you insisted on giving the Conner guy a pass?" Preppy asked, as I followed him into the back room of the house, where it looked like he was halfway done resetting up his operation. The other half of the room was still in shambles. Without being asked, I grabbed one end of the plastic tube he'd picked up and climbed the ladder on the other end of the room, setting it on the hooks. My robe fell open in the process and I quickly tied it back together, hoping Preppy hadn't noticed.

No such luck.

"What, it's not like I haven't seen you in your birthday suit already," he said. "I did witness your solo nudist party when we met, remember?"

"Guess it doesn't really matter," I admitted. "I look like shit anyway." I wasn't saying that I was ugly. I was never a girl who lacked confidence. I was just stating the truth. Heroin isn't exactly the drug of choice of models and pageant queens, and for good reason.

"Yep, you do look like shit," Preppy agreed, smirking like he was keeping a secret only he knew.

"Then why do you keep looking?" I blurted, remembering

his hardness against me on the water tower.

"Cause, maybe that's what I'm into," Preppy said, like it was nothing.

"Girls who look like shit?" I asked, not believing him in the least.

"Hey, some people like chicks with dicks, some people like to fuck dressed like Smurfs and painted blue. I look because you intrigue me, but I don't have a fucking clue why. I'll keep you posted, though."

"Are you always this brutally honest?" I asked. Finding his statements both offensive and oddly refreshing.

"Yes and no. There are times when a lie can't be helped. Honesty is a fickle bitch like that. I don't believe in filtering, though. When you start walking on egg shells around people, that's when you know that those are people you don't need to be around. Life's too short to pretend to be anyone else. I'm just me. I say what I want to fucking say. I do what I want to do and I don't fucking apologize for it."

"I think I need to adapt that kind of honesty," I admitted. "But I have a lot of apologizing to do."

"You can start your trip down honesty lane by answering my original question and telling me why you gave that guy a pass."

I sighed. "For now let's just say that Conner is someone I hurt." Oscar came running into the room, rubbing his head on Preppy's leg. "The kind of hurt that can't be fixed. That can't be brushed over with an apology or flowers."

"Must have been something real bad," he pointed out, leaning down to pat Oscar on the head.

I looked to the floor then back up at Preppy. "It was," I admitted, and like every time I thought about the event that lead up to me making bad decision, after bad decision, it was like I was bringing it back to life so it could stab me in the gut over and over again.

My thoughts quickly turned to using. The immediate euphoria. The relief from the guilt. Preppy cleared his throat.

I opened my eyes, although I didn't remember closing them, to find that Preppy was now standing next to the open window, lighting a joint and leaning against the ledge. "Where'd you go there, Doc?" He took a long drag. "You thinking about hooking up with your lover? I'll let you know that it's probably not a good idea. That bitch heroin gets around and in the end, the break up is brutal, but she'll never leave you, so you either dump her on the side of the road like a hitchhiking hooker, or you stay and she'll kill you."

"I know," I said, needing to desperately change the subject. The thought of using too fresh on my mind. "This said by the man smoking weed."

He held up the joint. "This shit won't kill me. You don't see anyone smoking weed and going on a murdering spree, or hitting a bong and going out to start a fight at a bar. Besides, weed's not a drug. It's a plant." He picked up one of the glass bowls and shook the leaves.

"Is that what you tell yourself so you can tell people you don't do drugs and actually believe it?"

"Fuck no, wouldn't work anyway. I do bowlfuls of blow when I feel so inclined," Preppy said, taking another long drag and blowing it out the open window. "There's a big difference between a party, and a problem, though, especially one that ends with an attempted high-dive off the water tower."

"Point made." I'd never needed a change in subject so badly in my entire life.

"Who's been taking care of Mirna?" I asked. I felt stupid that I had to ask this question from a virtual stranger.

"I look in on her and so do a few of her friends and a few people from the church. She's on a waiting list for one of those assisted living places in Sarasota. They could have an opening tomorrow or in six moths. They're not sure." He looked like he was thinking about something before adding, "It's getting worse and worse, you know. She'll have a few days where she's out of it, but then suddenly she'll go for weeks being just fine. This past week she was in and out, but mostly out. That's the most I've seen her like that for," Preppy said, confirming what I'd already thought but hoped wasn't the case.

My heart sank. "Can I have time with her? I don't deserve it. But once you tell her that I was one of the people involved in stealing from her, she won't want anything to do with me, but I just want some time." I paused. "Before it's too late."

"You can have time," he said, eyeing me warily. "But I'll want some stuff in return."

"What...what do you want? I'll do anything," I asked, immediately regretting my choice of words. His amber eyes reminded me of rich dark honey as he stalked across the room. He stopped in front of me and startled me by untying the sash at my waist and pushing my robe over my shoulders onto the floor. I felt the heat of his stare as he raked over my naked body, lingering on the place between my legs. I pressed my thighs together and he laughed, biting his bottom lip.

I shivered, unsure if it was because of his intense inspection of my body, the air conditioning vent kicking on above me, or from good old fashioned fear. "Just tell me what you want," I said, wanting whatever this was to be over.

Preppy chuckled. "Take care of Mirna. Help me fix this shit, too." The glimmer of something evil sparked in his eyes, the same spark I'd seen on the water tower, and that time my shiver was because of fear. "And get yourself together. I need you to not look like the kid from the *Jungle Book* for what I have planned for you. Think less Courtney Love, more Jennifer Love."

"Haha, funny. Is that all?" I asked, wary that I was getting off too easy and trying to avoid the need to knee him in the balls.

"Oh, that's far from all, Doc." He stepped back, and I bent down to gather my robe, covering myself quickly. "Far, far from all."

Preppy went back to his work, and I left to find some real clothes. I was looking through drawers in my old room, hoping to find a t-shirt or pair of sweat pants, when Preppy appeared in the doorway.

"I forgot to tell you something," he said, punching numbers on his cell phone and placing it back in his pocket.

"What?" I asked, pulling out an old boy band t-shirt from the bottom drawer.

"You remember what I said about using H again, right?"

"You mean when you said that either I break up with her or she kills me?"

"Yeah, well I forgot to add one tiny little thing," he said.

"What's that?"

He stepped into the room and lowered his voice. He stood over me, leaning on the dresser. His shoulder brushed mine. "If you do use again, make sure you're far, far away from Logan's Beach and Mirna first, because if you fuck her over again, I'll kill you long before the heroin will." He smiled happily, as if he hadn't just threatened my life. "Mmmm...kay?"

CHAPTER TEN

DRE

PREPPY HAD TOLD ME to take care of Mirna, but he still stopped by every afternoon to check on her before locking himself in the grow-room for at least an hour. Either, he wasn't up for conversation, he was purposely avoiding me, or he hadn't figured out exactly what it was I could do for him, in return for giving me time with Mirna. But then, I realized that wasn't it at all. He wasn't avoiding me.

He was toying with me.

Every time he was near, he found a way to touch me and make me jump. He winked at me when Mirna wasn't looking. He undressed me with his eyes every chance he got, and he'd laughed when I squirmed uncomfortably under his gaze.

But talk?

Nope. Not to me, anyway. Although, with Mirna he happily chatted and made small talk, like he wasn't there to torture me with his presence, the lingering favor looming between us.

I should have been happy he didn't want to talk to me but was oddly annoyed by the whole thing.

I'd been out of society for too long. That must have been the real problem. My need for social interaction was probably the very thing that led me to believe that the psycho killer growing pot in my grandmother's guest bedroom was someone I could have a conversation with, when in actuality I should've just taken a page from Preppy's book and start talking to the damn pig.

Mirna and I had used our gift of time wisely, and over the course of several days we unburdened our souls and told each other everything there was to tell. Well, everything that wouldn't have her tossing me out just yet. She hadn't slipped back into her alternate state of confusion, and I was beginning to think I overreacted or made it more than what it was in my head.

Mirna now knew all the events that led up to me being back in Logan's Beach, and she told me about being diagnosed with Alzheimer's the year before.

There was a lot of crying. A lot of laughing. A lot of looking at old photos, and a lot of grieving over my mother, even though she'd passed when I was just a baby.

Mirna also told me that she wished she were still close to my father, but they were both in a lot of pain when my mother passed and it was too hard on both of them to continue being a family without her.

Physically, I was feeling better, although I was still fidgety. The want for heroin was there, but it no longer had its hands on the wheel. Thanks in large part to Mirna and her keeping me good and unconscious during the worst of my withdrawals, and the vitamin shots she insisted on giving me twice a day.

"There you are!" Mirna exclaimed as she came out on the front porch where I was fixing the third step, setting it back in place. The top had warped and arched under the harsh Florida weather, and the nail had rusted out from the bottom, making it the perfect height to trip anyone coming to the house. A few well placed screws would keep Mirna from tripping over it like she had the day before, but luckily I'd been there to soften her fall. I'd also rehung a cabinet that had fallen from its hinge in the kitchen. Tacked the falling gutter back to the side of the house. And then tackled the pesky step. Mirna had told me that keeping busy was good for a healing soul, and I think she was right because I'd began to feel lighter. Like my old self again. She clapped her hands together. "I was just looking for you."

"What's up?" I asked. Mirna followed me as I carried my grandfather's old fashioned toolbox over to the one car garage, placing it safely back onto his old workbench like he was going to be home any minute and would be mad if I misplaced it. He might have been long gone, but his anger over his tools being mistreated lived on.

"You've always been good at fixing things," Mirna pointed out. "And speaking of fixing, you seem to be doing much better."

"I've only been up and about for a week," I pointed out. "But thank you. Dad taught me how to do this." I held up the drill.

"I know he did," Mirna said, glancing around the garage at my grandfather's half finished projects. She never even pretended like she wanted to get rid of them. "Did I ever tell you that when your dad married your mom that it was your grandfather who showed him how to be handy around the house?"

"Really?" I asked. It sounded pretty unbelievable. There wasn't anything my dad couldn't fix.

"Yep, your Grandpa Rick wanted to make sure your dad could take care of your mom, so he taught him everything he knew." She smiled as she recalled the memory which was obviously a happy one. "When Becky first brought him home, your poor dad couldn't so much hang a picture on the wall."

Of course I believed her, but the entire scenario was pretty hard to imagine when my dad's workshop at home looked like something out of a handyman's dream. My heart fell when the memory of my dad fixing the roof of my dollhouse came to mind. It was then he taught me how to use an electric drill. He'd always been my hero. There was nothing he couldn't fix.

Until me.

"I wrote him a letter you know," Mirna said, breaking the spell.

"I appreciate that Mirna, I do. But you know Dad, once he decides something, he doesn't change his mind. Maybe someday I'll reach out and try again, but it's probably for the best that I leave him be for a while. I'll try to fix things when I can back up my promises with some good old fashioned proof."

I wondered what my father would think when he read her letter, or if he'd even read it. My money was in the middle, him reading a few sentences, realizing what the letter was about, and tearing it into a million pieces. I'm sure he wouldn't be putting that one in my old blue shoe box, where I'd kept all Mirna's letters in my room back home.

But you don't have a room back home anymore.

One step at a time, I reminded myself.

"If nothing else, at least my letter will let him know that you're safe."

If you're not on that bus, then we're not family anymore... My fathers voice rang in my ears.

"Now, come, come!" Mirna said, the excitement back in her voice and the spring back in her step. She grabbed my hand. "I want to show you something." She was practically bouncing as she dragged me back up the newly fixed porch steps.

Mirna didn't do casual. Her mental state might have been slipping, but her style was as strong and bold as ever. Looking very much like an older pinup, her white hair fell right above her shoulders in large barrel curls. Heavy bangs with a slight bend on the ends stopped right above her perfectly symmetrical eyebrows. Her eyes were always lined, but just on the top with a dramatic cat-flare on the ends, making her already large gray eyes appear doll-like. Dramatic Red was the color of lipstick she wore daily, regardless if that day only consisted of gardening at home.

Many times in my early teens I tried to copy Mirna's style. Many times I ended up looking like a child who colored outside the lines, where as Mirna was a walking piece of fine art.

Mirna yanked me down the hallway to her bedroom. Much to my surprise, she led me to her closet and opened the double bi-fold doors in dramatic fashion. "Ta da!" she exclaimed, taking a step back and waving me forward.

Mirna's closet itself wasn't anything special. A small walk-in with a few rows of shelving. It was what was IN IT that had me gasping and holding my hand over my rapidly beating heart. Dresses. Not just ANY dresses, but dresses from an era long forgotten. Halter necks with flared skirts. Floppy hats. Platform heels that had me falling to my knees in the center of the room.

"Where did you get all this?" I asked, clutching the most perfect high-heeled, black, platform pump to my chest. It was complete with a large white bow across the rounded toe and the heel. Holy hell, the HEEL was incredible. Laced up from the bottom like a corset. "I don't remember you ever wearing any of this."

"Some things I've worn only once. Some I've never worn at

all."

"Why?" If I had a closet with these dresses in it I'd make every occasion a special occasion. Laundry. Getting gas. Watering the marijuana.

"Your grandfather loved it when I dressed up, so I wore something nice for him every single day. When he was overseas he sent back some of the european styles that were trendy at the time. Sometimes as many as a dress a week. When he came home I was pregnant almost immediately." When I gave her a knowing smile, she simply stated, "There was no television in the bedrooms back then, dear," before continuing on. "I still planned to wear them, even three babies later, even after you were born, but when Rick died I couldn't bare the thought of putting them on ever again. However, I also couldn't bring myself to throw them away." Mirna laughed. "Of course, there is no way on God's green earth that these would ever fit me now." She sighed and plucked a hanger from the rack, shoving it into my hands over the perfect shoe I was still cradling.

"I'm sure you could get them tailored. Or better yet, I've always wanted to learn to sew, maybe I could do it for you," I suggested.

Mirna shook her head. "No, my sweet girl."

"No? Why not?"

"Your grandfather risked his life to buy me dresses and ship them back to me. Feels wrong to change them now. Besides, I think they'll fit YOU just fine."

I pointed at my chest. "Me? Mirna, I can't." I held out the beautiful shoe, and the hanger, for her to take them back. "No. I don't deserve this. Any of it."

She ducked around my outstretched arms. "Andrea, I don't

know how much time I've got left, or how long the lights are going to stay on upstairs before they burn out for good, so I'm going to tell you this now while I still have a chance." She placed a loving hand on my shoulder and squeezed. "You are a good soul. A good person. We all make mistakes. Lord knows I've made my fair share of them in my day. You have to forgive yourself. LOVE yourself. And for Christ's sake girl, you have to grow some balls. Men want a strong woman who can give it as good as they get it." She winked.

I groaned. "We're not talking about clothes anymore are we?"

"Nope. Just remember. Lady in the street and a wild cat between the sheets."

"Mirna, seriously. I think my ears are bleeding," I said with a laugh. "Besides, men are the last thing on my mind."

"What about Samuel?"

"Mirna!" I said, "You want to hook me up with the guy who grows pot in your guest bedroom?"

Mirna shook her head. "No, my dear. But I wouldn't mind if you considered the man who's a lot more than he seems on the outside."

"What exactly is your arrangement with him anyway?" I asked.

"That's not my place to say, dear. That's part of our arrangement. But I will say that you shouldn't be so quick to judge. You only really know someone's true heart when they really want to show it to you." She squeezed my arm. "He reminds me a lot of your grandfather, you know. I just hope one day you find someone who takes as good care of you as he did of me." She plucked another dress from the rack and held it up to me. I hooked my fingers into the top of the hanger so she could take a step back to appraise her selection.

"I'm sorry," I said, Mirna waved off my apology. "I just want to make sure that you know what you're getting into with him and that…"

"That's not something you need to worry about. Samuel is a good man."

Who killed Eric. "Are you sure about that?"

"Because he's shown me his heart." Mirna sighed. "Good people can do bad things, Andrea. You've told me yourself that you've done some bad things. That doesn't make you a bad person, right?"

"I'm not entirely sure it doesn't," I admitted.

"Oh phooey, you're not at all a bad person. You've got a big heart, and your grandmother's eyes." She opened her arms wide. "And with that you can conquer the world." She added the dress, plus some high waisted shorts and some crop tops to the pile in my arms.

My hands started to shake, aftershocks is what Mirna had called them. I dropped the clothes, and when I bent over to pick them up, she shot me a concerned glance. "It's getting better," I reassured her. "I swear."

"You need to go to a proper rehab facility so you can make sure this sticks. Professionals can get you through this better than I can. I'm a nurse, not a counselor. I know there's more to this addiction thing than the physical part."

"Proper rehabs cost a lot of money, and the government funded ones are more like jails or mental institutions," I said, trying to gather the clothes back up. "And besides, I can't go because you wouldn't be there."

"Then here is what we are going to do," Mirna said, again clapping her hands together. She took the clothes from my hands and walked out of the closet, setting them gently on her bed. "We are going to get you all fixed up proper, and then we are going to go outside and meditate in the fresh air."

"We're gonna what?"

She put her hands on her hips. "Don't tell me you've never meditated."

"Not...recently?" I squeaked. "Meditation wasn't really something I'd manage to squeeze in with all the shooting up and letting people down I had going on."

She rolled her eyes and returned her attention to sorting the clothes. "Your sense of humor can be as off-colored as Samuel's. I have a book you can read, and I will teach you. The world is a tricky place. Meditation is a vehicle that will help you navigate through it better, you know, avoid the potholes."

"In my case that vehicle better be a tank," I said, bumping her with my hip and dropping a precious shoe in the process.

"Don't you sass me young lady. I may be losing my marbles, but I'm still your grandmother."

"Yes, Ma'am," I said, with a shoe salute.

"Meditation is like...stretching after a run, but instead of your muscles, you're stretching your soul," she said, pinching my cheek like I was a child, making me yelp. "Now, you're going to take these clothes as my gift to you and you're going wear them. For ME. For as long as you love them. And right now, we are going to play a little dress up," she ordered. "Is that clear?"

"Yes, if that's what you want. But...why?"

"Because, dear, I've been waiting what seems like a hundred years to see these dresses on a real person again, and what seems like even longer to see what they'd look like on you. These belong to you now."

My heart squeezed in my chest. There was no arguing after she said that, even if I'd wanted to argue. Which I didn't. Not even a little.

An hour later Mirna spun me around to look in the mirror, and I gasped at the reflection before me.

The green and white sundress Mirna had picked out for me had thick halter straps that snapped around my neck, and a squared neckline that pushed up my breasts and gave them a fuller, more rounded, look. The middle was corset-tight and accentuated my waist, while the bottom flared out slightly in an a-line, ending right above my knees.

And, of course, I was wearing THE platform, black pumps with bows. "Who says love at first sight doesn't exist?" I whispered as I turned my foot from side to side, to better admire my new lovers.

Mirna set my long hair in a style I wasn't sure I could ever duplicate myself. One side was tucked behind my ear, and the other side fell in cascading waves over my shoulder. Decadent Red was now on my lips as well, while black liner on my eyelids topped off the look. For an every day look, I'd prefer a more muted version of the pinup in the mirror. But, right then, I couldn't even believe that girl was me.

For the exception of the scars on my arms, the junkie was nowhere to be seen.

"I look… I look like…" I stammered. *A human being.*

Mirna stood behind me. Her eyes glazed over. Pride filled her expression as she joined me at appraising my reflection. She rested her chin on my shoulder and smiled. "A woman," she said. "You look like a beautiful young woman. Which is exactly what you are."

I angled my head so I was resting against my grandmother. "I was going to say that I looked like you." I turned around and held up my arms. But it had only been two weeks since Preppy brought me to Mirna's, so even though most of the scabs were gone, the scars, both new and old remained. "Except for these."

She cupped my cheek. "We all have scars, my dear." She grabbed my wrists and lifted them to her lips, pressing a kiss to each of my forearms, patting them when she was done, as if the matter was now settled and Grandma's kisses solved all. And in a way it did. "Some of us on our arms." She pressed her palm over my chest. "Some of us in our hearts."

Some of us on our face. I absently ran my hand down the jagged raised scar on the side of my face.

Mirna walked over to her dresser and grabbed a silver frame from one of the many crowding the surface. She looked from the picture to me. "Well, what do you know about that." She handed me the frame.

The picture was of Mirna wearing a very similar style dress, except she topped hers off with gloves and a white floppy hat. She was arm and arm with my grandfather as they smiled for the camera. My mother was young, standing at her feet holding a lunch box. Her blond hair and light features favoring my grandpa, while I was a spitting image of Mirna. I held up the picture frame and looked again at the similarity between a younger version of my grandmother and myself. It was like nothing I'd ever seen before. "You do look like me."

"It's like we were twins separated by...decades," I said as Mirna nodded and chuckled, taking the frame back from my hands and setting it back, exactly in the position it was before on the dresser, tweaking it left, then back right a few times before she was satisfied. "Mirna, exactly how old are you?" I asked, trying to do the math in my head.

Mirna sighed. "Four hundred and seventy seven," she dead-panned. We both broke out into a fit of laughter so hard I thought I'd rip the seam of my dress. When we reined it in she looked me over again, a look of satisfaction on her face, her lips twisted up into a beautiful smile. "You look breathtaking, my dear. Your grandfather would have loved to see you in that dress. You know, it was the very first one he sent me," she said, waving off the emotion that had her temporarily at a loss for words. Her eyes watered and reddened, but she stood strong. Sniffling and straightening her back like she was daring the tears to come back.

"Mirna..." I started, reaching out to comfort her, but she stepped back and waved me off.

"Oh, don't be silly. I'm just an old woman, which makes me just about as emotional as a pregnant woman," she said with a sniffle, lightening the mood. "Samuel is going to love the way you look," Mirna lamented.

"What does he have to do with anything?"

Mirna quirked up a white eyebrow. "Didn't I tell you, dear? He's the reason I remembered to give you the clothes I'd kept for you. They're for your new job."

"My new job?"

"Yes, your new job working for Samuel." Mirna took one last look at my reflection and sighed with satisfaction. "It will be good for you. Give you a chance to clean your soul, start fresh."

"Is that even possible?" I asked, but I wasn't sure if I was directing the question at her or me. "What if the stains are too great?"

"No, you'll see. It's the stains that make us human," she said, and with that I fell a little more in love with my grandmother. "I tell you what, you go water the plants while I go and find that meditation book for you. When you're done, you can meet me in the backyard. We are going to have our first meditation session, and you are going to focus on the future and what you want out of life. We're gonna clean that soul you think is so dirty."

Mirna could try her damnedest, but I was pretty sure that a soul as dirty as mine would need a lot more than some new clothes and meditation to be cleaned. I pointed to the stranger in the mirror, a girl who looked like she ALMOST had it together, I muttered, "At this point, bleach might be a lot more useful than a book on meditation."

Maybe I'd ask Preppy about how to clean a dirty soul, because although Mirna had enlightened me as to what he'd done for her, she hadn't seen his eyes up on the tower.

None of it made sense. A guy who helps old ladies in their time of need couldn't possibly be the monster I thought he was. Maybe he didn't have a dirty soul, after all.

Maybe it was just me.

LATER THAT DAY, Mirna gave me my first lesson in meditation. I was sans shoes in the grass, but every so often I'd open one eye and check to make sure they were still on the deck where I'd placed them, lovingly, in the shade.

We sat Indian style across from one another in front of her flower box, our hands on our knees, palms up. Oscar grunted around the backyard. Both Mirna and even Preppy seemed to care for the animal, so much that I'd yet to ask why the heck my grandma had an enormous pig as a pet, but when he nudged my shoulder with his dirty wet nose I shooed him away, pretending to be annoyed at his interruption. I placed my index finger across my lips and Oscar got the message, trotting back up to the fence and sniffing under the gate, like a dog smelling for other animals. Were all pigs that smart?

I took a deep breath and attempted to rein in my thoughts and concentrate on the meditation. Mirna's chin was tipped up toward the warm sun, her famous cat eyes were simple perfection in the bright light that made her wrinkled, yet flawless skin, look as if it were glowing.

Unable to help myself, I snuck another peek toward the back deck to check on my new shoes for the hundredth time, and for a second my heart stopped beating. One was missing. I was about to bolt to the neighbors house to call 911, or the fire department, or poison control, or the president himself, when a shadow fell over me. I shrieked and tried to jump away, but he grabbed me by the arm and held me down. I fell sideways across the intruders lap, all the while Mirna remained in her meditative pose.

The intruder laughed. And I glanced up to find Preppy holding the missing heel over my head.

"Nice shoes, wanna fuck?"

CHAPTER ELEVEN

PREPPY

WHAT IN THE fuck was she wearing? Her dress was hugging her tiny waist and pushing out her tits, and suddenly it was as if I'd gone deaf because all I could hear was the blood rushing to my cock. Everything in me was shouting at me to bend this girl over and fuck her until we both fucking DIED.

I didn't care that Mirna was sitting right there. I didn't care if the Pope and the Dalai Lama were watching on the sidelines with Jesus himself. All I wanted was to see that glossy red lipstick smeared all over my motherfucking cock.

Rein it in shit-head. I scolded myself, you have more important things to be focusing on, other than her tits.

But those tits…

It looked like Mirna had roped in another one. I was glad too because as much as I liked her, when she'd insisted on teaching me to meditate I mostly played a recap of *American Ninja Warrior* in my head until she told me we were done. Her current pupil had been shocked and amazed by how good I fucking looked and had fainted across my lap, unable to get a grip on her swoon.

OR, I'd scared the shit out of her and she fell onto me.

It was definitely one of those two things.

Regardless of how it happened, what stood out most to me was where her hand had landed when she tried bracing her fall. I'm not gonna lie, it was actually kind of cute when she blushed after realizing it was right over my cock.

I admit that when I first saw her sitting there in that dress, with her hair all done up in shiny waves, and her lips painted bright red like the star in my favorite fifties porn, Rosie the Rectal Riveter, I didn't even recognize her. My first thought was very caveman. Must put cock in pussy. But when I realized it was Dre behind that get up, it added a whole new layer of intrigue to the girl who already had me intrigued.

I had tasted that pussy, and I liked it.

No, I fucking loved it.

A fucking lot.

I wasn't going to tell her that, but omitting information isn't the same as lying. I wasn't a liar. I would even go as far as to say that my strength had always been in my amazing ability to be completely and brutally honest. Of course, the gift of honesty was in addition to my sense of humor, wit, charm, character, striking good looks, phenomenal—yet classic—sense of style, and last but not least, the tribungus slab of man meat dangling between my legs.

But I motherfucking digress.

So when my phone vibrated, and I found myself listening wordlessly to some guy, who I quickly realized was Dre's dad, launch right into an apology for turning his back on his only daughter, followed by a plea for me to tell him where she was so he could bring her home, my first instinct was to tell him the truth and take all the glory and credit for being the individual who successfully reunited the estranged father and daughter duo.

After all, that's what Dre had said she really wanted more than anything, to go home to her dad. And there I was—holding the capability to do just that in the palm of my hand.

Dre plucked the fuck-me heel I'd taken off the porch from my hands. I was about to tell her that it was her dad on the line when I remembered the reason I came over in the first place. I froze with my mouth open and the phone to my ear, like Zack Morris had paused time, *Saved by the Bell* style.

If Dre went home, then I'd lose my one last chance at getting Max back for King. I mean, it's not like I hadn't done anything for this chick, I reminded myself. I'd let her live and all.

Motherfucking generous is what I really was.

King had saved my life, several times over. Shit, he's the one who gave me a life to begin with. And as far as heterosexual life-mate's go, I'd won the fucking lottery when he showed up on the playground that day and knocked the fuck out of a bully, who I may or may not still have egged his mother's house on a regular basis.

I walked off and waited until I was at the back gate, far enough away, where I was positive there was no chance of Mirna or Dre hearing me before I uttered a single word. "Who the fuck is this?" I asked, inserting as much annoyance as I could into the question, interrupting Dre's dad, who hadn't stopped talking, his fast speaking made it almost impossible to make out his frantic plea.

"This is Adnet Capulet. Who...who is this?" he echoed my question, anger and confusion replacing the desperation in his voice.

"Adnet, I'm the guy who picked up the ringing phone," I sang, "And you're the guy who called and made the phone ring.

Go ahead, ask me another one. This is fun." I bent over to pick a sand spur from the side of my boot. One of its unholy devil points stuck into the side of my finger. I shook my hand several times before it finally detached from my flesh, flicking it into the brush where it would undoubtedly find another unsuspecting victim to torment, with their ability to cause just enough of an injury to throb mildly in the middle of the night and wake you out of a deep sleep. Those little cunt-seeds were so annoying, they were like the plant version of *Dancing with the Stars.*

Again, I motherfucking digress.

I sucked the drop of blood that pooled on my fingertip. "My daughter," Adnet started, "her name is Andrea. She called me a while ago from this number. I want to talk to her. Please, if you know where she is. I made a mistake. I just want her to come ho…"

"Let me stop you right there, man. You sound like a nice guy, maybe a little high strung, but nice. Unfortunately, I have no fucking clue who you're talking about. The payphone I was about to use started ringing, so I answered it. Sorry, man. Might want to look into getting her on the side of a milk carton, STAT."

I hit END and was about to shove my phone back into my pocket, when it vibrated again. "Listen," I snapped, the irritation in my voice no longer fake. "I told you that this is a public phone and I don't know where the fuck your daughter is but, I'm trying to make a call here…" Bears booming laughter interrupted me.

"Oh, it's just you," I said, and if a voice could snarl, that's how I spoke to Bear. Snarly. I held the phone under my chin and picked at the tall grass that had grown over from the connecting field and wrapped its way around the gate latch.

"Whatever's going on, you got it handled?" Bear asked. "Or is this gonna end with me finding half-burnt body parts in the fire pit?"

"Jesus Christ. You put one fucking body in the fire pit and suddenly it's a big thing."

Bear must have been somewhere near a highway because I could hear passing cars and honking truck horns. "Seriously Prep, everything okay down there? We just hit the Mississippi state line and stopped to gas up. Figured I'd check in while I could." Motorcycles roared to life. Men shouted to one another over the noise of their engines.

"You don't need to check in on me. I'm not a toddler," I pointed out, sucking on the tip of my finger, where blood had pooled into a drop from the sand spur from hell.

"Yet, I can hear you pouting through the fucking phone."

"I just got a lot of shit going on," I muttered, pulling the gate closed behind me. *Understatement of the fucking year.*

"Like someone calling and asking the whereabouts of their daughter? Yeah, I'd call that a lot of shit. What did you get yourself into now?"

"No, it's not like that," I argued. "It's just some guy looking for a girl who doesn't want to be found," I lied, and if lying to Dre's dad didn't feel quite right, lying to Bear felt like I was coming down with a case of something I didn't know how to cure.

Guilt. A disease I wanted no part of.

Telling Bear about Dre. Or my new plan to have her help me with the growhouses while I took care of the Max situation, was off the table, at least until I knew it could actually work.

Getting him or Grace's hopes up, only to crush them if it all turned to shit, wasn't something part of my plan.

Again, omitting isn't technically lying.

"You sure you're not just shacking up with some chick, Prep?" Bear asked, laughing at his own ridiculous statement.

"Yeah man, forgot to tell you. Me and Sylvia got something going on. It's real serious, too. I think she might be pregnant," I shot back, rolling my eyes like he could see me.

Sylvia was a one of the other founding Granny Growhouses.

She was also ninety-two-years-old.

"But seriously, Prep, this girl, the one who don't want to be found. She in some sort of trouble?" Bear asked, raising his voice above the background noise, which had only grown louder.

"She's Mirna's granddaughter. She showed up out of the blue, all strung out and shit, and beat the fuck up. She's gonna stick around with Mirna and watch over my plants until the facility in Sarasota has a spot." Which was sort of the truth.

I took the file out of the back waistband of my pants.

Bear was now yelling above the noise, when he asked, "You fuck her?"

"No."

Although, I think about it. Although, I've gotten a taste.

"She's fucking strung out, has the shakes all the time. One eye is like way bigger than the other and she's got this huge hump on her back. I mean, I'm not against it, but it's not like she's first on my to-do list."

"Does she live in a bell tower, Prep? 'Cause your girl sounds a lot like Quasi-Moto."

"She's not my girl. Don't try to do that thing you do where you make this into something it's not. I just made the shitty mistake of letting her use my phone, and now I gotta get a new fucking number so her daddy stops fucking calling me wanting to know where his junkie daughter is."

Suddenly, I was very grateful that Mirna didn't have a phone. If I were him, and just as desperate to get in touch with her, Mirna's house would've been one of the first places I'd call.

"Whatever, Prep." Bear laughed, like he knew something I didn't, which pissed me off and was probably the reason why the need to defend myself had me spewing my next line of bullshit.

When did life get so fucking complicated?

"You guys are looking for new BBB's over at the clubhouse, right? Didn't Puerto Rican Fury and Robert Dinero leave recently?" I asked.

"Yeah, Jessica and Ivette left. Jessica is knocked up and marrying some dentist, and Ivette disappeared into thin air, but you know how that goes. We could definitely use a few new faces around the MC." Bear ignored my use of two of the nicknames I'd come up with for his club girls over the years. I'd named the one girl, Puerto Rican Fury, for good reason, she was in fact Puerto Rican, and always pissed off about something. The other I called, Robert Dinero, because like the actor, she could pass for either Spanish, Italian, or Jewish. However, her smokin' body was a lot more banging than her male counterpart. "Why? You think the junkie girl would want to give club life a go?" Bear asked, before telling me to "hang on a sec." He didn't bother covering the phone when he barked orders out to his men. I held my phone away from my head, in order to avoid permanent damage to my ear drum, as he yelled out for everyone to be ready to ride out in five. "Okay, so yeah. The girl," he said when he came back on the line.

"She's got Daddy issues and a drug problem to boot. Think this one was actually born to be a BBB," I pointed out.

"All right, bring her over to the clubhouse when we get back." There was a commotion in the background, rowdy voices and crunching metal. "Fuck me. Gotta head out, natives are getting restless." Engines revved and became so loud I either A) didn't hear him say "bye" or B) Bear hadn't said it at all and just hung up on me. Knowing Bear and his stellar manners, plus the fact that the guy was allergic to shirts and all that went along with that, I went with B.

Dre jerked her head down when I turned back around, like she hadn't been caught staring at me.

She might have been the one to try to kill herself, but I was the one on borrowed time. It was time to show Dre what else I needed out of this deal of ours, before she found out the truth about her dad and Conner.

It wasn't like she gave a fuck about her life, I told myself.

So why should I give a fuck about ruining it?

CHAPTER TWELVE

PREPPY

"SAMUEL, WOULD YOU like to join us?" Mirna asked, without opening her eyes.

Dre shot me a narrow glare.

"Sorry for the interruption," I said, sitting down on the grass, "Mirna, but your granddaughter looks like a younger, less attractive version of yourself, so I couldn't help but stare."

"Samuel!" Mirna scolded, but I could hear the hint of laughter in her words.

I closed my eyes and took a deep breath, feeling Dre's stare on me.

Her body heat.

A hand touched my shoulder and my eyes shot open. I looked up to find Mirna hovering above me. "Samuel?"

"Yeah?" I turned to get another look of Dre's tits, but she wasn't there. The sun wasn't either. It had been early afternoon when I'd gotten there.

Hadn't it?

"Did I fall asleep?"

Mirna laughed. "You've been in the same position for three hours. I don't think you were asleep."

Mirna helped me up off the grass by my elbow, and I tucked

her arm under mine as we walked back to the house. "I believe they call it transcendence," she said, extending her hand toward the sky and making the shape of a rainbow, like she was talking about something out of this world.

"Transcendence?" I asked, scratching my beard. "Oh yeah, I know what that is."

"You do?" Mirna asked.

"Yeah, I had it once after a bad batch of shrooms, had to get my stomach pumped."

"You're a smart ass just like my Andrea," she said, pinching my arm. I took a seat at the table while she opened the oven and used her finger to check on one of the cookies on the tray. The kitchen filled with the sweet smell of chocolate that made my mouth water. "Don't let the state you found her in fool you, my granddaughter is a lot more than just a screwed up kid." She pulled a photo album from the shelf above the table and tossed it onto the counter in front of me. "Look for yourself."

I opened it up and discovered that it was full of report cards. All with the name Andrea Capulet.

"Wait, Capulet? Like Romeo and Juliet shit?"

Mirna smiled and nodded. "Yup, exactly like that. When Becky married Andrea's dad, Rick and I thought it was quite endearing, not realizing it would end almost as tragically."

Although the colors of the report cards, as well as the teachers names and the subjects changed, the letters of the grades remained the same on every page of every card.

All A's. Not a single B. Not even an A-.

"Wow. My report card was a lot more diverse than this one," I said, flipping pages.

"Diverse?"

"There was a lot more of the alphabet used." I closed the album and slid it back across the desk.

"Yet, you are the smartest young man I know." She opened the cabinet and took out her favorite teacups.

"Awe shucks, Mirna," I said, dramatically batting my eyelashes. She swatted me with an oven mitt.

"But if those grades don't show you how smart she is, this should," she said, lowering her voice to a whisper. She opened a drawer and pulled out a large envelope. She slid a thick stack of paper over to me.

"Why are we whispering?" I asked.

"She doesn't know that I know this. Look." It was pages upon pages of cancelled checks, stapled to reports. All the checks were made out to cash. A stamp over them read *FRAUD* in bold red.

"I assume that these are the ones she forged?" I asked.

"You would assume correctly."

"Forging signatures doesn't prove she's smart. It proves the opposite, actually," I pointed out.

"Samuel," she said, sliding the papers back to me. "She didn't just sign the checks. She MADE the checks. Security seals and all." And, although Mirna should be pissed that Dre ripped her off, there was no mistaking the pride in her voice.

I looked closer, ripping one out of its stapled hold and sure enough, security seal and all, watermarks, account code, it was a masterpiece. "Wow," I said, impressed.

"If you're not pissed, why don't you tell her that you know?" I asked.

"The same reason I haven't told her that I know she had a part in robbing your plants." She breathed deeply. "Because I'm losing my mind, Samuel, and I refuse to lose my granddaughter again before it's gone completely. There isn't enough time for anger or alienation. Not anymore."

"You know, if Grace hadn't already sort of adopted me as her own, I'd totally cheat on her with you," I said.

"Oh, no. Grace is one tough bird. She's been dealing with you boys for a long time, and I'm not sure I could have done half as good of a job as she has." Mirna checked on the cookies again, this time removing the tray and replacing it immediately with another uncooked batch. "Besides, I'm pretty sure she could kick my ass."

"Yeah, I don't want to fuck with Grace either," I said, reminding myself to call the cancer center when I left to check up on her.

"Why are you telling me this? Why is it important that I know that she's smart?" I asked.

Mirna grabbed my hand in hers. "Because I want you to know that I'm losing my mind. I'm not stupid. I know the way business works. I know the way your business works. She's around because you showed mercy."

"I wouldn't call it mercy, exactly," I said, although, I didn't know what I actually would call it. "She gets a pass because she's your granddaughter and that fucks with business on a different level. It's not a big deal."

"What did you do to the person who did that to her?" Mirna asked, her forwardness taking me off guard.

I sat back in the chair. "What do you think I did?"

"You forget that I'm a perceptive old bird. Been around the block or two myself," she paused and sighed. "From what she's told me, I think you saved my granddaughter and did what you had to do to protect your business and her…and I thank you for it. You didn't know she was my granddaughter when you did that and it is a big deal to me, even if it's not to you. The reason I need you to know how smart she is, is because I need you to know who you've given a second chance to." She nodded to the stack. "Look in the back."

I did what she said and realized what she had me looking at was two documents. A power of attorney and a last will and testament. Leaving every decision and every possession of Mirna's to me. "What is all this?" I asked.

"You've given me so much, Samuel. This is me giving you the only things in this world I have left to give. I'd give everything to my Andrea, but it's too much for her to handle right now on her own. There are some stipulations, but you don't have to decide on them now. Not right away, anyway. Those copies are for you. Take them. Look them over."

"Mirna, this isn't why I…"

"I know. I know," she said, opening the refrigerator. She cleared her throat, "Doesn't Andrea look beautiful? The dress she was wearing today. That was mine you know."

I stood up and rounded the counter planting a kiss on the top of her head. "She doesn't hold a candle to you."

She blushed and busied herself pulling plastic covered plates from the fridge and handing them to me. "Can you set these on the coffee table? The ladies from the church are on their way over for tea."

I did what she asked and was about to go find Dre when Mirna handed me a clear syringe. "Do me a favor, Samuel, and give Andrea her vitamin shot for me? I need to go freshen up."

"She can't do it herself? Insert joke about her already knowing how to use a needle?"

She frowned. "That's precisely why she SHOULDN'T be handling one."

"Okay, you're the boss, Mirna. One shot coming right up." I had an idea. "Where do I give her this?"

"Any muscle, dear. It's a bigger gauge then the one I've been using, so anything fleshy will work," Mirna answered, flitting about the kitchen with a knowing smile on her face. She wiped her hands on a towel and tossed it into the sink. She patted my cheek as she passed me and went into her room.

I didn't know what Mirna was up to, but I didn't have time to think about that or the now overflowing file weighing me down, in more ways than one.

I held up the needle and smiled. I had a motherfucking job to do. I pushed open Dre's door, without knocking. "Paging Dr. Clearwater."

CHAPTER THIRTEEN

DRE

"WHERE'S MIRNA? WHY isn't she giving this to me?" I asked. I'd been lying on my stomach on the bed, flipping through the brochure for the assisted living facility Mirna was on the waiting list for, when Preppy barged in. It looked like a nice place but it wasn't somewhere I thought she belonged.

Not yet, anyway.

"She's getting ready for some ladies from church to come over, so she asked me to do it. Now, come on. Time to strip. You need some music? Make sure you start slow. Teasing is key," he rambled.

"I don't have to be naked to get a shot," I argued.

"Well aren't you just a fun-sucker." Preppy held up the needle, smiling confidently. "Don't worry, Doc. I've seen like three episodes of *Grey's Anatomy,* so I'm practically a licensed doctor. Now, be a good girl and bend over, show Dr. Preppy that ass."

"Mirna gives it to me in my arm."

"This is a new one. Different needle gauge or some shit," Preppy answered.

Reluctantly, I did what I was told, but only because I wasn't feeling all that well and I knew the shot would make me feel better, regardless of where it was shot into.

I bent over the bed and hiked up my dress, dramatically. "You're a horrible junkie and an even worse stripper," Preppy commented. I felt his heat as he approached the bed. My lower spine tingled as his legs brushed up against mine. I held my breath and started counting in my head, when the sudden need to push back against him surged through me. My nipples tightened, and I was glad he couldn't see my face because I was sure I was flushed. "Why does it have to be administered this way again?" I managed to choke out.

Preppy chuckled. "It doesn't."

Before I could push off the bed, he pulled the cotton of my panties over into my crack and plunged the needle deep into my skin. It burned, but only for a second. When he pulled it back out I went to get up, but he pushed me back down onto the mattress. "Got to make sure it goes into the muscle," he said, his voice a deep rasp as he expertly massaged the injection site with his fingers in a circular motion that had me moaning inwardly, and even more mad at him all at the same time.

My breath caught in my throat when his hand started roaming over my ass cheek, slowly tracing circles on my skin, nowhere near the injection site, heading further and further toward the place between my legs that was suddenly tingling with awareness. "I love those fucking heels," he said, his voice lower than I'd heard it before. Raspy.

Fucking heels. That could be taken so many different ways, but my mind couldn't process any of them because his fingertips grazed the trim of my panties, just as Mirna walked in the room. I jumped up, covering myself again with the skirt of my dress. Where I was frantic and looked guilty, although I didn't know what I felt guilty about, technically nothing happened, Preppy smiled and plopped down on the bed, bouncing on the mattress like a little kid.

"It's not what it looks..." I started, but stopped when I noticed there was something different about Mirna, about the way she kept glancing from me to Preppy with her eyebrows drawn tightly together. The doorbell rang. "Samuel, when did you get here?" she asked. "And who's your friend?"

★ ★ ★

PREPPY

MIRNA SAT WITH three ladies from her church in the living room. I stood behind Dre, who leaned up against the wall of the hallway just out of sight, listening to Mirna tell stories about her past as if they'd happened that very day and not decades before. With each passing minute Dre's shoulders fell further and further as she watched her grandmother, in the grips of her dementia, introduce herself to women she'd known for decades.

"Why does she always remember you?" Dre asked, without turning around, a hint of jealousy in her voice.

I scratched my head. "Fuck if I know. When she's like this she'll forget an entire week's worth of our interactions, people she's known for fifty years, but she usually knows who I am. Your guess as to why is as good as mine."

I came up to stand next to her, she brushed her hair from her eyes. "Come on," I said, grabbing her hand. "I want to show you something."

"But," Dre glanced back at Mirna.

"Ladies," I announced. "We are going to step out for a moment. You cool here for a bit?"

Hilda, a woman bigger than Bear, turned around and nodded. "Take your time. We'll be fine."

"Hear that? They're having a lovely tea." I grabbed Dre by the hand and pulled her out the front door to my car. I opened the door and gestured for her to get in, but she stood there staring at the passenger seat. "It's not going to bite you," I informed her.

Dre looked back at the house. "What if she needs me in there?"

"She'll be fine. Get in, I have something I want to run by you."

She shook her head. "I can't."

I was growing irritated. "Don't pretend like you're the doting grandchild now. You kind of missed the boat on that one."

"Pretending?" she said, pointing at herself. "You're the one who puts on this fucking act so you can get elderly women to do your bidding. You're the one who's pretending. Not me!"

"Careful," I warned. "You don't know a god damn thing about me, Doc."

She crossed her arms over her chest. "I know you've got Mirna fooled into thinking that you're some great guy she thinks is her savior, when you're just using her to get what you want."

"Guess you got me all figured out then," I said sarcastically, rounding the car to the passenger side and closing the space between us. "Now get in the fucking car."

She took a step back, as if she had to prove her defiance. "Does she really even know who you really are? And I'm not talking about the guy who makes her laugh and listens to her stories, I'm talking about the other side. The side I caught a glimpse of on the water tower."

"You don't know shit about me, and now you've just proved you don't know shit about Mirna, either. Your grandmother's got dementia, she's not fucking stupid."

"Does she know you killed Eric?" she asked, staring me right in the eyes, challenging me. Fully expecting me to tell her no.

I put on my shit eating grin. "She sure as fuck does, Doc."

"Bullshit." She put her hands on her hips.

"Mirna not only knows, but it's been Granny approved, Doc. I have a feeling I could have taken out half of Logan's Beach and she wouldn't give a flying fuck as long as you were still alive, because unlike you, Mirna knows what family and loyalty is all about." Dre's eyes widened at my admission and her shoulders fell, but just for a second, before straightening again and assuming a defensive stance. "Wait, never mind, you do know something about loyalty if you count giving that shit-bag Conner a pass for some obscure reason you refuse to share. I mean, I could say you were loyal to heroin too, but here you are two whole weeks sober, one conscious, so I guess you fucked that bitch over, too."

Dre drilled me with her eyes, her plump red lips a hard line. We were standing so close I could feel the warmth radiating off of her skin and smell her light flowery shampoo. "And you know so much about being loyal?"

"Fuck of a lot more than you do."

"I don't have to listen to this!" Dre shook her head. "You don't know a fucking thing about me!" She turned back toward the house. I grabbed her wrist, digging my fingers into her flesh.

"You're not going anywhere," I said, spinning her back

around.

"Let me go!" she said, arching her back and planting her feet for leverage, but it didn't matter how hard she was pulling, I wasn't letting go.

"No! Not until you tell me why you're being such a fucking cunt right now."

"Fuck you!" she spat, her face reddening as she pulled harder and harder.

"Always a possibility, Doc, but stay on the fucking subject."

"You want to know why I'm being this way?" She stopped struggling and stepped up to me, so close she had to crane her neck. "You!" She jabbed her finger into my chest. "My problem is you! You grow your plants and make your confusing sarcastic remarks and think that because you've got this unique beautiful charm thing going on, and you smile a lot, that you can do whatever you want. Well, newsflash. You can't. You got the old ladies fooled but you aren't fooling me. You don't own me." She tried to wedge her fingers under my arms to loosen my grip.

I pulled her against me, roughly. I leaned down, my lips at her ear. "That's where you're wrong."

"You think you're better than me," she said. "But you're not." Her voice took on a serious tone. She lowered her head and stepped back. I allowed her the space but didn't let go of her. "When you've gotten what you want from Mirna, you're gonna pack up and go without another thought for her or her feelings, and she's going to worry about you when you're gone. She's going to hurt when she doesn't know where you are." Her step faltered. She dropped to the ground and looked up at me with glassy eyes. "And it's all because you caused her a kind of hurt that you can't take back." I released her wrist, and she rubbed the red mark on her arm and looked to the ground, shuffling her feet.

"I don't think we're talking about me anymore, Doc."

"I don't know what the fuck I'm talking about anymore," she said, running her fingertips over the marks on her arms. "I did things. More than leading Conner and Eric here, knowing what they...what *we* intended to do. To my dad. To Mirna. I can't erase what I put her through, but that's all I think about." She bit her bottom lip and shoved her hands into the pockets of her skirt, bringing the neckline down lower, exposing more of the top, rounded part of her tits.

"You're talking about the checks?"

Her lips parted in surprise.

"Mirna told me," I said, before she could ask. I purposely left out the other part Mirna had told me she knew. "I told you, she's not stupid."

Dre dropped her head to her knees. "What the fuck am I going to do now? I have to apologize." She looked up to the house where Mirna was sitting by the window laughing with her friends, that glazed look easily noticeable even from the front-yard. "But I can't."

"Doc?"

She spun her head around and quirked a brow at my out-stretched hand. I held the file in the other. "I think I know how we can help each other."

"How?"

I crouched down in front of her. I tapped her on the fore-head with the file. I flashed her my best reassuring smile. "First..." I brushed a curl off her shoulder, and she stiffened at my touch, "...you need to get your ass in the motherfucking car."

CHAPTER FOURTEEN

PREPPY

"**W**HY IS IT so important to you to get King's kid out of the system?" Dre asked after I explained to her the situation with King and Max.

"Because he can't do shit while he's locked up, and because he's not just my best friend. He's family, and family fights for one another," I said, turning onto a dirt road. It was pitch-black out, and where we were at there was no such thing as streetlights. Thankfully, I could find the place we were going drunk, high, and naked.

And I have.

"You make it sound so simple," she said.

"It is. When I was a kid there wasn't anyone around to fight for me. My mom was a piece of shit and so was every single man who found their way into her fucking bedroom." I shrugged like it was nothing, but I'd rather take a spike to the eye than talk about my childhood, but I needed Dre to understand the situation. "She was a junkie, a loser, a deplorable human being. I learned from her. She was a walking 'what not to do' guide to family."

"A junkie loser," Dre repeated softly, looking out the window.

"Ain't no other way to describe her because that's exactly what she was," I said.

"Go on."

I tapped my fingers to the beat of the Kane Brown song playing on the radio. "Mommy dearest was the worst of the worst, and not like she outright beat me or anything, but she wasn't exactly a member of the PTA. There was this one guy that she married, well maybe she married him, she called him my stepdad, but I don't remember a wedding or anything. Anyway, his name was Tim, he was the worst of them all."

"What did he do?" she asked, hesitantly, no longer looking out the window but at me.

I cracked my jaw as I recalled the day King walked in and found Tim rutting into me like a fucking barnyard pig. "He beat the living shit out of me...amongst other things."

I heard her sharp intake of breath.

"Don't pity me." I glanced over at Dre, who was picking at her nails and looking down at her lap. "I sure as shit don't. Listen, life isn't about what happened to you in your past, it's about where you are now and where you're going. Onward and upward and all that jazz."

"That's very poetic," Dre said. "But I'm surprised you moved on without seeking justice or revenge."

I smirked. "Oh, I got revenge. That fucker is very VERY...let's just say what he is rhymes with, shed."

"How?" She shifted so she was sitting sideways. I leaned into her as well, until I was only inches from her face.

"That's not important," I said, not able to help my smile as I recalled a teenaged King taking that fucker out of this world, like the fucking trash he was.

"That's actually kind of extraordinary," Dre said after a long pause, her words taking me by surprise.

"Why do you say that?"

"Because, most people wouldn't be able to recover from something that crippling." And again, I didn't know if she was talking about me or herself.

I scoffed. "Nah, I just don't let what that cocksucker did dictate my life. If I do, then he wins. Besides, him and my mom made my life so fucking miserable that now I appreciate every damn good thing that comes my way, and even some of the bad. If it weren't for them, I wouldn't have recognized King as my brother that first day on the playground at school, or taken to Grace when she showed a kid wearing wrinkled pants a bit of kindness."

"WRINKLED pants?" Dre asked, dramatically opening her mouth in mock surprise, and my mind immediately went to something else she could do with those lips that could make her gasp.

Or gag.

I cleared my throat and looked away. "Yeah, now THAT would probably go down as the biggest tragedy of my childhood. By far."

Dre giggled, and the sound did something to suck the heaviness from the air like a vacuum.

I pulled in between two pine trees and killed the engine, leaving the radio on. I flipped off my headlights and the still waters of the Caloosahatchee appeared spread out in front of us. To the right was the causeway, its high back out of the water like the Loch Ness monster doing stretches. The shore, on the other side of the river, twinkled with lights from hotels and condos.

Occasionally, a set of headlights would appear from the other side and travel over the causeway like a slow moving shooting star over the beasts back.

"It's beautiful here," Dre said, leaning over the dashboard and looking out over the water. "I forgot how much I love it here. My summers here with Mirna were the best of my life."

"Me too," I admitted.

She sighed and sat back against the seat. "So you need to get Max out of the system. How exactly can I help with that?"

I picked the file up from my center console and set it on her lap. I leaned over to her with my chin resting just above her shoulder. I wet my thumb on my tongue when a few of the pages wanted to be assholes and stick together. When I got them separated I plucked the paper I needed out of the file and held it up, only to find Dre staring at my mouth when I handed it to her. "What?"

She put her hands on the seat and shifted like she couldn't get comfortable. "Nothing," she said, pointing down to the file again. "What is all this?"

"I'm going to need your talents if I'm going to make any of this work."

"Talents?" she asked, looking confused. "Did Mirna tell you I had some sort of talent? Because I think you might of caught her during one of her bad times. The only talent I have is sabotaging my own life." She tapped her index finger a few times against the seam of her lips. "Oh!" she exclaimed with a snap of her fingers. Leaning closer, she placed a hand on the side of her lips as if she were warding off lip readers. "When I was in kindergarten I ALWAYS colored inside the lines. Although, I'm sad to say I never pursued it professionally." She sighed deeply.

"One of my many many regrets in life."

I found myself smiling back at Dre, and it sure as shit wasn't as a result of her joke, because it wasn't nearly as funny as she seemed to think it was. But if smiles were infectious then Dre's was the plague of smiles.

Extremely contagious.

"Listen, Doc, I have no doubt that you were a coloring badass at one time. A Crayola savant, if you will. Unfortunately, that skill isn't really going to work in this particular situation," I said, nodding to the papers on her lap. "I need to create a paper trail so I look like an exceptional citizen in every way." I leaned back against the door. "Like Martha Stewart."

Dre lifted her head and scrunched up her nose. "Martha Stewart did time for insider trading."

I sat back up. "Then John Stewart, or Tony Stewart, or whichever Stewart looks like someone the state would want to give a kid to. Fuck, even Kristen Stewart would do," I said. "Although, I hear she's a lesbian now, which is awesome by the way, but if she lived here they might not give her a kid 'cause Florida's southern and very conservative," I said, repeating Grace's words.

"Well, we are in Florida, it doesn't get much southern then that," Dre said.

"Yeah," I agreed. "We're so southern that we're below the bible belt. We're like...the cock of the south." Dre laughed.

"Did you know that gay marriage isn't a thing here yet?" I asked.

"I actually did know that," Dre said, tilting her head to the side while she went over the papers. "Well, I *knew* that. I can't exactly say I'm up to date on current events just yet."

Normally, when I went off on a tangent, especially to someone who didn't know me very well, most people liked to call me out when I've veered off track and would try to and rein me back in. I was beginning to notice that Dre didn't do that. In fact, every time my brain steered me off course, she'd let me go with it until I found my way back around on my own.

It was…different.

"Long story short is that I need to be a model citizen, and the list in that file tells us what we are going to need to make that happen. Since I can't exactly prove a lot of that shit the legit way, I need your skills to create them." I got out of the car and she followed, file in hand. I leaned against the hood and lit a joint, inhaling the smoke along with the salty air. Dre's head was still in the papers as I continued, her bottom lip between her teeth. "At first, before Mirna told me what a diabolical genius you were with the forgery, I was going to get you a job at the clerks office and see what you could do to move things along. You know emails, files, signature stamps. Whatever might help," I explained. "But when she told me you created the check itself, watermark and all…I figured we could use that talent to make a big dent in that list a lot faster."

She didn't answer, instead her face twisted like she was in pain. She shifted sideways pulling up one of her knees and unknowingly exposing a strip of white panties between her legs before rearranging her dress. The memory of her smell, the taste of her on my tongue, flooded my senses and had me momentarily forgetting why I was there, because Dre's stunning-as-fuck pussy had shoved aside the red velvet rope and stolen the first spot in line at a club I desperately wanted to shove my cock inside.

If it was beautiful when it was battered, I couldn't imagine how perfect it looked pink, puffy, and wet with excitement.

"Okay, but how the hell does it fix this shit with Mirna?" she asked. I offered her the joint and she rolled her eyes.

"Tell me, Doc. What are your plans when the assisted living place has an opening and Mirna moves to Sarasota?" I asked, blowing smoke rings out into the night.

She shrugged. "I hadn't thought too much about it. I can't go back to my dad."

Actually, you could.

"Okay, let me be more direct. Where do you plan on living? Mirna's?"

"Maybe. If it's okay with her. I wouldn't make any assumptions, though. I'd have to ask her."

"See, that's where you're wrong. You can't stay at Mirna's when she moves."

She pushed off the hood and stood in front of me. Any closer and I could pull her between my legs. "I think we should leave that up to Mirna to decide."

"But it's not up to her."

She threw up her hands in frustration. "Then who is it up to?"

I grabbed the file and pulled out the warranty deed Mirna had given me earlier. "The big-dicked, well dressed motherfucker who owns the house, of course."

DRE

"YOU'VE GOT TO be fucking kidding me," I said, not believing what I was holding in my hand.

"Doc, I'm hurt. You know how very serious of a person I am," Preppy said with his hands over his heart.

"So you're saying if I do this, forge the documents you need, then what, you'll let me stay there when Mirna goes to Sarasota? That's blackmail."

"I know you're upset but there's no need to be racist."

"Seriously!" I said. "What, you want me to rent it from you?" I asked, shocked by what I was holding. I didn't give a damn about Mirna's possessions or her house, and I could understand why I wouldn't be the best choice to handle her affairs, but that didn't mean it still didn't sting.

"No, not like rent it from me." Preppy shook his head. "If this works and we get Max back, then the house is yours, free and clear. I'll sign it over to you and you'll never have to worry about not having anywhere to stay ever again. And before you jump to any conclusions, I didn't weasel the house from Mirna in some scam where I forced her to marry me or anything. I didn't even know she was transferring the title. She just sprung this on me today."

I was quiet for a moment. Glancing down at the paper, then out at the water again and again, without a single clear thought about what had just happened registering.

"If it helps any, your forgery skills are top notch. Where did you learn all that shit?"

"Wowed?" I asked at his strange compliment.

"Yeah and I've never really been WOWED before. Okay, maybe once, but it was during *American Ninja Warrior,* and that guy who won was an amputee and god damned war hero. You'd have to be made of fucking stone to speak during the commentators touching tribute while the camera zoomed in on his prosthetic leg and the star spangled banner played in the background."

Her face contorted like she was about to be sick. "It's not a wow at all. It's not something I'm proud of, one of many things."

I scoffed. "We've all done shit we're not proud of, but for most people that involves getting drunk and doing something fun that someone else disapproves of. Most people's 'shit their not proud of file' doesn't involve forging complicated documents, though. I mean, is forgery the new thing all the kids are doing? Maybe not, because if it were a new thing then there would for sure be a porn parody about it already and since I haven't come across anything titled *Teenaged Asian Forgers Take it Real Deep,* I don't think the forgery trend is going to be all the rage anytime soon."

"It was mostly Conner. He was always trying to literally print money. I just picked up a few things along the way," I admitted. "I'm going to pay her back every last cent, plus interest, you know," I said. "I know that's THE lie a lot of users tell themselves and others in order to follow through with whatever bad idea they had in mind, but I really am going to pay her back."

Preppy pushed off the hood. "I believe you," he said, with actual sincerity in his voice. "Think of how much faster you'll be able to do that when you don't gotta worry about a roof over your head." He held out his hand. "Deal?"

Preppy was right, as much as I hated to admit it. I took his hand. "Deal." When I tried to let go, he pulled me between his legs and wrapped his hands around my waist. "A handshake is so informal. We should seal this deal with a fuck. That sounds much more official don't you agree?"

I shook my head.

I pushed off his shoulders. "You know, sometimes I'm not sure when you're serious."

"Oh, well that's easy to figure out. I'm always sometimes joking in a way that's honest."

"Totally cleared that up."

"Glad I could help," Preppy said as we both got back in the car. He started the engine.

"I could go to prison for this you know," I stated, and although I intended for it to be an argument, I found myself smiling.

Preppy blew out a breath. "Minimum security, doesn't even count."

"I can't believe I just agreed to forge documents when I told myself I'd never do it again," I lamented.

Preppy put the car in reverse. "Don't think of it that way then."

"How would you have me think of it then?"

He wagged his eyebrows. "Think of it as coloring outside the lines."

CHAPTER FIFTEEN

DRE

"W HERE ARE THE SHOES? I thought we'd agreed that you'd wear the FUCK-ME heels?" he asked, when he saw me sitting on the rocker on the front porch in a pair of 50's style, denim, high-waisted cut off's with buttons on the front and a white 'wife-beater' style tank top that showed a small sliver of skin on my midsection. I'd opted for plain white Keds instead of my precious heels, which I seriously considered bubble wrapping for safe keeping.

"We didn't agree to anything of the sort." I stood up, and Preppy's eyes dropped to where my shorts stopped high on my thigh and instantly, I regretted wearing them. "Besides, they didn't really go with the outfit."

"In my head you agreed to wear them. Actually, you agreed to a lot of things in my head. You want me to tell you about it?"

"Nope."

"You really are a fun-sucker, Doc."

Ten minutes later, he was dragging me through the woods in the back of Mirna's house. The same woods I'd ran through when I ran from him weeks ago. "And you wanted me to wear heels?" I asked, stepping over a fallen tree branch. "Where are you taking me, anyway?"

"NOW you ask?" Preppy asked, turning around with a look of surprise on his face. "There is a man dragging you through the woods, with god-knows-what on my twisted mind, and now you think to ask where we're going? I hate to say it again, Doc, but you're kind of shit at this life thing."

"Working on it," I muttered.

"I'll help you," he said, ducking under a low growing bush. "First lesson, don't go into the woods with men you don't know because more than likely they have plans that end with your parts being scattered across several counties."

"No following strangers into the woods," I said, summarizing his lesson. "Check."

"Number two, no candy from strangers."

"What if they're in a really cool van and parked by my playground?" I asked, with mock stupidity. "And they have Reese's?"

"Well, then that all depends."

"Depends on what?" I asked, as we finally found our way clear of the jungle of foliage.

Preppy stepped out into the clearing, turning his face up to the sun. "If the creepy guy in the van is me or not."

Where most of Logan's Beach is flat, the clearing was rocky on all sides with a large pond in the middle. Jagged rocks and piles of hard shell created a slope to a rocky perch ten feet or so above my head and twenty feet above the water below.

Preppy took off running up the slope but I stayed put, wondering what on earth he was up to.

I thought our funny banter about life lessons was a good step toward having a good time. I was ALMOST looking forward to the rest of the day, but the second Preppy pulled off his shirt I knew it was all a big fucking mistake. Even with only his naked back in view while he set his shirt neatly on a nearby rock, I knew I was screwed. But when he turned around and I was given a full view of his upper body, I considered heading back to the tower for another dose of a life reality check.

Because he COULDN'T be real.

He was complete and utter…perfection.

PAINFULLY so.

Colorful tattoos were inked over most of his skin. His defined abs flexed when he stretched his arms over his head. His biceps and forearms were lined with veins. He even had one of those V things that ran into his jeans and had me licking my lips like he was a steak and I was a hungry lion.

Which I wasn't. I was the weak hurt lamb, wasn't I? How the fuck did that movie go again?

You've got to be fucking kidding me? I thought, unable to tear my eyes away from the man, who with the removal of one item of clothing, had turned from looking like a hipster-professor type…into walking sex.

"Why am I kidding you?" he asked. That's when I realized I'd not exactly kept that thought to myself.

There was no way to hide my staring, and since I couldn't rip my eyes away from his body I decided to go with the truth, no matter how painful it was. "Seriously, THAT'S what you've been hiding under your *LEAVE IT TO BEAVER* clothes?" I asked, as he stood on the very edge of the ledge where the sunlight highlighted every bit of his perfection. He looked like one of those tattoo models on the cover of INKED magazine. Was it too much to ask that he have lopsided nipples or a beer belly?

"Like what you see, Doc?" Preppy asked, rubbing his chest, slowly sliding hands down his abs, gyrating his hips like some sort of erotic dancer. A move I'd never found attractive...until right then. Shit, there wasn't much I'd found attractive before Conner and I started on our road trip to hell, and the first stirring of any kind of desire in over a year comes courtesy of the devil in a bow tie.

Man, I really was fucked up.

"God, no" I said, finding my voice. "I mean, what kind of person would like that?" I asked, twisting my face in disgust. "What I meant was that you're like *seriously* disgusting. You should just cover..." I waved to his bare chest, "all that up," I said sarcastically, rolling my eyes. "If we were in public, there would be people puking everywhere at the sight of you. So gross." By the time I was done with my rant, Preppy's smile had grown so big it was blinding.

Without warning he shoved down the waistband of his pants. I quickly turned around so he wouldn't see the redness creeping up my neck at the thought of him without his pants on, and I kept rambling, "Do a sit up for Christ's sake, before you go flashing your flabs all over the place."

Preppy's chuckle echoed over the water. "What was that, Doc?" he called out, "You want to sit on my face?"

"I am so fucking screwed." I muttered, keeping my voice low, but he heard me anyway.

"Not yet, anyway," he said.

"What the fuck?" I asked, turning around. "Do you have fucking sonic hearing? Or maybe sonar, like a dolphin?" Preppy was perched at the edge of the ledge, dressed only in a pair of black boxers.

With one last wag of his eyebrows in my direction, he held his nose and jumped off the rock, hugging his knees tightly to his chest. "Cannnnnnon Baaaaaaaalllll!" he yelled, until he connected with the water, sending a huge splash raining down over me. I guess I wasn't staying dry after all.

I was wiping the water from my eyes and realized that was a huge mistake when my eyes began to sting. "Shit!" I said, stumbling around blindly.

I heard the water dripping onto the rocks and Preppy's feet as he padded over to me. "Here, stop," he said, taking my face in his hands and tilting my chin up so he could inspect my eyes. "The pond is salt water, it connects underground to some of the canals around here and salt water is a bitch on the eyes. Open your eyes and blink as much as you can and as fast as you can," he ordered, and I listened. It stung at first, but after a minute the stinging sensation eased up as a mixture of salt water and tears dripped from my eyes.

"Thanks," I said, focusing on the man above me, his hair and beard dripping with water, droplets beading on his chest.

He kept his hands on my face. "You're next, Doc," he said, in a low suggestive voice. "I want you to get nice and wet."

"Do you ever say anything that's NOT dripping with innuendo?" I asked, pulling away from him and turning around to pull my now wet hair into a high ponytail. I heard Preppy padding back up to where he'd hung his jeans, and then the sound of his buckle as he got dressed.

I made the very big mistake of whipping around too quickly, not realizing that Preppy was standing right behind me, and again I slammed right into his hard wet chest. Even worse, when I put my hands out to cushion the impact, they landed low. TOO LOW. And right on something very large and VERY hard in the front of his pants.

He shrugged. "Probably not, but I can't say for sure, being as I don't really keep track of that kind of shit," he answered, following my gaze which was still locked on the crotch of his pants and the huge bulge pushing out the fabric.

"Ummm…" I said, diverting my eyes.

Preppy laughed and reached into his waistband. Just as I was about to turn tail, thinking that I was about to come face to face with little Preppy in all his glory, he pulled out a pistol. "It's just my gun," he said, tucking it back in then wringing the water from his hair. "Although, the other weapon I'm packing down there is just as impressive."

"Why do you have a gun?" I asked, without thinking of how stupid my question really was. Maybe, if he ever put his god damned shirt back on, my case of stupid would turn back off.

"Why do I have a gun?" he repeated, like it was the ridiculous question that it was. "'Cause throwing bullets by hand isn't exactly effective."

"You carry that all the time?" I asked, curious.

"Every day that ends in Y."

"Why? Because you're a criminal?"

"Really? We going there, Doc? 'Cause last time I checked, heroin wasn't exactly legal." He leaned in closer like he was sharing a secret, whispering, "Neither is robbing your grandmother."

"Fuck you," I spat, the lightness between us growing heavy in the span of a few words, like an anvil had been dropped on top of us.

"Gladly," he responded. "But you're just as much of a criminal as I am."

"No. I don't do the things you do," I argued.

"No, but you know about the shit I do. That makes you an accessory. Keep them coming. This is fun."

I growled, growing frustrated with both the company and the fact that I couldn't find the break in the brush where we'd come in. I set my sights on the rocks protruding from the perch where Preppy had just jumped in the water and started climbing them. I didn't know where they lead, but anywhere else was the only place I needed to go. "I knew this entire day would be a mistake."

"You can't go anywhere, Doc," Preppy said, sounding bored.

"Oh yeah? And why the hell not?" I asked, finding my footing and pulling up. One step down. I looked up. About seventy to go.

"You can't go anywhere 'cause you've got nowhere to go," he answered. Although, I knew what he was really saying, that without him keeping my secret from Mirna, I couldn't stay there. "Truth hurts, don't it?"

"The truth?" I asked, growing more irritated by the second. I growled when my foot slipped from a rock. Holding on tighter I tried again, this time landing my foot on a smooth rock that felt like it would hold. "What would you know about truth? About honesty?" I asked, looking back over my shoulder where, unfortunately, he was still shirtless, his thumbs tucked into his pockets as he watched me climb. Even though we were arguing, his gaze was fixated on my ass until he finally decided that my face was also worthy of his attentions. "All you've been doing is playing games and toying with me. First, you act like you want to kill me, and then you act like you're saving me, then you're ignoring me completely, and now you want to take me out and pretend like you haven't been playing some sort of game with me that I never agreed to play!" I shouted, just as the rock I thought would hold gave out and I slid the foot and a half I'd climbed back to the ground. I hit the rock with my closed fist and surprised myself when I made a dent.

"First, I said you couldn't go anywhere not because I was being a dick, but because that type of rock you're trying to climb crumbles like chalk and doesn't hold much weight." I let my forehead fall against my rock nemesis.

"SECOND, I think I liked you better when you were all crying and weepy over your shitty life, because this stubborn-chick thing is starting to be a real pain in my dick," Preppy said. "And last, but not motherfucking least, I may be a lot of things, Doc. A criminal. Sure. A very good dresser. Absolutely. A man with a huge cock. Fuck, yes." His face grew serious. "But I'm no fucking liar." For the first time, there was no joke behind his words. No cocky smile or punchline to follow.

"Yeah?" I asked, just as an idea hit me. He'd put me in my place by throwing the H back in my face, and maybe it was time I put him in his. "Then let's find out," I said casually. I hopped back down the rocks and marched right back up to Preppy, who looked amused as all hell as I crossed my arms over my chest and tapped my foot on the ground.

"Oh yeah? How do you think you're gonna prove that?" I couldn't wait to wipe that smirk right off his face.

"SHOW ME." I demanded, pointing to his crotch.

"Now we're getting somewhere," Preppy said, biting his bottom lip.

I shook my head. "I don't want to fuck you. I want to see it. ALL of it. NOW. Since you say you're not a liar, and I've been hearing about this monster cock, this thick dick, this whatever the fuck you seem to want to call the third man living in your pants, it occurred to me that you're probably only talking about it so much because you have some sort of complex about it. Like the way short men are aggressive, or the way older men buy sports cars." In my head, I'd already won this challenge and was well on my way back to Mirna's where we could pretend the entire day never happened. "The way I see it, this is me." I took a step toward him, pushing my index finger into his chest. "Calling your bluff." I lowered it and pointed again to his pants. "Now strip."

Preppy took a step back and, for a second, I thought he was going to tell me to fuck off. I was already planning my victory 'flipping of the bird' when he slowly tipped his chin up to me, accepting my challenge. He again removed his gun and set it on a rock.

"What do I get if you're wrong?" he asked, hooking his thumbs in his pants and boxers, like he was about to pull them down. Yeah, definitely a move by someone who was bluffing. I was calling him out on his, and now he was calling me out on mine.

"What do you want?" I asked, curious as to what he would even want.

"Three minutes," he said, without a second of hesitation.

"Excuse me?"

"Not to fuck you," he said, and I let out the breath I was holding. "That would at least take four." He taunted me more by lowering his pants, stopping just above what the fuss was all about. "Three minutes, and I can do whatever I want to you."

"What do you want to do?" I asked.

"Whatever I want."

I swallowed hard. Oh, he was good. He was really good.

I wasn't buying it.

"Deal," I said, taking a step back and waving for him to continue. "But when you say BIG, I do mean it better be BIG," I said, although I didn't exactly know how big was big. "Should we get a ruler or maybe call in a second opinion?" I asked, finding it easy to tease the man who'd been dishing it out to me for weeks now. "Or maybe some tweezers?"

Any second, I was sure he was going to fold. I could feel it. I just knew I was right and that he would…

"Oh, Doc," he said, slowly shaking his head from side to side and making a "tsk tsk" sound. "You've just made the best mistake of your life." Without another word he dropped both his pants and boxers, letting them fall around his ankles.

HOLY. FUCKING. SHIT.

"We done here, Doc?" And although it was him who was naked and exposed, it was also him whose voice was thick and laced with desire. "We good?"

I just. I mean. "Yeah, yeah we're…done here," I said, turning my head from side to side to avoid looking, but it was…wow. I didn't even need a point of reference to know that what he was packing was monstrous.

And hard.

Preppy cleared his throat, and I was mortified that I'd been caught open-mouthed gaping at his dick. So I did what any respectable junkie would do. I turned and bolted.

"Oh no," Preppy said, catching up to me in a few short strides before I'd even reached the first boulder.

Damn these short legs.

"Let me clarify," he said, pulling me back against his bare

chest. "YOU are done here, because you lost." He spun me around in his arms and pushed me back against the rocks. His nose almost touching mine when he leaned down and said something that sounded eerily like a warning. My entire body went on high alert. "But WE are most definitely not done here, because I WON."

"Fuck," I muttered.

"No, Doc. Not with only three minutes." He lowered his lips to my ear as he added, "But you best fucking believe that I'm going to make the most out of every single second I have."

He pushed his naked hips against my backside, and I gasped. And this time, I knew for a fact that the hard prodding against my lower back had nothing to do with his gun.

No.

It was much MUCH bigger than that.

He shifted his hand so it was flat on my stomach. He dipped his fingertips inside my shorts.

"Time starts now."

★ ★ ★

PREPPY

THREE MINUTES.

I chose that number for two reasons. One, because fucking with Dre was everything I dreamed it would be and more. Two, because the other bets I thought of throwing out there all ended with being balls deep inside of her, and since I was pretty sure she wouldn't agree to that, I played it safe.

Or, so I thought.

After Mirna had given her a little makeover I found myself panting after her like a dog left out on the porch in the middle of the day. Then, I'd shown up to pick her up and she was wearing shorts so short her long thighs were on full display and her ass cheeks were teasing me, playing a game of peek-a-boo, every time she swayed her hips or took a step. Her hair and makeup weren't as styled as the day before and her lips were a softer pink, instead of the bright red, and I thought just then, for the first time in my life, that a girl was beautiful. I'd thought hot. Or fuckable. But beautiful was as new a thought to me as restraint.

Not to be confused with restraints.

Those, I was familiar with.

On the water tower, when she was on the verge of ending her life, it was her frailty that piqued my interest. When I brought her unconscious body to Mirna's, it was her weakness that had me stealing a taste of her pussy. And when she'd turned to me and crossed her arms over her chest, pushing up her tits, challenging me to show her my dick so she could verify the size, I thought I was about to come in my fucking pants, right then and there.

If I'd thought her weakness was a massive turn on, it was absolutely jack-shit compared to the the surge of pure want her show of strength sent, shooting straight through my spine into my ridiculously hard cock.

Dre wasn't some random chick at a party who knew what the price was for the all-you-can-snort-buffet I so generously provided. She also wasn't one of Bear's BBB's who knew what they were getting into when it came to the bikers and their familiars.

All joking and heroin aside, Doc was just an ordinary girl.

Only, she wasn't.

As much as I wanted to leave her alone and pretend we'd never met, it was impossible. Lately, I couldn't even jerk off without picturing her.

The whole restraint thing was new, but I still remembered the way she tasted and wanted to know how tight she was. How warm.

Dre was always flushed for one reason or another. Anger, sadness, confusion, frustration. I wanted to see what she looked like when she came. I'd pictured it. Jerked off to it.

I kept her pinned up against the flat rocks with my hips. This wasn't about me, but there was no way I was putting my jeans back on or wasting another fucking second before I put my hands on her. I circled her waist with my other arm, and pushed my fingers into her shorts. I heard her quick intake of breath and my cock responded by hardening even more. There was something about her reaction, whether good or bad, that had me on a level of excitement that surpassed my discovery of U-porn.

"What do you want from me?" she said, and although I knew she was looking for something deeper than the answer I gave her, I couldn't help myself.

"Your tits. Your ass. Your pussy," I answered honestly, shoving my hand down the front of her shorts with such force the buttons popped open, allowing me more access.

"That's not what I meant," she said, trying and failing to turn around in my arms. My fingers dipped lower until I came in contact with her clit, and I left them there without movement until I felt her squirming for more contact. "I mean, why do you want to do this? Why do you even want to touch me?"

The words came out before I could stop them. "I have no

fucking idea, but I only have three minutes to do what I want, so shut the fuck up and stop trying to stall me," I said, gliding over her clit and farther down into her panties which, much to my delight, were soaking wet. "What's got you all wet and worked up, Doc? Did you like what you saw?" I drawled. When she opened her mouth to answer, I shut her up again by rocking against her lower back, the only thing that came out of her mouth was a throaty groan. I rubbed my shaft up and down against her denim covered ass crack and decided that I hated her little shorts after all.

I pulled my hand away and took a small step back, but only to give me enough room to yank down her shorts and her white cotton panties in one move. The naked flesh of her ass was exposed to me and my mouth watered with the urge to bite it, but time was running out so I settled for a stinging slap.

"What the fuck?" she yelped, jumping at the sensation but settling against the rocks when I kneaded the raised red flesh in the shape of my hand print with my fingers.

Standing behind her, fully naked, with her ass in front of me and her pussy peeking out from between her legs with Dre bent over had me questioning this new found restraint, but, remembering my task, I slipped my hand between her legs and stroked the opening of her pussy a few times, before finding her little hardened clit and strumming it with my thumb, like I was fucking mad at it.

I felt her entire body tighten under my hold. I groaned when she pushed back into me in search of her release, but I had something better in mind. At least, something better for me. "We only have thirty seconds," I said, continuing to thrust my cock between her ass cheeks as her movements for more grew bolder, pushing back against me harder and harder, as everything inside of her body seemed to tense. She was so fucking close. As one hand continued to stroke her clit, I used the other to gather her wetness dripping down her legs onto my fingers, swiping only briefly over her pussy and gathered what I needed to make this bet all the more interesting. There was nothing that could distract me from the task at hand.

Not even the dark urges from the depths of my mind trying to claw their way to the surface.

CHAPTER SIXTEEN

DRE

EVERYTHING INSIDE OF ME was hot and tight, and I felt like I was about to explode. When Preppy's hand swiped over my entrance, I knew I was only seconds away from something that excited and scared the shit out of me.

"God damn, Doc. I can feel how close you are. This pussy of yours wants to come all over my fingers."

"Time's almost up," I managed to groan out, even in my state of ecstasy I needed to put him in his place.

"Fuck time," he growled, pushing one long finger deep inside me.

"Aaaaahhhhh," I called out, leaning against the rock for support.

He was now grinding against me, sliding his cock through the crack of my ass over and over again as he pumped his finger inside me, angling it so that he was pushing against my front wall with his fingertip when he pulled out.

I lost my cocky attitude, suddenly, when he lowered his cock and slid the shaft between my legs, through the wetness dripping down my thighs. A flash of Conner holding me down by my head, while Eric raped me from behind, flooded my mind. I was there again. In that dirty motel room. I could smell his stench and relived the fear as they laughed at my cries for help. "Stop stop stop no!!!!!!!" I screamed, it was no longer Preppy behind me, but Eric. There was no more pleasure. Only pain.

With all the strength I had, I jabbed my elbow into my attacker. Preppy stumbled back with a grunt, holding on to his ribs with one hand, his thick cock purple with his arousal, bobbing up and down as he bent over in pain.

I felt an overwhelming tug of guilt when I realized what I'd done, and that it was not Eric but Preppy that I'd done it to.

Guilt quickly turned to fear.

Preppy stood, straightening his spine and his eyes darkened. He glanced down to where he was covering his torso and pulled his hand away, revealing the bright red spot where my elbow had connected with his ribs. He LAUGHED, and in my head it sounded just like Conner's laugh, sending a trickle of fear rippling down my spine. "Oh, Doc. You did it now." And then there it was, for the second time, I saw it. The spark of evil living behind his cocky smile.

Fear crashed into me and the need to escape was overwhelming.

I tried to run, but I forgot where I was and just as I was about to turn, my back connected with the rock wall. I was trapped. He was on me in a second, towering over me, his face up in my face, his cheek against mine. His cock still hard and hot between us, jutting onto my lower stomach. He reached under my shirt and took hold of my nipple, pinching it hard. A bolt of pleasure shot straight to my core.

I didn't like it.

I didn't want him, but yet I wanted him. I felt excited and nervous and strong and weak and I wanted to give in, but not as much as I wanted to get out.

My head was a cloud of confusion, a mixture of fear and want, delivered courtesy of the man glaring at me as if he were about to eat me alive.

There was no doubt in my mind that he wouldn't.

"Stop! Stop! No!" I cried. Preppy watched as a tear fell onto my cheek, following it as it rolled down my face and dripped off my chin onto his chest. That's when I noticed that, in an odd way, he reminded me of Mirna, except instead of being unfocused, it was as if he was almost hyper focused. He reached between my legs and I pushed them together, trying to keep him out. Trying to make it all stop. It was too much. He was too much. I was scared. More scared than I'd ever been, but there was nothing I could do to stop him when he pushed his knee between my legs, spreading me wide open. "No! Nooooooo!" I slapped him across the face as hard as I could, but wherever it was he'd gone, it was like there was no coming back from. He didn't even flinch.

I pushed against him as hard as I could. Pounding on his chest with my closed fists, kicking him with my legs. "Then you're just like them!" I screamed. "You're just like them!" I said, wailing against his chest.

He stilled.

Slowly, Preppy lifted his head and when his eyes met mine, it was as if whatever spell he was under had been broken. "I wouldn't..." he said, and then he stopped like there was more to say, but he didn't know how to say it.

Suddenly, he reared back, slamming his fist into the rock above my head with a roar tearing from his throat. The soft rock crumbled into tiny pieces, falling over us in a cloud of dust and debris. He released me and I dropped to the floor, pulling my knees up to my chest and sobbing out my relief.

Preppy moved back hesitantly, one slow step at a time. He watched me cry with confusion written all over his face. For someone who was so aggressive only seconds before, he now looked defeated. Vulnerable. He grabbed his jeans and quickly tugged them on.

"I'm not just like them," he said, his jaw tight. His fists clenching over and over again. "Because they didn't stop did they?"

I shook my head.

Preppy ran his hand through his hair and punched the rock for the second time. I yelped. His muscles across his cheek and neck tensed. He was breathing erratically. His look drilled me to the rock. "I'd kill him all over again if I could." He grabbed his shirt and darted through the opening I wasn't able to find, its location now ridiculously obvious.

It made sense that his body was built for sin, because the hold Samuel Clearwater had over me was something straight from the depths of hell.

CHAPTER SEVENTEEN

PREPPY

PRESENT

I WAS BEGINNING TO think I'd never again see the light of day. Or light at all.

I didn't even really know where I was being held. All I knew for sure was that the walls and floor were both made of dirt and were cold and damp to the touch on some days and dry and dusty on others. The ceiling felt low although I couldn't see it.

My voice echoed all around me when I talked to myself. "There isn't a damned thing a chick could wear that's hotter than high heels. That's a motherfucking fact," I said, into the darkness. "You can hold on to them when you fuck, too, so they serve a practical purpose. It was I who coined the term 'handlebars,'" I coughed up dust, choking on it when I breathed it back in.

Surprisingly, the darkness answered me back and a dim light walked toward me, growing brighter with each step. "Shut the fuck up, asshole," Chop muttered, shining his flashlight into my eyes.

"You know, if you didn't look like Bear's older, uglier doppelgänger, I would never think that the two of you were even related. 'Cause even when Bear is PMSing and in a bitch-ass mood, he's still all there upstairs." I pointed at the gray-haired man, staring hatred down at me. "You sir…have a few pumpkins missing from your patch." I swayed and my vision blurred, when it came back into focus a few seconds later, Chop's hovering image shifted from one to three, then back to one.

One was still too fucking many.

I was lying over the threshold of death's door, yet it was Chop whose eyes held no signs of life, void of anything other than his constant anger. If I didn't want to shove a rock through his skull so badly, I might have pitied the motherfucker and his sad existence. Which was fucked up because I was the one bleeding all over the dirt at his feet.

"No more talking, boy! It's time to SHUT THE FUCK UP!" Chop roared, slamming his hand against the wall beside my head.

I didn't flinch. Not because I was being a badass, but because my reflexes were shot to shit. I could tell by the way his nostrils flared that my lack of reaction was taken as yet another act of defiance. He swallowed hard, like he was holding back. From where I was sitting, that was a fucking first for the sadistic bastard.

A few seconds passed where we just stared at one another. If the motherfucker wanted a contest of wills he was going to lose, because it wasn't like I had anywhere else to be but hell, and from the looks of things I was pretty sure I was already there.

After a moment a smirk crept onto his face, deepening the wrinkles around his eyes. He seemed satisfied that I was going to do what I was told, which was basically shut up and bleed. He turned around and started walking away.

He was wrong.

"Just one more question, and it's a serious one," I managed to scratch out, my throat feeling as if someone with sharp nails was trying to claw their way out from the inside. Chop paused mid stride, and I could almost see the hairs on the back of his arms stand on end. I coughed. Warm, coppery fluid filled my mouth, coating my teeth. I was used to the taste at that point and knew exactly what it was before it poured past my lips and dribbled down my chin, falling onto what was left of my shirt. "Does this place have wifi?" I asked, spitting blood as I spoke. "Because if not, I'm seriously going to have to take that into consideration in my **Yelp** rating. I will say, though, that the torture is excellent." I went to lift my arm and a wave of pain assaulted my ribs. I winced but kept talking, enjoying the look on Chop's red face as he slowly turned around, cracking his knuckles and stomping his way back toward me. "However, the staff doesn't give me that warm tingly feeling I've come to expect from such an establishment, not to mention they're ugly as all fuck."

Chop picked up the bat leaning against the wall and turned it over in his hands. He crouched down beside me and pointed at my head with the thick splintered end. "Are you done now?" he asked, white knuckling the handle.

"Nope," I said, shaking my head, slowly, from side to side, ignoring the dizziness from earlier that again threatened to take hold. I slid my hand from my thigh to my crotch, grabbing my dick over my torn khakis. "You can also suck my cock, bitch."

Chop's goal in life was to hurt me, little did he know that nothing he could do to my body could match the pain in my broken heart.

If only I would have listened to her when she told me no. When she told me to stop and stay away, then I wouldn't have felt like the torture Chop doled out was a pain only secondary to the hurt in my heart, put there by a little junkie. A pain that hit a lot harder than Chop ever could.

CHAPTER EIGHTEEN

DRE

SLEEP DIDN'T COME easy. Or at all. I was restless, my thoughts on what had happened in the clearing. Preppy had said that he was over what happened to him as a kid, and although I was sure he believed it was the truth there was no way it was reality.

I rolled over, tugging the blanket with me, when I suddenly felt an awareness as if I wasn't alone. In the darkness, I caught a glimpse of the reflection in the full length mirror behind the closed door and, for a second, it looked as if someone was standing over me. At first, I thought it was just the haziness of sleep lingering over my eyes that caused the shadow.

Until it moved.

I sat up with a start, preparing to scream when a large hand covered my mouth, muffling my attempt to call for help. "How many times?" Preppy asked.

I couldn't answer him if I wanted to because his hand was still covering my mouth. He lifted it off my lips slowly, like he was waiting to see if I'd scream or not. When he was sure I wouldn't he stood up and wandered about the room, looking over the pictures on the dresser. "What are you doing?" I asked. "Why are you here?"

Preppy stepped up to the bed, turning around a picture of Mirna holding me as a baby. "I like this one," he said, placing it on the nightstand next to the alarm clock. He sat down next to me on the bed. "How many times, Doc? How many times did they fuck you when you didn't want them to?"

My chest tightened as the panic set in. I shook my head. "I don't want to talk about..."

"Just tell me!" He rubbed his temples and looked more tired than I'd ever seen him look. "Please," he said, lowering his voice to a whisper.

"I don't really know. It didn't start until the end, before that everything was about the H. I wasn't awake for all of it," I said, hating to hear the words come out of my mouth because it made it even more true.

Preppy nodded and in a move that surprised me, he reached out and took my hand linking his fingers in mine. I went to pull away, but changed my mind when he said, "Please."

"I was just a kid when it started," he said, in a very serious and solemn voice. "At first, I didn't know what was happening or why, but I knew it was wrong. The fucked up part was that I began to think it was normal. That being made to suck cock was just like taking out the trash or doing your homework."

I felt sick, wrapping my arms around my mid section.

"Tim?" I asked. Preppy gave me a small nod.

He swung his legs up on the bed, so he was sitting next to me with his back against the headboard, his hand still in mine. "By the time I was actually old enough for my dick to get hard, I began to like it." He pinched his bottom lip and his shoulders shook in a small burst of sad laughter. "That's the part that made me sick to my stomach. I'd throw up all the time, could barely hold anything down. I was like a walking skeleton. Told the nurse at school I had some weird disease that I looked up in an encyclopedia so she wouldn't ask too many questions."

I squeezed his hand and he squeezed back.

"I was nine when he first fucked me. Actual penetration. I hated him for it, but then when I was alone I couldn't even get my dick hard without thinking about him, of all people." He adjusted his bow tie. Something that I learned was pretty much his only nervous tick.

"Where was your mom?" I asked. "You said she was neglectful. Did she work a lot?"

"The bitch was right there. Right fucking there, under the same tin roof of the same piece of shit trailer. Tim, he was the guy who had his card punched the most in my mom's ever revolving door of losers she needed to support her own habits."

"Where is she now?"

Preppy shrugged. "She left me. With him. Just ran away and left me with Chester the Molester."

"You don't need to joke."

"Doesn't matter, it's not fucking funny." He ran a hand down his beard.

"Do you know where she is now?"

"Fucking rotting in the ground, hopefully. I don't waste a lot of time thinking of someone who's a waste of space on this earth."

"After Tim…" he glanced over to me, "left?" I smirked and this time it was Preppy who squeezed my hand first. "I was a wild kid and I was free. King and I got our own place and things were great. I realized that what Tim did hadn't changed who I was deep down inside." He smiled. "I especially knew this the moment I saw April Trenton, from ninth grade, in a tiny blue bikini top. That was life changing."

I laughed and nudged his shoulder.

"King's the one who told me that living with regret and hatred would just give Tim the power he wanted over me. Said it was no kind of life to be living, so I decided to embrace the good along with the bad and I did, never looked back. Stop being alive and start living, he'd told me and it stuck. Never even felt a shred of guilt for a damn thing I did since that very day until…"

"Until when?"

"Until today." He looked me in the eye. "I didn't mean." He blew out a breath and looked at the wall. "I didn't mean to scare you."

"It wasn't just you. I freaked out. I saw," I sucked in a breath. "It's just all so fresh."

He let go of my hand and rolled over onto his side, propping himself up on his elbow to face me. "I want us to be friends, Doc."

"Friends? Why?" I said, unable to help my smile. "Because your other friends aren't around?"

Preppy reached over and pushed some hair out of my face, his fingers lingering, tracing my cheekbone and then my lips. "I have no fucking idea. But what I do know is that I've never been friends with a girl before, so you'll have to walk me through it."

"I don't know how much help I can be. I pretty much ran all my friends off," I said.

"Good. Then we can learn together. Especially, since we're kind of stuck with each other since I'm blackmailing you."

"That you are."

"And since we are going to be working together."

"Working together on what?" I asked.

"Tomorrow, bright and early. I'll show you what I mean."

Preppy stood up and I thought he was going to leave, but he kicked off his shoes and took off his shirt, folding it neatly on the nightstand. He tugged off his jeans revealing black boxers underneath. "What are you doing?"

"We're friends now, right?" Preppy asked, with an excited look in his eyes.

"Yeaaaaaaahhhhh," I drawled, suspicious of why he needed to be undressed for us to be friends. "But we're not THOSE kinds of friends."

"The kind that have sleepovers?" he asked.

"Are we twelve?" I wasn't able to hide my laugh as Preppy maneuvered his body into the twin bed. I had no choice but to either scoot over or be crushed. The only way for him to fit was for both of us to lay on our sides. He laid his head on the pillow facing me, his thighs pressed up against mine. Our noses only inches from one another as our knees and thighs tangled together.

"I don't sleep much," he admitted.

"I don't either," I admitted. "Too much on your mind?"

"That and the blow." Preppy's arms moved under the covers and suddenly a large warm hand was covering my breast. "Good night," he said, closing his eyes and taking a deep breath. I grabbed his wrist and pushed it back. "Friends don't fondle one another."

"Bullshit, sure they do," Preppy argued, his eyes popping back open.

"Do you fondle Bear and King?"

Preppy yawned, closed his eyes again, and settled into the

pillow. "Ummm. Sure. Every day and twice on Sunday's."

"You make me laugh, Preppy," I said.

"You make me confused as fuck, Doc, but I realized something today."

"What's that?"

Preppy's voice was a distant whisper as his chest rose and fell in a steady rhythm. "That we're the same."

Oscar chose that moment to grunt his way into the room. He nudged Preppy with his snout. "Preppy?" I whispered.

"Yeah, Doc?"

"Will you please tell me what's up with the fucking pig?"

CHAPTER NINETEEN

DRE

O SCAR WAS A service pig.
          This is not a joke.

Apparently, a pigs sense of smell is better than that of a dogs and they're smarter too, but since they aren't as convenient as a dog they'd been passed over for that position and instead used for other things.

Like bacon.

"So you bought Mirna a pig?" I asked. We'd spent the morning in the grow-room and Preppy was showing me the ropes. And by ropes, I mean hoses. There were a million yards of different hose that needed to be installed in each of the rooms. The ventilation aspect of the operation was of Preppy's own design and very impressive. It was disguised as a window air conditioning unit and it kept the smell of the plants not only from the inside of the house so the Granny's wouldn't be bothered by it, but it also kept passers by from smelling what was going on inside the house. He showed me how to install a basic system, while explaining to me how the recruitment process worked.

"I did buy her a pig," he said, laughing like the notion was ridiculous even to him. "I read an article online about service dogs for people suffering from dementia but those motherfuckers are expensive and the waiting list is years long. So I looked up alternatives to service dogs and BOOM. Now Mirna has Oscar."

"What exactly does he do?" I said, and as if he knew we were talking about him, the cow-colored pig came traipsing into the room as if he was supervising and checking on our progress.

Preppy patted him on the head. "In a nutshell, he'll alert us when the shit's about to hit the fan." He unraveled yet another plastic hose and opened a small tool box.

"Where did you learn all this?" I asked.

"From a fucking ten-year-old on Youtube," Preppy said, unloading equipment from a box marked as dog food.

"Shut the fuck up!" I said, covering my mouth. "There's no way."

"It's the truth. We've been having issues with our source, guys a real douche. When King was sentenced I wanted to come up with a plan B, so I set this in motion. I first thought about buying a house and setting up our operation in there, but growhouses are kind of obvious. Usually, a guy that looks like a thug coming and going is kind of a tip off. The smell is harder to handle on a mass scale, as well. So I wound up on Youtube, watching videos of how these young kids were growing it in their closets and using these intricate filtration systems they set up with tubing from hamster cages and science projects. Figured we could do the same thing. Smaller scale of growing scattered around the town."

"Ahhhhh, so that's when it all started."

"Yes, it is. So we look for older women. Someone who lives alone. Not a lot of family to ask too many questions. Someone needing to supplement their social security check. It was actually a lot easier than I thought to get people to agree."

"Why women? Why not an older man?" I asked, dropping the drill I was holding when Oscar ran into me like a bull from behind, taking out my knees and knocking me to the floor. "Thanks, buddy," I mumbled.

Preppy helped me off the floor, and I rubbed the spot on my tailbone I'd landed on. "Want me to get that for you?" he asked, eyes gleaming with mischief.

"I think I can handle it."

"Report back if that situation changes." Preppy went back to his tools, and I drilled another hook into the wall.

"There are a few types of people my charm and wit doesn't work on. Old men being one of those kinds of people. Besides, old ladies make the best cookies. We have four now, but in order to stop getting supply from the asshole we get it from now we're gonna need more. A lot more. That's where you come in."

"So not only am I forging documents for you, but you've somehow roped me into co-conspirator of your drug ring?"

"Yep."

"Sneaky bastard," I said, pointing the drill at him and pushing the trigger, giving it a few spins. I looked around at the progress we'd made. "This is actually kind of a genius idea."

"Yeah, I think so, too," he said with a cocky smile. "It doesn't raise suspicion and the Granny's are compensated well. It's win win all around."

"So you make your pitch and they hand you the keys to their house?"

"Something like that. Some prefer not to know what I'm doing in their guest bedroom. For those who want to know, I try and make them see that I'm not dragging them into a torrid drug trade."

"How do you prefer them to see it?" I asked.

He grinned from ear to ear. "Subletting."

Preppy passed me one end of a tube and we each climbed one of the ladders set up on opposite ends of the room.

"Was Mirna your first?"

He scoffed. "Far from it."

I flashed him a middle finger salute with my free hand. "That's not what I meant, although I wouldn't doubt that your first time was with an elderly woman who seduced you with cookies and reruns of the *Golden Girls*."

"It was *Jeopardy*," he deadpanned, before his face cracked open into a smile. "Would have been cooler if that were true, but if you must know, the truth was I was fourteen when a woman stole my precious virtue." Preppy got down from his ladder, and crossed the room to pass me the nail gun.

"And what was this lucky lady's name?" I asked, tacking my side up with a lot more finesse than Preppy had.

"Her name?" He laughed. "Anything I wanted it to be."

"You lost your virginity to a hooker!" I said. Preppy grabbed me by the waist and brought me down from the ladder.

Preppy opened the top of the filtration system. "I sure did. Best birthday ever, thanks to King. Turned into kind of an annual thing after that."

I stood there gaping. Not that he'd done it, but that he admitted it.

"What?" he asked, when he saw me staring with my mouth open. "Your family doesn't have traditions?"

"Something tells me that you don't have a lot of skeletons in your closet."

Preppy shook his head. "Nope, I don't keep evidence."

Oscar darted out of the room. "Are all pigs that fast?"

"Not sure. He's the only pig I've gotten to know on a personal level." Preppy stripped some wires while I sat on the floor untangling extension cords. "So what about you, Doc? When did you lose your virtue?"

"What is this, *Pride and Prejudice*?" I asked. Preppy narrowed his eyes at me. After his admission last night, the least I could do was come clean. "It was..." The look on Preppy's face told me that I didn't need to continue, he knew exactly what I was about to say, that I'd lost it when I was raped by Conner and Eric. His jaw tightened and he was white knuckling the screwdriver in his hand so hard, I thought his knuckles were going to pop out of his skin. Suddenly, his entire demeanor shifted.

"So that's the only time you've ever fucked?"

"Way to beat around the bush about it," I said dryly, biting my lip as embarrassment and shame washed over me. Suddenly, Preppy was crouched down in front of me. He lifted my chin so I could face him. "What?" I asked, as he searched my eyes.

He cleared his throat and for a second I thought he was having a stroke, because I'd never heard him go quiet for so long. He took a deep breath and held my gaze. "Doc?"

"Yeah?"

"I volunteer as tribute."

Oscar came darting back into the room, running around and bumping into everything, squealing this high-pitched death scream, like he'd just escaped the slaughterhouse and was running for dear life. I was about to ask what was up with him, but before I could form the words Preppy was on his feet running down the hall. I was close on his heels, but felt like everything was moving in slow motion, including me. Frame by still frame, the realization of what was happening was revealed. Preppy's voice calling out Mirna's name. Oscar's squeal as he pushed passed me in the hall.

Mirna, laying on the kitchen floor.

Blood pooled around her head.

CHAPTER TWENTY

PREPPY

D RE WAS QUIET when we followed the ambulance to the hospital. She was quiet when we sat in the waiting room. She was even quiet when the doctor came out from behind swinging double doors, calling for Mirna's immediate family. We followed the doctor back through the doors to a room with a glass wall, the pale blue curtain peeled back, revealing a complicated web of tubes and what could have been Mirna somewhere underneath. Dre pressed her forehead to the glass. "We're going to monitor her," the doctor said. "She's stable for now, but the next forty-eight hours will tell us more. She hit her head when she fell and we stitched that up." She was a young Asian woman with a high bun in her hair, and at least three pencils sticking out of it. She didn't look much older than I was. "But just know that even if she survives, the chances of a full recovery at her age, with her pervious diagnosis of dementia, isn't likely. If the next two days go well, then she'll be here for a couple of weeks. If she's still stable after that then we'll discharge her, but she'll need around the clock care." She looked up from her clipboard to Dre, whose eyes were still on Mirna, and then to me. "Probably for the rest of her life."

"She's been on the waiting list for Sarasota Assisted for

months," I explained.

"I'm going to the ladies' room," Dre muttered, hugging herself. Her Keds squeaking against the linoleum as she headed toward the hall with the restroom sign hanging from the ceiling.

The doctor scribbled something down on her clip board. "I know some people over at Sarasota Assisted. I'll give them a call, tell them about your grandmother's situation, see if we can get her moved up the list." She tore off a page from her note pad and handed it to me. "Here is the name and number of another facility. It's a little farther away, but it might have an opening sooner if SA doesn't work out."

"Thanks," I said, folding the paper and tucking it into my pocket.

"And I know it's not my place," she started, glancing to where Dre just disappeared. "But I saw her arms. I wrote down the number for another place. Just in case it could help."

I know the doctor was just trying to help, but for some reason her suggestion that Dre wasn't okay infuriated me. "Mind your own fucking business," I snapped, leaving the doctor and heading down the hall. I passed the elevators and waited across from the restroom.

After a few minutes, I knocked on the door. The elevator dinged and a sad looking couple got off and checked the room numbers on the wall. The doors closed again, and that's when I knew that when I burst into the ladies' room that Dre wouldn't be there.

I was right. The single stall was empty. No windows. She was never even there.

I jogged to the elevator and frantically pressed the button. I didn't know where the fuck she went, but she had a five minute head start, which if she wanted to run from Mirna, from me, wasn't nearly fucking enough.

CHAPTER TWENTY-ONE

DRE

THERE WASN'T ENOUGH TIME. Not in this life or the next. There were still a million apologies owed, a trillion cookies to be baked, a lifetime of hugs to be had.

Life is short. Death is final.

Dementia is a purgatory in which nothing matters.

There just wasn't enough fucking time.

The voice in my head grew louder. The one that started as a whisper. A suggestion. A voice that told me that they knew what I needed to stop the pain. The one that told me that escape was only a needle away.

I swallowed down the lump in my throat and pushed open the back doors. I ran across the parking lot to the shell road behind the building, picking up speed, running with no destination in mind until I could no longer see the lights from the hospital behind me and my tears dried on my cheeks. I passed a few scattered houses before stopping when I came to a cemetery lined in wild growing hedge.

My heart was beating fast from exertion, but suddenly it started to pound erratically but it wasn't my heart. It was bass from music. Some poppy dance tune. Laughter floated in the air from behind the bushes. A house slowly came into view. A three-story run down Victorian that looked as if it had been abandoned. The hedge gave way to an open iron gate. A sign reading DO NOT ENTER was hanging from a cut chain. Young people, around my age, were scattered all over the lawn and the porch. Candles lined the railing.

"Hey," someone said, startling me. I spun around to find a petite red-headed girl with a glazed over look in her eyes. "Do I know you?" she asked, her words slurring slightly.

"I don't think so. I just heard the music."

"Well if you're looking for a party, you've found it!" She raised the bottle of vodka she was carrying in the air and took a swig, splashing some of it onto her face.

I shook my head and was about to turn away, when the breeze rustled the trees and a very familiar scent snaked its way from the house, through my nose, and into my brain. The sensation of awareness that followed was like smelling the cologne or perfume of an ex-lover. With one little sniff, I remembered every touch, every taste, every euphoric feeling, almost like we'd never been apart.

My ex-lover, the only real lover I'd ever had, was calling to me.

And the bitch's name was Heroin.

I DON'T REMEMBER moving my feet. I don't remember entering the house. What I remember is the couple having sex against the wall of the foyer. The smell of body odor and feces. The graffiti marking the walls. The peeling wallpaper.

A small room off to the side, what could've been a sitting area at one time, was aglow in candlelight, the scent of my lover stronger, sticking to the inside of my nostrils. A group of four sat around in a circle, in various states of chasing their dragons. One, slumped over against the wall. Another, smiling with anticipation as he flicked the syringe with his finger. There was one person that stood out to me above the others. I could only see the top of his greasy brown hair as he tied off an elastic band around his arm. I didn't see his face until he was tightening it with his teeth. His eyes met mine, and I gasped. Shock. Pure fucking shock shot through me. My stomach rolled and my heart pumped wildly. Every single hair on my arms stood at attention. I took a step back and shook my head because there was no way what I was seeing was real.

Eric.

It couldn't be. He was dead. *Wasn't he?*

I heard a bang, which turned out to be someone tripped over a chair. When I looked back into the room, the man was gone. Either I was seeing things or my Eric picked a really shitty night to start haunting me.

"Come on out back," the girl said. "We got a taste of every-thing out there."

I followed her through the house and into the backyard which butted up to the cemetery. We hopped the small gate where a larger circle of people were gathered under a large tree, sitting on the big bulging roots which had upturned several headstones as they grew through to the surface.

"That's Dom," the girl said, pointing to a dark haired guy unrolling a ball of foil. She cast me a knowing smirk then glanced down to my arms. I folded them around my chest, instinctively protecting my scars from her knowing gaze. "He'll hook you up with whatever you want." She clucked her tongue.

"My guess is that you like to chase the dragon."

I didn't say anything, there was no use in denying something I wore the evidence of.

A few minutes later, I was sitting next to Dom, Indian style, while he fired up the heroin, getting ready to reintroduce me to my old lover. I salivated for a taste of her. I already felt her in my blood. My knees bounced anxiously. The second he held the needle up to my arm, I pulled it back. "Second thoughts, pretty girl?" Dom asked, leaning close enough to me where I could smell his rancid breath.

I didn't get a chance to answer. Not him. Not my own question about why I'd hesitated. Because the needle was yanked from Dom's hand and plunged into his neck by a masculine arm covered in tattoos.

"Good shit, right?" Preppy asked Dom, pulling his gun from his waistband and pushing it to the back of Dom's skull. Screams erupted, and the partiers scattered like cockroaches exposed to light. Dom's face was contorted in both fear and pleasure, which proves that even with a gun to your head, heroin wins.

Heroin always won.

I untied the elastic from around my arm and let it fall to the ground. Preppy's hair was mussed. His face was red and his eyes were angry and determined.

"Get the fuck out of my town. I see you here again and it will be a bullet in your neck instead of a needle next time," Preppy warned. "You understand me motherfucker?" Preppy pulled Dom's head back by his hair so he could see the seriousness in his threat. He then released him, and Dom nodded sluggishly until his eyes rolled back in his head and he fell over in a heap onto the grass.

"You don't know what else he's had. He could die!" I said, standing up.

Preppy shrugged, his face uncaring and hard. "Oops." He scratched his head with the barrel of his gun. "You know, it's not very nice to run off like that. You could have at least said bye first. Maybe a 'Hey Prep, just gonna go shoot some dope into my fucking veins. BRB.'"

I couldn't deal with the possibility of never having Mirna back and Preppy's sarcastic bullshit at the same time. "Fuck you!" I spat, taking off into the cemetery, jumping over thick roots and tripping over small triangular shaped headstones, barley visible over the grass which was the same height. It was pitch-black and my eyes weren't adjusting well. I fell into half a dozen statues and headstones, like a ping pong ball, before I stopped to catch my breath under a crumbling mausoleum.

My head was on my knees when I heard Preppy approach, his heavy footsteps a hard thud on the wet ground. "You know what the really fucked up part is?" I asked. "Well, I'll tell you. The really fucked up part is that I thought I saw Eric in the house when I got here." I lifted my head and glanced at Preppy, who had his arms crossed over his chest. His biceps flexing. "I mean, I know he's dead so it's impossible, right? But I'm fucked up, more than I ever thought. So much so that I imagined I saw him. But even after that, during that split second when I thought he could really be alive and there in that house, ready to shoot up, I'd made the decision that I was going to stay, anyway." I ran my nails up and down my calves. "That's how badly I wanted it." I paused. "WANT it." I corrected.

The desire was so great inside of me I groaned out loud. Preppy crouched down in front of me, his gun hanging from his hand between his legs, pointed at the ground. His finger stroking the trigger.

"Look at me," he demanded, tilting my chin up so I was looking into his eyes. "There are no old junkies, Doc. You either make the decision to stop inviting it into your fucking veins or it kills you."

"I…I know," I stammered, staring up at him through a curtain of my own dark hair. *But I just don't care.*

Preppy pushed the hair from my face, tucking it behind my ear, and trailing his fingertips over my cheek in a sweet gesture that both thrilled and frightened me. I wasn't expecting that, especially after what he'd just done to Dom.

Preppy sighed and withdrew his hand. "I need to point out that letting the H kill you is the same as leaping off that tower, because it's still you making that decision to die." He trailed the barrel of his gun up my leg, from my ankle to my knee. The cool metal set my skin to prickles and made me shiver so hard, my teeth chattered. I sucked in a breath. Preppy's voice slowly turned from an eerie calm to a violent rage. "You were going to use," he said, but it wasn't a question, it was an accusation. A fact.

I nodded, my eyes on his gun as he rested it on my thigh. "And you still want it?" he asked. I nodded again, too ashamed to speak the words out loud.

"Say it!" Preppy demanded, turning the gun so it was now pointed at me, but his finger wasn't on the trigger. "Tell me you still want it. Tell me that you want to die."

"It's not that simple," I tried to explain.

"Tell me!" Preppy demanded.

"Why?" I asked, trembling. I scattered backwards until my

back hit the cold marble of the mausoleum, but Preppy crawled over the step and hovered over me before I could get any further.

"Because I've been holding back." He leaned forward and grabbed a handful of my hair, yanking me up to him roughly, his lips hovering above mine, his cool breath on my face. "So I need to know if you give a shit about your life." He pulled me up to a standing position by my hair, my scalp screamed in agony. He slammed me back against the wall. "Because the way I see it, is if you don't give a fuck about your life," he leaned in and ran his nose along my jaw and chuckled deep and dark, the sound vibrating to the depths of my soul, "then I don't have to give a fuck about it, either."

I looked over his shoulder, scanning the cemetery to see if there was anyone nearby. Anyone I could call to for help. No such luck.

Preppy must have been reading my mind. "Nobody's here to save you. Nobody can save you, except you. So fucking tell me, Doc. Do you want to fucking die?"

"I told you! It's not that simple. It's just that I feel..." I started, but the words wouldn't come.

"Tell me damnit!" Preppy roared, pushing his knee between my legs to better pin me to the wall.

"I feel like I'm fucking bleeding out!" I screamed. Preppy's face remained hard and impassive as his eyes frantically roamed my body for wounds. But he wouldn't find any, not on the outside, at least. "No!" I said, grabbing his wrist and bringing his hand still holding the gun to my chest, pressing it between my breasts. "Here. I'm bleeding out here, and I don't know how to make it stop. You told me before that you could make the call. You said you could get me what I need. I need it. I need it so bad. Can you? Can you give me what I need?" I hated the desperation in my voice. I hated the weakness. One brief encounter with my ex-lover, even though I'd only watched her across the room as she seduced others, had me falling under her spell once again.

"Oh, I can give you what you need," Preppy growled, pinning me to the wall with his hips. His erection hard against my lower stomach, taking me off guard. My pulse spiked with fear, then fell with disappointment. "But no fucking H." He ground his hips against me, his hardness taking me off guard. I pushed against his shoulder, but I might as well have been attempting to lift a car because he only held me tighter.

"Why? Why won't you help me? You can help me! You said we were friends. Friends help each other, right? And this is how you can help me." His stare grew more intense, which infuriated me because he didn't say a thing. Instead, he let me cry and wail and pound my fists against him. "Why won't you help me!" I screamed. My throat was tight and sore. "Pleeeaaassssse!" My yell turning into a sob. "I don't want it," I cried, my head falling back against the wall. "I don't." I shook my head. "But I don't know how to stop the bleeding and make the pain go away. I don't know how to dull the edge that makes me want to scratch off my skin without running back to that house and sticking a needle in my arm." I met his furious dark eyes. Preppy's body as unyielding as his drilling stare. "So, pleeeeeaaasse," I cried, bouncing slightly on my knees as I begged. I covered his gun with my other hand. "Please help me."

I don't know if it was me touching his gun, or the begging that did it, but the spark was back, glistening wickedly in his eyes. His pupils grew large. He licked his bottom lip and ground his hips against me. I gasped, my blood turned red hot. I instantly regretted everything I'd said. He rocked his knee against my core and a flush of wetness soaked through my panties. I didn't want this, there was too much going on in my head. Too much to sift through and process, but my body didn't seem to care about what I wanted, because my nipples tightened under my tank top. "Do you trust me?"

My brain wanted heroin.

My body wanted Preppy.

"No," I answered honestly, my chest heaving from fear and anxiety and anticipation. "I don't trust you."

He pulled his gun back and turned it over in his hands, examining it as the moonlight glinted off the metal. He smirked. "That's good, Doc." He leaned in close, his beard bristling against my cheek, his lips brushing against the sensitive spot behind my ear as he spoke. "You shouldn't," he said as he held the barrel of his gun to my head.

Finger on the trigger.

CHAPTER TWENTY-TWO

PREPPY

"YOU WOULDN'T."

"You want to die that can be arranged, but don't be a pussy about it and use the heroin excuse to end it when you can man up and I can just pull the trigger and it will all be over."

"That's not what I want!" she said, and instead of fear her anger boiled over. Her face turned red. Regardless of my gun to her head or not, she drilled me with her stare.

Good girl.

I pulled her off the wall by her shoulder and shoved her further into the cemetery. She stumbled on one of the overgrown roots the place is full of, bracing her fall on a lopsided tombstone. "What are you doing?" she asked over her shoulder, her words shaky, fear in her eyes. She was bent over at the waist, arms stretched over her head, her hands gripping the stone as she gulped to catch her breath. The bottoms of her ass cheeks teased me from right under the hemline of her shorts.

"Giving you what you want." I paused. "No, what you need."

"What is it that you think I need?" she asked, the fear turning to unbridled lust when she realized I was staring at her denim covered pussy.

I chuckled, yanking her back by her jet-black hair tangling in my fingers. I licked the side of her face and pushed my hard cock into the seam of her ass. "You want to be high? You can be high on me. You want to take the edge off? I'm gonna do just that, baby."

I flipped her over and brought her to the edge of the stone, keeping her in place by pulling tight on her hair when she tried to wrestle away from me. All her struggles stopped when I ran my hand up the inside of her thigh, into her shorts, grazing her soaking wet pussy. I groaned and tamed down the voice inside my head that wanted to take her right then and there. This wasn't about me. This was about Dre. This was about teaching her a lesson. I worried about taking it too far again. About scaring her off. But those thoughts disappeared the second I pushed a finger inside her tight heat and her head fell back and her mouth partially opened. Her eyes closed. "No, you look at me while I fuck you with my fingers," I commanded, forcing her head forward so she had no choice but to look at me right in my eyes as I added another finger. With my gun still against her head, her hips bucked against me as I brought her closer and closer to the edge. I heard footsteps and laughter but couldn't care less if we were caught. All that mattered was Dre and that look in her eyes, like she wanted me and hated me all at the same time. My cock was rock fucking hard and as I pumped my fingers into her over and over again she moaned and cried out. Again, she tried to look away, but again I tightened my grip on her hair and forced her to look at me with those big, beautiful, dark eyes of hers that always seemed like they were looking right inside of my head.

"So what? This is some kind of sick lesson you're trying to

teach me?" she asked breathlessly. Her pussy clenched around my fingers, milking them, wanting more than I was giving. I pumped faster, hooking my index finger inside of her. "You think making me...come is going to make everything better?" she asked bitterly, a stammer in her words.

"Who said I wanted to make anything better?" I asked, running my nose along her neck and biting down on her earlobe, inhaling her vanilla scent. "Maybe I just want to be the one to ruin you," I said, against her skin. With one last thrust of my fingers her pussy clamped down, and she cried out into the night with my suspenders twisted around her hands. I didn't know if she was trying to pull me closer or push me away. Her wetness dripping down my fingers as she rode out her climax. Her head fell forward against my shoulder. "I can't keep you," I whispered into her hair, echoing the voice inside my head, reminding me of the same thing over and over again since the day I brought Dre back to Mirna's.

"I'm not yours to keep," Dre spat bitterly between heavy breaths. Her words may have been harsh, but she didn't move her head from my shoulder.

"No," I said, pulling my hands out from her shorts and licking her taste from my fingers. Finally, lowering my gun. "But this pussy is all mine."

CHAPTER TWENTY-THREE

DRE

I WAS JUST coming down from my orgasm when it occurred to me that we weren't alone. The sound of grass rustling and whispers floated over the air from somewhere nearby. I lifted my head from Preppy's shoulder. "Stay here," he ordered in a whisper. With his finger on the trigger, he turned around, stepping over roots and headstones before disappearing behind the mausoleum.

The sounds of angry shouts burst from where Preppy had just gone and before I could think about what I was doing, I was running in that direction until I came upon Preppy, the barrel of his gun against someone else's head. Someone with his chin on his chest and a needle hanging from his arm. The girl who invited me into the house was standing next to him, crying for Preppy not to shoot him.

"He owe you money or something?" the girl asked, her words slurring together, her steps faltering. She grabbed onto a headstone for support. There was no real concern in her voice. "What did Eric dooo to you?"

That's when I knew what I'd seen in the house was real. It was Eric.

"How?" I asked, taking a step back and tripping over a root.

Falling onto my ass. Preppy and the girl turned to me, and Preppy took a step toward me. "No, no," I said, standing up on my own. Just then, Eric lifted his head and his glazed over eyes met mine.

"Hey Dre," he said. "I knew you'd come back." Preppy took a step back to him and smacked him in the head with the barrel of his gun, sending him back into unconsciousness. The girl started screaming, but it was as if I couldn't hear her over the blood rushing in my ears. Over the questions. Preppy had lied to me. He hadn't killed Eric.

Preppy made a move toward me, but the girl jumped on his back with a high-pitched screech. I left him to fight her off as I took off through the cemetery answering my own question as I ran.

Conner.

Conner was dead.

CHAPTER TWENTY-FOUR

PREPPY

'M IN SO much fucking trouble.

Dre knew it was Conner I killed and not Eric. She probably hated me even more now, as if she needed more reasons to. Yet none of that mattered because regardless of how she felt, regardless of how *I* should've felt, the pure primal need to shove my cock deep inside her frail body was like nothing I'd ever experienced before in my entire fucking life.

Yup, so much fucking trouble.

After what had happened in the cemetery I was sure of one thing.

I didn't just want to *fuck* her. I wanted to *ruin* her.

By the time I shook off the spider-junkie, Dre was gone. I searched everywhere before finally finding her in the first place I should have looked. In Mirna's backyard. That's where I found her lying in the grass, scribbling furiously away in a notebook.

I took a moment to admire her. I was glad I stopped her from shooting up but for a reason I couldn't begin to explain I was fucking FURIOUS that she even wanted to. She'd just gotten over the most severe part of her withdrawals, the shakes fading to slight tremors. Her bruises had faded from angry purples, blacks, to pale yellows, but after I found her at that house I realized how rough of shape she was still in.

Too rough.

God damn it. She was fucking perfect. Flaws and all.

She'd gained weight, enough for her ass and tits to become all curvy and touchable. I should just fuck her and get it over with, but I still needed her help more than I needed a quick fuck.

I adjusted myself, trying to shift my dick so it wouldn't be so painful, but it was pointless as it strained against my unyielding zipper. Getting my cock to go down now would be like talking a lion out of his dinner, when he already had the lamb in his mouth.

Dre had the same constant sad look about her as she stared up into the cloudless sky. I felt downright feral and was overcome with a need to possess her, OWN her—even if only temporarily.

Even if it was just for tonight.

My throbbing cock agreed.

I watched her profile as she bit down on the end of her pen, deep in thought. She might have been fragile in body and spirit, but her mouth...her mouth was an entirely different story. Cocky, snarky. Maybe it was the contrast between that bold attitude and her weakness that had me imagining all the things that mouth could do if she were on her knees looking up at me.

She paused her pen and was staring up at the stars. With her back to me she sat up on her knees, her t-shirt rode up on her, exposing her concave stomach and a flash of white cotton panties, the outline of her pussy lips clearly visible through the thin fabric. I palmed my aching cock through my pants and mentally reminded myself that it wasn't a good idea to come in my pants like some fucking kid.

I couldn't stay away anymore. Whether she hated me or not... There was no staying away. Not anymore.

Dre didn't see me coming as I stepped out of the wooded backyard and into the light.

She wouldn't see me until it was too late.

I shouldn't fuck her.

I knew I shouldn't.

But I'm going to anyway...

I came up behind her and peered over her shoulder as she's yet again scribbling away in the notebook. That's when I realized she was crying. Her shoulders were shaking and the ink on the page is smeared with her tears...and her blood. A small razor blade in her hand as small droplets of red fell from her wrist and onto the pages of her letter to someone named, Mellie.

My blood was full on boiling, anger taking over running operation Preppy where lust had just left off when I read the next sentence.

Mellie, I'm so sorry. I can't go on like this. I won't. I think I'm ready for it to all be over. This time for good....

After everything, she still wanted to die?

A growl tore from my throat. I gnashed my teeth together, leaning over I ripped the notebook out from under her. She yelped in surprise, but I ignored her. I was dragging her through the back gate into the field before she could utter a single word in protest.

"What are you doing?" she asked, tumbling under my grip. I continued to pull her along side of me through the field.

"You'll see," I spat, venom in my usually happy voice.

"Fuck you. Get off of me. You killed him! You killed Conner!" she yelled. "Why? Why didn't you just leave me there to die when that's clearly what you want?" Dre asked, her eyes narrowed at me, her posture tight.

"You want to know why I killed him? I'll fucking tell you why. I pumped three bullets into that motherfucker's chest because he was touching you, trying to ruin you..." I searched her eyes and ran the backs of my fingers across her cheek. "I was jealous," I admitted.

"Why?" she asked, anger and confusion marring her beautiful face.

"Why? Because, if anyone is going to ruin you, it's going to be me."

"You're sick," she spat.

"Oh, Doc. You have no fucking idea," I said, tightening my grip on her arm. "He hurt you, and he paid for it."

"*You* are hurting me!" Dre screamed. I dug my fingers harder into her skin.

"So make me pay."

"I don't want this. I don't want you," she said, sounding like she was arguing with herself instead of me.

"You have a sick need to kill yourself. I'm going to help you with that." I lowered my voice to a deep growl. "Meanwhile I have my own sick needs I think you might be able to help me with."

"No! I hate you," she spat, as I continued to tug her beside me.

"Good, you can hate me while I fuck you," I said. "But first things first. My lesson obviously didn't take in that brain of yours. You want what you want and I can't stop you," I said, as we approached the train tracks which were elevated on a mound of gravel several feet off the ground. The warning lights flashed orange, the neon reflective barriers dropped down to cover the service road, while the bells indicating an approaching train clanged away. "And since I can't stop you, I'm going to help you out. Bullet in the head was so three hours ago. I've got something even better in mind now."

"Wait. What?" she asked, her teeth chattering. "You...you wouldn't."

"Wouldn't what?" I said, turning around to face her, almost losing my footing when I noticed the trail of dried tears on her cheeks. I looked away for a fraction of a second to regain my composure. "You think I wouldn't kill someone?" I cocked an eyebrow. "You already know that I've been there, done that, bought the motherfucking t-shirt, doll." Her eyes went wide and she made a move to step back. "Oh no, Doc, I read your letter and I saw what you wanted. And remember, I'm nothing if not accommodating."

When I pulled her to climb the gravel mound her knees locked up so I bent over and picked her up by the waist, tossing her over my shoulder, carrying her onto the tracks while she beat on my back with her closed fists. When I got to the top I set her down roughly and she fell backwards onto her ass, bracing herself with her hands against the large pieces of gravel under the tracks.

The whistle of the train blew in the distance. It wouldn't be long now. Dre made a move to stand up, but that wasn't what I had in mind. I bent down and pushed on her chest, spreading her tiny frame across the tracks. I crawled on top of her, pinning her down with my thighs. I leaned over her, my chest to hers as we both breathed rapidly. She struggled underneath me to get up, pushing at my chest, but I wouldn't budge. "Why the struggle, Doc? This is what you wanted, isn't it?"

She glanced up at me as the train whistled again. Her gaze flipped to her right, where the single yellow light from the train emerged from around the corner, shining brighter and brighter as it chugged closer and closer. For a moment she stopped struggling, looking back and forth from the train to me.

"So what, you're gonna die too?" she asked, hoping to appeal to my sense of self preservation.

I shrugged. "I get bored easily, maybe the devil will make me his errand boy or something."

"Preppy, this isn't funny. Get up and get off the fucking tracks," she said, her concern shifting from herself to me.

I shook my head and yawned. She wiggled underneath me, and although there was a train barreling toward us my cock once again stirred to life. Maybe I should just rip down her panties and push inside of her. Train or no train, it would be one fuck of a way to go out.

"You have to choose, Doc," I said, making my voice as serious as I was capable. "Life?" I asked, screaming over the sound of the train screeching against the track. I pushed my hard cock against her core and she gasped. Her trembling turned into a shiver, her mouth fell open. I glanced to the side at the blinding light of the approaching train as it bathed us both in a tunnel of light. I leaned down, so close that my lips were a whisper above hers, as I shouted, "Life? Or death? What's it gonna be, Doc?" My hair blew around my face as the light grew brighter and brighter. "Answer the fucking question!" I demanded, my hands squeezing her shoulders, my fingers digging roughly into her skin. "DO YOU WANT TO FUCKING DIE?"

With only seconds left until we became shredded under the train, Dre closed her eyes and sighed. When she opened them again they were glistening, fresh tears spilling from the edges.

She started to speak, her lips forming the beginning of the word, but before it could fully leave her lips I stood, pulling her up with me. I lifted Dre into my arms and took a running leap off the tracks, my legs flailing in the air as we fell the seven or so feet. Dre's decision still on her lips, her scream surrounding the air around us as we crashed down into the field.

"I wanna liiiiiiiiiiiivvvvvveeeeee."

★ ★ ★

DRE

"GET OFF OF ME! You're fucking crazy!" I yelled, wailing against his chest with my closed fists. Preppy only laughed. "You're insane!"

He grabbed me roughly, his fingers biting into the delicate flesh of my wrists as he raised them above my head. "Oh Doc," he said, his voice low and deep, his eyes gleaming wickedly. He leaned over, lowering himself so his lips brushed the corner of my mouth when he spoke, a chuckle vibrating from deep within his chest. "You have no fucking idea." He grazed my earlobe with his teeth. "By the way, I love this look on you," he added.

"What? What look?" I asked. His eyes met mine and something dark flashed across them, something that caused the hair on the back of my neck to stand on end and my nipples to stand at attention.

"Helpless."

"Let me go!"

"Oh, no, Doc. You made your bed, now you're going to live in it."

Before I could ask him what the fuck that meant, he leaned down and pressed his lips to a spot behind my ear that made me close my eyes and almost forget that just happened. Almost. I pushed at him again, just enough to separate his mouth from my neck, which instantly felt cold at the loss. "I wasn't even trying to kill myself!" I huffed, still out of breath.

"You could have fucking fooled me, Doc," Preppy spat, his eyebrows knitted tightly together and he looked down at my arms.

My chest heaved up and down. "I don't want to die," I tried to explain again, but the anger etched in the lines of his face only grew deeper. I needed to talk faster. "I wasn't trying to kill myself, I was just...I was trying something because I don't know how to make the pain go away," I admitted in a rush, suddenly feeling very ashamed of the self harm I was trying on for size.

"Doc," Preppy groaned, stepping forward he weaved his his fingers through my hair, his hand firmly gripped the back of my neck. He pulled me closer, and I stumbled forward until our chests were pressed together. His eyes were dark—pupils huge. His eyelids hung heavy and red. He sucked in his thick lower lip. "Why didn't you say something?"

"What do you mean?" I asked, more out of breath at that moment than I was with a train heading straight for me.

"Because, baby girl. If hurt is what you want, hurt is what I can do."

"What...what are you doing?" I asked, as he reached for his belt and buckle, freeing it of his pants and tossing it aside.

"I'm going to hurt you," he said, undoing the top button of my shorts and pushing his hand into my panties, cupping my sex in his warm and powerful hand. He squeezed, just a little, a show of power. "I'm going to hurt you with my lips. With my fingers. With my cock. It's going to be the best fucking pain you've ever felt."

"No!" I said, a knee jerk reaction to his words. I tried to sit up but he squeezed again, and I fell back into the grass as a sensation washed over me that had me pushing my thighs together, trapping his hand between my legs.

Preppy held my hands tighter over my head to keep me still. With a crooked smile on his face, he leaned down so his lips brushed my ear. "No doesn't mean shit to me, baby girl." He followed his words with a sharp bite to my earlobe that sent a jolt of pleasure pulsing through my body, tightening my nipples which rubbed painfully against my shirt. A tightening sensation ripped through my lower stomach and I felt a flushing from my core. Preppy abruptly pulled his hand from inside my shorts, obviously aware and probably repulsed at whatever had just happened down there. My face reddened when he held up his glistening fingers and stared at it in wonderment, shocking me even further when he licked his palm slowly, from wrist to fingertip, closing his eyes and groaning.

"That was the best NO I've ever fucking tasted," he said, and without another word he was yanking down my shorts and underwear in one move, before climbing back up my body so we were again eye to eye, his hand back between my legs. I yelped when he pinched my clit, and although my mind was protesting, my body wasn't, my legs falling open at his rough touch. "I'm going to own this tonight."

At the word "own" my entire body stiffened.

Preppy leaned down and pushed my shirt up to my neck, his mouth finding my nipple and sucking it between his lips, biting harshly down on the tip and blowing on it as he made his way over to the other. Still I remained stiff. "Just tonight," he muttered to himself. "Just tonight, this is mine." He breathed over my nipple before sucking it into his mouth and rolling his tongue over the tip before releasing it. "I CAN'T keep you."

"You've said that," I breathed, as he pressed two fingers inside of me. "I can't be owned," I cried out and bucked my hips, reveling in the sensation that was even more powerful than in the cemetery just an hour before.

Preppy continued to assault me with his fingers. "No, but you will be fucked." He worked his own pants with his other hand. Withdrawing from between my legs again, I shifted at the loss of his touch. He lifted off his shirt and there we were, in a field, completely naked with critters chirping and branches snapping. He grabbed my thighs and pulled me forward, his huge throbbing erection was pressed up against my core, hot and impossibly hard.

I tried to roll over and scramble away because I finally realized what Preppy meant by hurting me. "No!" I said, crawling only a foot or two before he was on me, his chest to my back, his mouth on my neck. He pushed my legs apart, and I groaned when he slid his length against my opening. I lunged forward but only managed to land on my stomach in the grass. Preppy fell against me, his hold firm. "But I said no," I huffed out.

"It's adorable that you think that can stop me." He ran his length against me again, and I couldn't help but buck back against him, needing more.

"But you're going to hurt me," I panted, referring to the massive size of his cock, which stretched well above his belly button, the tip thick and purple.

He chuckled low in his throat. "That's the plan, Doc." He pulled back, but only to grab me by the waist, lifting me up so I was on my hands and knees. I felt his throbbing heat and another flush of wetness left my body. Preppy hissed and again covered my body with his own. He reached around and without warning, painfully twisted one of my nipples as he roared out, thrusting hard and deep inside of me, fighting my tight entrance. It did hurt like fucking hell, but I never wanted to feel anything else ever again. It was an exquisite pain. A torturous pleasure. It was nothing I'd ever felt before.

"Is this still a no?" he taunted, pushing inside again, this time much harder, hitting a spot that made stars dance in my eyes. "Is this cock enough hurt for you, Doc?"

I couldn't form the words to attempt to answer when he yanked me back by my hair and covered my throat with his hand, squeezing just enough to allow me to still breathe. He turned my head so we were looking right at one another as he started moving again. "Tell me 'no' again," he dared, continuing to twist my nipple with one hand and choke me with the other as he pulled in and out slowly a few times, dragging his shaft against something inside me that felt like when the tip of a sparkler is ignited. A flash of light and heat that grew brighter and bolder. Stretching everything inside of me. It was painful, but it was the pain I was seeking. The release from my own thoughts. Preppy was right. His kind of pain was one I wanted, a pain that made me cry and buck back against him. "You need more? Don't you?" he whispered, the chords of his neck strained.

He released my throat and nipple, and pushed me back down onto my hands. "Tell me 'no' again, and I'll give you what you want. I'll give you more," he said, grazing his teeth over the skin of my shoulder and thrusting hard inside me, stilling when he was buried as far as my body would let him in. "Say it," he hissed, grinding his hips against my bare ass.

"No!" I managed to yelp. My body was alive. So fucking alive. Every fiber of my being wanted to be touched, licked, fucked. The aching in my core became almost unbearable, needing to be released or stopped or something. "YES!" I cried out, finally admitting what I'd been trying to deny for so long. Telling him what he wanted to hear so he'd give me more of what I was seeking.

I wanted more and he gave me more.

He didn't just fuck me, he took command of me. An all out assault on my body. Hard and long he fucked me, like he was punishing me and his cock was a lesson I needed to learn. The hurting became real in a way that had me pushing against Preppy. "I think you need to stop. Please stop. It hurts too much. I can't keep..." The words fell away from me as I was answered with a furious thrusting, his hips slamming against my ass, his hands digging into my shoulders as he fucked and rode me all at the same time. Ignoring my requests for a reprieve from this new kind of suffering, I felt Preppy's abs contracting over my back and his muscles tense. He was tense, giving me his all, but he was still holding back.

"Give me...all," I muttered as I felt something turn from pain to pleasure, igniting a heat around my stomach and pussy, reaching to other places in my body. The sound of another train approaching dinged nearby. The skating of the metal against the tracks. The horn wailing, grew louder and louder as it came closer. I was there, right there, but couldn't find what I was looking for. "I can't..." I said, pushing back against him, meeting him thrust for powerful thrust.

"I know what you need. I got you," Preppy said. He reared back, something clicked behind me, followed by a sharp scraping sensation against my lower back, giving me just enough pain to bring me over to the pleasure I was seeking.

The train whistle blew, the ground around us shook like a thousand thunderous horses were about to stampede over the top of us. I screamed loud and long, the sound swallowed by the high-pitched scratching of the passing train, its wind blowing my hair around my face as I crashed over the fence I'd been climbing, giving the fluttering feeling inside of me wings. Wings on fire, flying all over my body in a degree of pleasure that had me lingering on the border of unconsciousness as I sank further and further into wave after wave of pure, unadulterated pleasure I never wanted to end. My pussy tightened around Preppy, holding him still with one last chokehold I never wanted him to escape from.

"So fucking....ahhh" Preppy roared, and with one final thrust he pulled out of me and I felt the loss, my pussy clenching at nothing but the space he'd filled. He spread my ass cheeks with one hand and I turned my head just in time to watch him take his cock in his hand, stroking himself as he spurt hot streams of white, directly into my most private of places. Preppy groaned, as he watched his cum drip from my ass over my swollen pussy. His groaning, his sounds of pleasure, sounds that I caused, was like music, a song I never wanted to end.

The train passed, leaving an echo of screeching metal in its wake. Preppy flipped me over and collapsed on top of me, between my still spread legs. His cock resting over my pussy, still pulsing against me as he recovered from his own orgasm.

"Your pussy," Preppy said, trying to catch his breath. He was hunched over my body with his chin resting between my breasts, looking up at me through eyelashes so long, it wasn't fair for them to be on a man. "Fuck, it's so fucking good," he muttered, thrusting against me with his still hard, yet softening cock like he couldn't get enough.

Preppy may not have been able to keep me, but I'd been wrong on the other account.

Because after that night there was no denying that he owned me.

CHAPTER TWENTY-FIVE

DRE

"TELL ME ABOUT CONNER. Tell me why he didn't deserve what I did to him."

I rolled away, but he grabbed my shoulder and rolled me back. "Tell me and I promise if I can help take away that hurt I will," he said, in a moment of sweetness that surprised me.

And I was tired of living with the burden. As much as I didn't want to ever recall what happened in my head, never mind speak it out loud, the words just started to flow.

"My dad's just a regular guy. He was always kind of lost. He's an engineer but never stayed with the same firm for too long, a few years at most. Then he found Jan and everything changed. They got married and he was happy again. Jan wasn't my most favorite person but I guess stepmom's never are, but she was nice enough and she made him smile, that's all that mattered. What I liked best was who she brought with her."

"Who?" Preppy asked, tracing lazy circles around my belly button.

"My stepsister, Amelia. I called her Mellie. That's who I was writing the letter to. I really wasn't trying to kill myself, just unburden my soul. After the cemetery and Conner and everything, I didn't know what to do so I just started writing."

"You said you don't have anyone. Why didn't you try calling her?"

"I can't," I admitted, choking down a sob. "She's dead."

Preppy nodded in understanding. "People die, Doc."

"They do," I said, inhaling a shaky deep breath, "but she's the only person I've killed." And before I could convince myself that it was a bad idea, I was rubbing the scar on the side of my face and was telling Preppy the story that's haunted me since the day it happened. The story that started and ended it all.

I don't drive.

I never learned how. Well, I never finished learning.

My stepsister. She was older. She was eighteen and just about to leave for college. She was going to be gone, she didn't need to be nice to me, she didn't even need to ever see me really. We were only going to be living together in the same house for a few months.

She was pretty. Tall, blond, huge blue eyes. She turned down modeling contracts because she wanted to focus on her education. She wanted to be a doctor, not just any doctor, but one of the ones that traveled to other countries and treat people without access to medical care. She was a good person and that's what makes this all so much worse. If she was a bad person, someone like, someone like me, then maybe it wouldn't be so bad but it is and every day it hurts more, even though they say it's supposed to hurt less.

I'd just gotten my driver's permit. My dad was supposed to take me driving that Saturday, but he called and couldn't make it. Work stuff. When Mellie saw how disappointed I was, she volunteered to take me.

We went to this abandoned parking lot next to the highway. She was so patient and I was such a brat. Nervous laughter. But then I got the hang of it, or so I thought I did. We sang along to the radio and must have gone around that damn parking lot a hundred times.

We were almost out of gas. I put the car in park and reached for the handle so we could switch and go get gas. Mellie said that it was close and I could drive.

I should have said no.

I was nervous, I pulled out into the road without looking and a car hit the passenger side. It didn't even feel hard but when I looked over, Mellie's head was all awkward and she was bleeding from her mouth.

The car isn't even what killed her, it was the air bags. Freak accident. But if she was driving it would have never happened. It was all my fault.

Our parents got divorced a few months after she died. My dad tried to keep a positive attitude, but he couldn't. Neither could I. He rarely ever came home early from work, and I stayed out all hours of the night doing whatever I could to get my hands on what would help me forget.

Soon a bunch of kids I was hanging out with suggested a road trip. There was a ton of us that piled into this van and headed south, but after a few months the drugs grew stronger and the party was over for everyone but Conner and me. The rest of them went back to their lives and I just couldn't. I mean, I tried a few times, but every time I was about to get on a bus or a plane or hitchhike, I just...couldn't.

Conner. You wanted to know why I wanted you to keep him alive. Conner was Mellie's boyfriend. They met when they were in kindergarten and were inseparable. He couldn't cope and neither could I, and I guess I let him rough me up and toss me around because I felt like I needed to be punished for what I'd done. I *needed to make it up to him. And in my mind, there was nothing he could do to me that I didn't deserve. Until it was all too much, and I took my dad's final offer and the bus ticket. That's when I met you on the tower. I stayed because I felt like I deserved it.*

Plus he funded this little adventure. Well, at first he did, until his credit cards were all maxed out. That's when we started forging or stealing or doing whatever to buy more drugs. I kept saying yes. Not because I wanted to keep going, but because of the guilt.

"It's bullshit you know." Preppy said, pulling me back to the present. I was shocked at how easily the story had flowed out of me.

"Guilt doesn't feel like bullshit. It feels like a rock on my chest. It hurts like it's real."

Preppy looked at me, studying me with intensity. He turned away and muttered something I couldn't quite make out, but if I had to guess it sounded very similar to "I fucking know the feeling."

CHAPTER TWENTY-SIX

PREPPY

PRESENT

"LOOKY HERE," I said, snapping my fingers, "It's the fucking bell boy. Has my luggage arrived?" That question was met with a blow to my jaw that rattled around in my head before everything went black.

When I woke up with a headache that seventy party patches couldn't cure, I heard whispers on the other side of the wall. Female whispers.

"Is someone there?" I asked.

"Yes, I'm here," a meek voice responded.

"Who are you?" I manage to ask as I set myself upright.

"Nobody. That's why I'm here."

"Nice to meet you, nobody. I'm Samuel Clearwater. My friends call me Preppy."

"I know who you are."

"Well then, this is a fun game. You know me, but I can't know you," I said, letting my head fall back against the wall.

"It's better if you don't."

"It would also be better if I weren't in some biker's home-made torture chamber, but we all can't get what we fucking want, now can we?"

She sounded better off than me, her voice clearer, although not by much.

"Are you always so comfortable around other people?" the feminine voice asked, reminding me of the question Dre had asked me when I'd taken her to Billy's place. "Is your glass always half full, even in here?"

I laughed and then coughed, "Lady, right now my cup is half dead so stop shitting on my parade and take your torture and rape like a fucking man."

"Why do you think you're here? Why do you think he's doing this to you?"

"Shits and giggles?"

"Power. He could have killed you, he could have let you die, but he let your friends think you're dead and keeps you teetering on the edge of life and death because he loves power above all else. What better way to gain power than to take control of the lives of others? Besides, now every time Able pisses him off, he can come in here and beat on his friend or kill you or torture you. But that's up to him. That's what he feeds off of."

"And here I just thought he was a sadist and went and jerked off with a belt around his neck after he delivered his beatings."

"No, when he's done he comes over to this side of the wall and he rapes me."

"See? Shits and giggles. I was totally right," I said, and for the first time in however long, the voice on the other side actually laughed. "Preppy, One. Lady Chop rapes on the other side of the wall, zero."

"I think I might like you Samuel Clearwater," she said.

"I don't think I care for you at all, whoever the fuck you are."

CHAPTER TWENTY-SEVEN

DRE

M IRNA MADE IT through the next two days and the assisted living facility called with an opening so arrangements were made to transfer her via ambulance to Sarasota, which was an hour drive away. When Preppy told me we had to go somewhere, I though it had something to do with Mirna's paperwork or the documents I'd started on but hadn't finished for King's file.

"What exactly are we doing here?" I asked, as Preppy pulled up to a small store with a neon sign in the window that flashed EVERYTHING IS ONE DOLLAR over and over again in different colors. I could still feel the effects of my orgasm pulsing inside of my body, like my core was searching for more. I crossed and uncrossed my legs, the unease I felt growing greater the closer our proximity.

"You'll see," Preppy said. "Stay here." He tossed me a wink and jumped out of the car before I could respond. He was only in the store for a minute or two before coming back out with a large black bucket which he placed in the trunk. When he got back in the car he tossed me a bag, something cold chilled my legs through the thin plastic.

"Hot dogs?" I asked, pulling out a generic package of hot

dogs marked 'miscellaneous meat product'. A star shaped gold sticker over the label advertised its $1 price tag, like the flashing sign wasn't enough.

"Yep, hot dogs," Preppy said, turning onto a side road between the trees covering the road sign.

"What exactly is *miscellaneous* meat product?" I asked, turning the package over and finding another curious label warning that the hot dogs MAY CONTAIN PEANUTS. "Is this our lunch? Because I have to say I don't even think that you can eat these," I said, feeling my stomach turn at the thought.

"They're actually not bad. When I was a kid I survived on those things," Preppy said with a smile, surprisingly not like it was a bad memory to recall, but one he looked back on fondly. My stomach flipped again but not because of the hot dogs, but because I realized how awful my remark had sounded.

"I'm sorry, I didn't mean..." I started. "I just...I can't wait to try one."

"No!" Preppy said, laughing so hard he had to hold his stomach. "First of all, don't pity my past. My past made me who I am and I love my life. Second, I should have been more clear, these aren't for US to eat, although they do have something to do with lunch."

I stared at him waiting for him to give me more, but all he did was smile. "I have no idea what that means," I admitted.

"Well," he said, parking the car where the small road was cut off by a wall of trees. "You're about to find out. Bring the hot dogs," Preppy said, opening the trunk and pulling out his bucket and another bag I hadn't noticed before.

I followed him through a maze of brush, glad that I'd changed my clothes as he suggested. Preppy turned and grabbed my hand and tugged me through a small opening onto a huge dock and seawall that had seen better days. It looked as if it had been abandoned for years, left to rot under the Florida sun.

"It's beautiful," I said, and I truly meant it. Even with parts of it heavily coated with layers of barnacles and other parts falling back down into the salty water, it had an eerie sense of beauty about it. Almost like I could imagine how it used to look with a long pier stretching out into the water. The pillars where the boats would dock were far apart so I could only imagine what kind of large boats were parked there at one time. "This must have been some place," I said.

Preppy set down the bucket and rope. He let go of my hand but only to spin me in the opposite direction of the water, up to where a large yellow three-story house was peeking above a fence overgrown with grass and weeds. It was in the same shape as the dock. Windows boarded with rotting wood. Siding streaked in dirt, run off from the constant afternoon summer rains. "Wow," was all I could manage to say.

"Yeah, it's pretty fucking great, right? It was built in the 1920's," Preppy said. "It was abandoned ever since I could remember. Kids used to dare each other to spend the night inside because rumor was that it was haunted or a witch lives there or some shit. It was always changing. Anyways, a few years back, when anyone and their Aunt Tilly thought they could make money in the Florida Real Estate market, a developer bought it to demolish it and turn it into canal front condo's but the market went belly up and it's just sat here rotting ever since."

"It would be a shame to tear it down. She just needs some work," I said, shielding my eyes from the sun. I could only see from the second story and up behind the brush, but if I squinted hard enough I could almost see what the home looked like at one time. Wrap-around balconies where families could sit and have lunch overlooking the water or entertain guests. A sitting area or reading room making up the entire third story loft area, lit only with natural sunlight in the evenings.

"That it is. There isn't anything like this around here anymore."

"Who do you think lived here?"

"I'm not sure, but Thomas Edison and Henry Ford had winter places not too far from here, so maybe someone who brushed shoulders with that crowd. It's definitely possible."

"Wow. There is a lot of history in this town." I never knew that. Slowly, I felt myself falling back in love with Logan's Beach.

"This town is not exactly historical, although hysterical might fit just fine."

I was still staring up at the house, imagining the boats that must have docked there and the parties the original owners must have had. It was a true piece of southern perfection. Like a southern bell with a dirty dress.

"One thing is for sure," Preppy said. I turned around to find him tying off small hooks to the end of each of the nylon ropes. "Whoever lived here, they probably weren't the type to do this."

"What exactly is *this*?" I asked.

"I'm taking you for lunch. Sort of," he said, opening the pack of hot dogs and breaking off pieces to set on the end of each of the hooks. "But we have to catch it first." Preppy dropped the hook in the water slowly. "Gotta make sure it's on the bottom," he explained, tying off the line at the top of one of the pilings, then repeating the process with the other three ropes.

"What are we catching?" I asked, whispering, like whatever was on the menu could hear us and be spooked by our voices. I stepped up to the end of the dock and glanced down into the murky water where I couldn't see anything but brown.

"You'll see." One of the ropes started moving and that's when I realized that whatever Preppy was catching, it wasn't fish because the line didn't just dart away like it was eaten by a fish, but rather looked like it was...walking away?

"Here," Preppy moved me in front of him so that his chest was to my back. He held up the line in front of his body for me to take so I did, but he didn't move away, just bent over so his chin was resting on my shoulder. "The trick is to pull it up slowly," he said, his breath tickling my ear. I tried to concentrate but I could feel his body, his nearness. It was like a low vibration or whistle that no one else could pick up on but me and it was so close I had to bite my lip to keep myself from pushing back against him. "Slowly," he repeated, dragging me back to the task at hand. I did as he said, crossing my hands over one another, pulling up the rope like Preppy had showed me. Preppy stepped back for a moment, appearing again by my side with the bucket. He crouched down just as a face appeared just below the surface of the water, staring back up at me.

The face of a crab.

"Now don't move or you'll scare him," Preppy whispered out of the side of his mouth, still as a statue. "The second you get him above the water, that's when you have to move him over to the bucket as fast as you can before he let's go and drops back into the water."

For the sake of staying still, I didn't answer. "You can talk," Preppy whispered, trying not to laugh.

"Oh, yeah. Got it," I whispered. Even slower than before, I raised the rope until the crab was free of the water. I quickly whipped the rope over the bucket, but a little too eagerly because Preppy had to dodge getting hit by the crab, who released his hold on the hot dog just a tad earlier then I expected him to. Preppy set the bucket back onto the seawall and I glanced inside at the blue crab who was only a little larger than the palm of my hand. He circled the bottom of the bucket, snapping at the plastic walls with his claws.

"Wow, how did you learn to do that?" I asked, looking down at my achievement with wonderment as he snapped at the air with his claws. Preppy didn't immediately answer, so when I looked up to the other side of the bucket I found him staring at me, his mouth partly open. "Preppy?" I asked, my voice sounding scratchy and rough.

"Oh," he said, coming back from wherever he'd gone. "This guy King and I used to sell weed to when we were kids taught us. There was one summer we ate so much of these fuckers we had to stop when we realized we started to smell like them too," he said with a laugh, recalling the memory.

"They're so small," I pointed out. "Hardly seems like enough for two growing boys."

"It's not. That's why we need more," Preppy said, yanking me by the hand back to the end of the dock. We caught seven of them before Preppy declared that was enough for our lunch. We drove to what looked like an abandoned shack in the middle of similar looking shacks in the middle of the causeway. The smell of freshly fried seafood wafted from the little building making my stomach growl. "Hungry?" Preppy asked, guiding us into the small space which only held a few mismatched tables and an old

Pepsi cooler.

"Starving, you?" I asked, surprised when we didn't take a seat. Preppy pushed passed the counter into an even tinier back room where a large man with silver hair was standing over a pot.

"Preppy, my good man, what do you have for me?" he asked, taking the bucket from Preppy's arms.

"The gift of crabs," Preppy announced.

The man chuckled and set the bucket on the ground next to the stove. "This might be the only time when crabs make a good gift," he said. "You want them the usual way?"

"You got it," Preppy said, tugging me by the hand out the back door. "Oh, and this is Dre," he called back my last minute introduction. "That's Billy."

"Like Dr. Dre?" Billy asked.

"Yep, she has a sister named Snoop," Preppy said, opening the creaking screen door. We sat on yellow chairs at the single rickety patio set that looked like it had been rotting in the sun for quite some time.

Preppy leaned in closer like he was studying me.

"What are you doing?" I asked, leaning back from his intense glare.

"Trying to figure you out."

"Huh? Me? Why?"

Preppy pointed to my face. "You have these huge eyes and although they're dark as hell, they're still bright somehow. You've got seriously black hair, so black it's almost blue, but your skin is only slightly tannish. What are you? Some flavor of Spanish? Oh! I got it, a little Asian? No, that's not it. Caribbean islander, maybe? Barbados? Antigua? Narnia?"

I shook my head. "Narnia? That's not even a real place. It's fiction."

"Have you ever been there?" Preppy challenged.

"No."

"Then how can you be so sure?"

"I guess I can't be."

"I rest my case."

I laughed. "Well, real or not, I'm not…Narnian. My mom's background is English if you go way back and my dad's side is French Canadian."

Preppy slid his sunglasses down his nose. "So…you be a white chick then?"

"Like, I totally be a white chick."

Preppy sighed. "Bummer. Here I thought we were all interracial and shit."

"Disappointing, I know."

"The struggle is real."

After a few moments of comfortable silence, Preppy spoke first, "What are you thinking about over there, Doc? I can see your wheels turning."

I shrugged. "You're just always so comfortable. Around everyone. You know, when you're not threatening me or trying to teach me a lesson or dragging me around somewhere."

"And?" he asked, swallowing hard.

"And I was wondering how someone…in your line of work can be so relaxed all the time."

"And what line of work is that?" Preppy asked, leaning in toward me and grinning like he was up to something.

"You know, dealing the drugs," I said, wincing when my sentence came out as awkward as I felt.

"Well, Doc, I can tell you that, although I deal in *the* drugs, the reason I look so comfortable is because I am."

"Don't you have enemies? Business deals gone bad? I mean, you carry a gun so you have to be worried about something."

"You've seen too many movies, Doc. Although sometimes I *do* have to use it for more than putting it to your head while I make you come," Preppy said. I blushed. "It's BECAUSE I carry a gun that I'm not worried." He looked out over the water. A rusted shrimp boat was slowly pulling up to the dock. One man jumped off onto the dock, while another shouted instructions and tossed him a rope. The gentle breeze blew Preppy's sandy-blond locks around the top of his head. He turned back to me "And you're wrong you know."

"About what?"

"I'm not always a hundred percent comfortable around everyone," he said, locking eyes with me. "There is this one person. This girl who I think…" Just then Billy pushed open the door.

"Hot plate!" he announced, setting down a huge platter of newly steamed crabs in the center of the table. The platter actually wasn't a platter at all I realized, but an upside down lid of a metal garbage can.

"What's that amazing smell?" I asked, leaning in over the crabs and inhaling the spicy-sweet scent coming off the crabs that were still steaming.

"Old Bay seasoning. It's great on any kind of shell fish. I make my own version of it. It's my secret ingredient," Billy said.

"Billy, I hate to be the one to tell you this but when you tell everyone about it, it's not much of a secret anymore. And copying a name-brand isn't exactly an original creation."

Billy smacked Preppy on the shoulder with his rag. "Touché, my friend," he said with a burst of laughter. He placed his hand on the back of Preppy's chair. "Listen, I wanted to thank you for helping me get the stoves working again. I'd be cooking blue crabs under a bridge right now if it wasn't for you making that call and getting me those stoves."

They shook hands and did the secret handshake all men seemed to know, the one that ended with a half hug and a clap on the back. "Couldn't have my favorite chef without a kitchen, who would feed me?"

"Oh, I don't know, maybe one of the dozen old ladies who make you whatever you want. Maybe Grace. Maybe one of the biker whores," Billy said, with a smirk. He turned to me. "Sorry about the language ma'am. I mean the ladies that are associated with the Beach Bastards."

"No worries," I said, deciding right then and there that I liked Billy.

"Dude, I wouldn't do you wrong like that," Preppy said. "None of them make seafood like you do. Nobody." Preppy reached for the crab with his hands and set one on a plate, handing it across the table to me. Billy gave him a knowing look. "So are we cool?" Preppy asked, adding, "It's not you, it's me?" He held up his arms in surrender as Billy swatted him again with a dishtowel. He thanked Preppy again and headed back inside, whistling along to a staticky version of the Billy Joel song playing through the small radio on the floor, where it was also keeping the door propped open.

"I almost forgot to give you these," Billy said. The door swung open and he tossed two plastic yellow crab crackers over my head and onto the table.

I'd successfully ripped the first leg off my crab and was doing my best with the cracker to rid my lunch of his shell when I looked up to find myself locked in Preppy's intense stare. "This looks so great, doesn't it?" I asked, trying to break the thickness of the air between us.

Preppy remained silent as he lifted a crab off the platter and set in on his plate. Then he made a show of lifting two very familiar fingers to his mouth to slowly suck the seasoning off, just like he had before. My panties dampened, instantly. I held back a groan and cleared my throat, turning my attentions back to my plate. "Are...are you hungry?" I asked shakily, trying to sound unaffected as my nipples pebbled through my shirt.

As if on cue Preppy's gaze dropped to my chest, lingering there, like he was admiring what he'd done to me.

"I'm fucking starving."

CHAPTER TWENTY-EIGHT

PREPPY

PRESENT

"THERE IS ONE THING you haven't thought of," I said, sitting up as straight as I could.

"Oh yeah, and what the fuck would that be?" Chop asked, crossing his arms over his chest and leaning against the wall with a shit eating grin on his face.

"You're a fucked up individual," I said, pausing to adjust to the sharp pain in my ribs.

"Is that it?" Chop asked, rolling his eyes.

I shook my head. "No, you didn't let me finish." I pushed against the floor and slid my ass against the wall, bracing myself into the corner. "What you don't seem to understand is that there ain't nothing you can do to me that ain't been done before. You're an amateur. A fucking hack. You think threatening to have me ass-raped is going to break me?" I laughed. "Think again cocksucker, 'cause my stepdaddy already had that honor."

"All you're doing is telling me that you're white trash. Like I didn't already know. Why don't you shut the fuck up so you can die with a little fucking pride," he said smugly. "Come to think of it, maybe I should call him up and invite him over for a visit?

Wonder what he's up to these days?" He was goading me, using what I'd told him to try and get a rise out of me.

Think again, motherfucker.

"He's just peachy. Rotting in the swamp right where I left him," I said without so much as a flinch, even though the pain shooting through my spine was crippling.

Chops face momentarily fell. He pushed off the wall and knelt down beside me. "So you killed a man? So what? Should I be impressed? You think some story about your pathetic childhood is going to make me feel bad, and then what? You think I'm just going to let you go?"

I shook my head or, at least, I think I did, all the muscles in my neck were numb at that point. "No, what you don't seem to understand is that all this is pointless. You can have me ass-raped and it's not going to break me. You can keep torturing me, but what you don't get is that half that shit makes my dick hard. You can have me killed…" I leaned in closer and smiled. "But I'm already dead, bitch."

Chop reared back and kicked me in the ribs with his heavy steel-toed boot, sending me crashing into the wall beside me, my teeth chattering with the overwhelming pain ripping through my body.

Either Chop left without saying a word or I passed out from the pain and didn't get to hear his last thoughts on what a piece of shit I am. Regardless, when I opened my eyes I was grateful to find that once again I was alone.

Except, of course, for the woman who wouldn't tell me her name. I should've been happy to not be alone, but every word out of her mouth made me cringe and every time Chop left she had a comment.

"You know, provoking him isn't going to make things any easier on you. I've learned that lesson the hard way," she said softly.

"Hello?" I asked, and when she didn't immediately answer I figured I was just hearing things, so I did what anyone losing their fucking minds would do and finished out the lyrics to the Lionel Richie song.

"*Hello? Is it me you're looking for?*" I sang out, grabbing my ribs as every word felt like I was stabbing myself in the gut, but the song needed to be sung or like a fairy would lose its wings or some shit.

"I never did like that song," the woman said again, and this time I was positive I wasn't hearing things. Or like, close to positive. Like, forty percent.

"Listen lady, I don't know if you're even real at this point but if you are real, then I'll forgive your temporary lapse in judgment when it comes to the greatness that is Lionel Richie."

"Do you ever shut up?" she said, annoyed.

"Yeah, I do this thing when I pass out where my mouth stops running," I said.

"No, actually it doesn't. Yesterday you were commentating like you were an announcer over some sort of competition," she huffed.

"Probably *American Ninja Warrior,* always thought I'd be good at that." I adjusted so it didn't feel like I would crack my tailbone under my own weight. "Well, now that the pleasantries are out of the way, are you finally going to tell me your name?"

"Names aren't important," she said.

"Sure they are. My name is Samuel Clearwater, but my friends call me Preppy," I said, although I was pretty sure I'd already introduced myself to this annoying bitch. "If you're not going to tell me your name you can at least describe your tits to me. Bra and nipple size if you please."

There was a brief pause. "He's not going to kill you, you know."

"That's...disappointing?" I said, although it came out as a question. I didn't want to die, but being tortured every single day wasn't exactly on my bucket list either.

"Chop believes in taking lives," she said, stating the obvious.

"I kind of got that. He been hitting you in the head?"

"No, you don't get it. There is more power in taking lives than there is in ending them. By keeping us alive and trapped down here like rats, he dictates how we live and if and when we die. And if a situation arises where he can use us, he'll toss our gaunt bodies at the feet of whoever he's trying to intimidate by showing them how much power he really has."

"That sounds like a lot of work."

"I think you had it wrong when you told him that you're more fucked up than him," she said with a sad sigh. "Pray. Meditate. Concentrate on what life was like before you came here, because Samuel," she paused. "Because you're never going to see that life again."

I didn't argue with her. Not just because she'd been there for years and I thought arguing with her would be a waste of energy, but because somewhere deep inside I knew she was right.

She went silent shortly after that, and I assumed she fell asleep in whatever hole she was placed in. Without a lot left to keep my mind from torture and death, I closed my eyes and used the simple meditation breathing technique that Mirna had taught me. I took a few deep breaths, well, as deep as I could without choking to death, and I tried to focus on what my life looked like before I was shot. I was happy-ish. I had family. I had respect. What I didn't have. Was HER. Even when I pictured the cast of characters in my life, King, Doe, Bear, and Grace there was someone else standing further off in the distance, overshadowing the people standing right in front of me.

She was overlooking the bay with her back to me. Her dark hair blowing around in the wind. She turned around to face me just as I got close, her dark eyes softening when she saw me, her smile tugging at the corners of her plump lips. When she spoke it made my heart beat faster and I drifted off into a state of semi-consciousness, surrounded by her words echoing in every corner of my brain over and over again on an endless loop of regret.

Keep me.

CHAPTER TWENTY-NINE

PREPPY

W HEN THE DOORBELL rang I thought it was Billy, who was supposed to be dropping off some fresh blue crab before I headed out to see Dre. I wanted to take her mind off Mirna and what better way to do that than a nice homemade crab dinner, followed by my face between her legs, and my tongue deep inside her pussy, for an undetermined amount of time?

When I opened the door, it wasn't Billy. It wasn't even a man. A woman stood on my porch, She had shoulder length bleach-blond hair and she smelled of hairspray. Her glossy lips were painted bright pink. She stared up at me with big golden eyes like she was waiting for me to say something. "You're the one that knocked on my door, lady," I said, wondering what the fuck was keeping Billy. The woman adjusted the short sleeved jacket of her white pant suite, gold bangle bracelets slid up and down on her wrist when she moved, clinking together loudly.

When she didn't say anything and continued to stare up at me, I raised the volume of my voice and spoke slowly, "Can I help you?" I wasn't even sure if she'd blinked. I knew I was a sight to behold but god-fucking-damn lady, I had places to be. Over her shoulder was a shiny white Cadillac SUV. The front window was tinted dark so I couldn't see anyone in it, but I could hear the engine running.

The sunlight glinted off of the humungous rock on her left hand and I flinched when the beam of light shot me directly in the fucking eye. "Oh, I'm sorry," she said, moving her hand behind her back. "And yes, yes you can help me. Although, the reason I'm here is because I didn't help you."

"But let me guess, Jesus can help me?" I asked, leaning up against the door frame. "'Cause I gotta tell you, lady, that you should stop before you even start 'cause you're waisting your time with me. It don't matter what kind of god you're selling today, I'm not buying it. I don't need to go to church to know I'm a sinner and whatever god up there that might exist is fully aware of who I am and hasn't struck me down just yet. So the way I see it, me and God have a good thing going and you know how that saying goes, don't fix it, if it ain't broken."

I went to close the door and call Billy to see when I could expect him, when the woman's hand shot out and grabbed onto it before it could click shut. "Samuel! Wait!" she shouted, and that's when the recognition slammed into me head first.

It couldn't be.

But it was.

I opened the door again, taking another look at the woman in front of me. "Mom?"

"Yes, Samuel," she said with a small smile. Happy I recognized her. "It's me."

I'd been angry a time or two in my life. I'd been confused. I'd been hurt. But I'd never been more murderously irate than I was right then. I balled my fists. The heat of my sudden rage threatened to boil me alive. "Get the fuck off my property," I hissed, taking a step out onto the porch. She had no choice but to drop down to the first step or be trampled. I glared down at her with all the hate that had been festering in my soul for years. "I thought you were dead."

"I'm not," she said, her hands shaking.

"Shame."

"I…I deserve that," she said, glancing back at the SUV where an older man in a sport coat got out of the car and buttoned his jacket. "Mitch, it's okay. We're just talking," she called out to him.

"No, we're not. Leave. NOW!" I demanded.

"That's my husband, Mitch," my mom said, pointing back to the man.

"You were always good at ignoring me," I muttered, feeling the pressure build behind my eyes. If she didn't take my warning, things were going to end badly for her.

"Samuel, I'll be quick. I promise. Two minutes, that's all I want," she said, raising her eyebrows and waiting for me to respond.

"You have one minute."

She spoke quickly. "I came here because it's part of my rehab. To make amends with those I've wronged and I've wronged you the most."

"No wonder I didn't recognize you. You're sober. Never seen that look on you before. And there is no need to make amends, there is only a need to get the fuck out. NOW."

She dropped down another step but still didn't leave. "Four years now. Four years, I've been sober."

"Congratufuckinglations! Took you four fucking years to want to apologize for the shit mom you were?" I laughed and leaned over. "Apology not accepted."

"I didn't know what to say to you four years ago."

"Oh, but you do now?" I asked. "This should be good. All right, let's hear it," I said, crossing my arms over my chest and waiving for her to continue.

"I'm sorry, Samuel. I was an addict. Still am, 'cause it's a sickness that never really goes away. I've made some bad choices and I hurt you. I'll never forgive myself and I don't expect you to either."

"You *hurt* me? You make it sound like you ran over my bicycle."

She took a deep breath, and I could tell she was trying to steady her nerves because her hands shook harder, along with her voice. "When I left I didn't know where you were or where you went. I didn't look for you. And for that, I'm sorry. I should have looked for you. I should have come back for you. I shouldn't have left at all, but most of all, I shouldn't have given up on you. I ignored you as if you weren't there and I don't expect you to want to have a relationship with me, but I thank you for letting me speak my peace. This is for you," she said, taking a small piece of folded up paper from her pocket. She held it up for me to take and when I didn't, she set it on the step by my feet and backed down the steps. When she reached the bottom, she turned around and her heel caught in the gravel. She fell sideways, catching the railing to right herself again. She straightened, adjusted her jacket, and was about to head back toward her awaiting car.

Suddenly, rage wasn't even a word. I was beyond rage. I was beyond anger. I was something that existed in another fucking realm and this bitch was not getting away with her half-assed apology.

"Fuck that!" I said, leaping down the steps and stepping in front of her, cutting her off from the SUV. "If you're going to apologize then you need to know what you should be apologizing for," I said, feeling the fire flaring out of my nostrils as I spoke through gritted teeth. I could strangle her, shoot the motherfucker by the car, and burn them both in the fire pit in the backyard, and still be on time to make Dre dinner.

Possibilities.

"You don't get to unburden your soul and walk the fuck away when I can't ever have that same privilege because of you!" I yelled. "What the fuck do you think was going on while you were doing all that ignoring you're so fucking good at, huh? You saw the bruises so I know that you know about the beatings, but what you don't know is that while you were too busy forgetting you had a son, Tim didn't forget. In fact, Tim was paying close attention to me. Very close." I was right up in her face when I added, "He paid me so much attention that he knew how I like my dick jerked. He knew what made me come before I even knew."

"Noooo," she said, her eyes going wide, she tried to take a step back, but I closed the distance between us again. There was no way I was going to let her back away from what I had to say.

"So much attention that he knew how tight my asshole was," I continued. She wrapped her arms around her stomach. "So much, that when he was too drunk to come, he blamed me then beat me until I passed out."

"That's not possible," she whispered, her hand covering her mouth.

"It's fucking possible and it fucking happened," I spat. "Over and over again it happened, in the very next room, under the same fucking roof. It happened BECAUSE of you. Because you did nothing to stop it. Because you weren't there or didn't care. So you see, you didn't just ignore me. You forgot you had a son and left me in the hands of a man who I'd wished forgot I was there."

She shook her head in disbelief, and either she really didn't believe me or she was processing the cement truck I'd just dropped on her head. Either way, it was her head shaking from side to side that pushed me over the edge I'd been teetering on. My vision became a blur and I couldn't see beyond the hatred that was either blinding me or making me see clearer than I ever had before. I pulled my gun from the front of my pants and pushed the barrel to her forehead. She dropped to her knees.

"Son, wait!" the man in the blazer called out, jogging up to us. I cocked the gun and he stopped in his tracks.

"Son?" I asked with a laugh. I looked down to my mother who was whimpering. "You might really want to rethink your choice of words there, motherfucker. 'Cause Mama and me aren't exactly having the friendliest of family reunions, so that word makes me a little twitchy." I tapped the trigger to show him what I meant and Mitch stopped behind my mother, raising his arms in surrender.

"Put your god damned hands down, man," I spat. "I'm not robbing! I'm killing, don't get it twisted."

"Please. No!" Mitch pled.

"Fuck off," I told Mitch. I looked down at the woman before me on her knees, her white pants dirtied by the driveway, and all I wanted was for her to feel what I felt. Live how I lived. "Maybe I'll have one of my biker friends come over and fuck you in the ass in front of your husband," I told her. "Rape you. Take what you don't want to give. Fuck what you don't want fucked, but unlike you, I won't ignore it. I won't turn my back on it. I'll watch. I'll cheer. And I'll fucking rejoice when he splits you in two."

My piece of shit mother wailed and shook as one would naturally do when they know they're about to meet their end. "Samuel, please…" she begged, her black eye makeup ran down her face and it seemed fitting that she was crying dirty tears.

"You know Mom…" I started, turning the barrel of the gun on her head, tangling it in her hair. "To me, you've never looked better than you do right now…at the end of my gun."

Billy's van pulled in the end of the driveway and he hopped out with the cooler in his arms. He took in the scene in front of him, glancing from me to my gun to my mom to Mitch, before landing back on me.

"You can't kill me," my mother stated on a sob. "He's, he's a witness."

"Oh yeah?" I asked. "Hey Billy, put the crab in my trunk, will you? I'm leaving here after I take care of this situation."

Billy nodded. "No problem, man. You need any help with that?" He jerked his chin to the bitch on her knees. "I got some time before I gotta get the girls from soccer."

"I'm straight," I answered.

"All righty then," he said, turning toward the garage and whistling as he walked.

I kneeled down in front of my mother and shoved the gun under her chin, jerking her chin up to face me. "Something tells me he wouldn't make a very good witness," I pointed out, Billy's whistle still echoing over the house.

"I didn't know," my mom wailed. "I promise I didn't know

what was happening. I swear."

"That's the fucking problem!" I shouted, standing back up. My finger leaning heavy against the trigger. Just a little more pressure and it would be over. SHE would be over. The burden on my chest would be lifted. Just a few more seconds, and I could make all the things right that she made wrong.

But no matter if I killed her a million times over, it couldn't turn back time. It couldn't make her a better mom. It couldn't make Tim unrape a scared and lonely kid.

"Go ahead, I deserve it," she said.

"Nancy. No," Mitch said, finally lowering his hands. I glanced up at the worry written all over his face. The guy actually seemed to care about the cunt, and suddenly I felt sick to my stomach. Not because I didn't want to kill her. I did. But because I wasn't going to.

"I want you to think about what I told you. I hope it's seeped into that bleached brain of yours. I hope it gives you nightmares and you think about him grunting over my back while you were passed out on the other couch." My mother cried out and her shoulders shook violently. "You both have ten fucking seconds to get in that car and get off my property, before I start firing. Mitch, you make sure this bitch stays far far away, because if I so much as find out that you've come within twenty miles of me, I will come for you, and I don't care if there are a thousand witnesses around. I will put a bullet in both of you, but before I do I'll seek out your friends. Your other family. Anyone close to you. Anyone you know, and I'll end them first so you'll know I'm coming for you. If you don't think I'm serious, all you have to do is cross me and you'll motherfucking find out. You have ten seconds." I leaned down next to her and ran the gun down her face. Oh, how it would be so easy. "RUN BITCH!" I shouted in her ear. She stumbled, falling backwards on the gravel. Mitch rushed to her aid, picking her up by her elbows and practically dragging her to the car as he ran and she struggled to keep up.

The tires spun as they fishtailed down the driveway. I ran after them, aimed my gun, and fired several bullets into their bumper, before falling to my knees on the road.

As their SUV drove out of sight it looked as if they were being swallowed up by a black hole that grew bigger and bigger until they were gone and there was nothing at all.

CHAPTER THIRTY

DRE

WHEN BILLY CAME over and told me what he'd seen over at Preppy's, I wasted no time hopping in Mirna's car. It was the second time I'd been behind a wheel in years, but the dread I once felt toward driving was an afterthought, far behind the one that told me I had to get to Preppy as soon as possible.

I hadn't put too much thought into where he lived so I didn't know what I was expecting to see when I pulled up to the address Billy had given me, but the three-story stilt home towering over the smooth waters of the bay, was not it.

There wasn't too much time to linger on the view, or on the siding in much need of repair, or the overgrown plant beds, because a crash sounded from somewhere inside the house and I bolted from the car, leaving the engine running and the door open. I tried the front door but it was locked. I banged on the screen, ringing the doorbell several times over, but my only answer was the squawking of a bird from a nearby tree. I attempted to open the window but it didn't budge. I hopped off the porch and darted around the back of the house, taking two steps at a time, losing my flip flops in the process. The back door was not only unlocked but had been left partially open.

"Preppy?" I asked, pushing open the door so hard it slammed

against the wall with a thud. I darted from room to room, finding them all empty. It was dark and musty, the curtains all drawn and not a single light was on. The smell of weed and something sinister hung heavy in the air. The shag carpet was old and stiff, stabbing the bottoms of my bare feet as I jogged down the hallway, stopping in front of a closed door when I heard movement from within.

"Preppy!" I called out, jiggling the handle but it didn't budge. When there was no answer I ran back to the kitchen and searched for something I could use to unlock it. I grabbed a knife from a drawer but dropped it when my eyes locked on the bar stools. I darted around the corner, picked one up and lugged it down the hall. I didn't stop at the door, but instead used every bit of my forward momentum to hurl the stool against it. Over and over again I bashed the legs of the stool into the door, splintering the wood around the handle until I made a hole large enough to fit a couple of my fingers through, the jagged wood slicing my skin as I felt around for the lock and flipped it open. I wasted no time opening the door.

I tried to prepare myself for the worst.

The worst was exactly what I found.

One look at him was all it took to realize how wrong I'd been. The spark I'd seen in his eyes that first night wasn't the sign of a monster. It wasn't the glint of an evil man.

It was a warning.

A warning that he'd been hurt and had never healed. It was the anger and the fear of his past lurking just beyond the surface waiting for him to finally break.

And break he did.

The room was dark, except for the green lava lamp on the

bedside table and a small reading lamp that was turned over onto the floor, blinking on and off. Preppy was pacing the room, shirtless. His jeans were open and hanging low on his hips, his belt dangling from the loops. His hair was disheveled. He carried a bottle of whiskey by the neck in one hand, a lit cigarette in the other.

"Why?" he asked, the pain in his voice cut through me, sharper than any knife. He kicked the closet door in with his foot, sending it careening off the hinges.

"Preppy," I said softly, taking a tentative step toward him. "Preppy, it's me. Dre. Doc." I stopped at the foot of the bed as he continued to pace, and although I was right there it was like he couldn't see me, his eyes glazed over. He let his cigarette fall onto the carpet, and immediately I stomped it out with my foot before it could catch fire. He threw the bottle into the bathroom where it smashed the mirror into pieces, sending shards of glass shooting around the room like shrapnel. He pushed down his jeans and took his soft cock in hand stroking up and down angrily.

"Preppy. It's me," I said again, taking another step toward him. There was no fucking way I was leaving him in that condition. I was either going to find a way to drag him out of it or we were going down together.

"Go away," he barked, his voice a strangled cry. He fell to his knees, bracing himself with one hand on the carpet as he continued to stroke himself furiously, growling in frustration until finally he stood up and stepped out of his jeans.

"I'm not going anywhere, Preppy."

He paced the room, yelling at the wall. He overturned the desk. He paced back to his nightstand, where he leaned over and snorted three lines of blow in a row. He ran to the closet and came out wielding a large pocket knife, stabbing it into the drywall and running it down to the baseboard with his teeth bared and his face turning ten shades of red. His knuckles were white. "I was a good boy!" he cried out. "Bad boys have wrinkled pants. Bad boys wear t-shirts and ripped jeans. I was a good boy. No fucking wrinkles. I was such a good boy!" he yelled as his fist sailed through the wall.

Preppy was in the grips of his own personal hell and I had no idea how to drag him back out.

"Fuck you! Fuck yooooooouuuuuuuu," he screamed to the ceiling, banging his head against the wall again and again, so hard his eyebrow split and blood trailed down his face, narrowly missing his eye.

"Don't do this!" I shouted. "Stop! Stop!" I cried, jumping up onto a coffee table that was pushed against the wall.

"Die motherfucker! You're dead, just fucking die you god damned asshole!" he screamed again, the tendons tight in his neck and the veins in his forearms popping at the surface of his skin. I reached for him, grabbing his face on both sides and pulled him toward me. Consequences be damned.

He swatted at my hands and pulled away.

"Don't you see? He broke me. I'm broken!" he shouted. His eyes were bloodshot and his voice raspy from yelling. "And that fucking bitch let it happen! She fucking let it happen!"

"You're okay. You're not there anymore."

"But I am! I'm always fucking there!" He pushed his hands through his hair and looked as if he were pulling it out. He spun in a circle and dropped to his knees again, tugging on his cock.

"No!" I screamed, "Look at me." I jumped off the coffee

table and got on my knees, pressing my forehead to his. "Samuel Clearwater, you are a good man. I see that in you. Everyone sees that in you. Don't let him take that away from you."

Preppy stared straight at the wall. "I hate him. I hate her. I hate them so fucking much."

"I do too," I said, not realizing that I'd started to cry along with him. "I do too," I repeated, because I truly meant it. "I hate that man and what he did to you. If he were still alive I'd kill the fucker myself and if I were here when she came I wouldn't have stopped you if you tried to kill her."

Preppy stood up abruptly, knocking me back onto my ass. He slammed his open palms against the wall, and dropped his forehead against it, the blood from his eyebrow splattering on the light blue paint. I jumped to my feet and again hopped up onto the coffee table, needing the height in order to put myself at his level. I grabbed his face again and when he tried to rip it away I dug my fingers into his cheeks and pulled harder, until he had no choice but to look at me.

"Go away, I'm just going to hurt you," he said, his eyes bulging from his head.

"Then hurt me." Preppy was staring right at me, but he was looking right through me. "Hurt me. Let me make this better for you."

I pulled him closer and felt his cock hardening against my thigh.

"I..." he started, wrestling with his words and feelings, and unable to communicate to me what he needed, but thankfully I already knew.

"It's okay," I assured him, tugging him back. "You need me?"

"Yes," he choked out. "I need you. So much."

"Then use me," I said, putting every ounce of determination I have into my voice. "I WANT you to use me." I took a step back and lifted my shirt over my head. I unclasped my bra and tossed it to the floor.

I stepped down from the table and stood in the middle of the room, my breasts exposed to him. I unbuttoned my shorts and Preppy's eyes roamed down my body. Up on the table he looked very much like an evil demon, a gargoyle high up on a castle wall. The moonlight from the window behind him casting him in an eerie shadow.

Preppy jumped down and stalked over to me like a crazed animal. He grabbed my hips and spun me around, pushing me roughly against the wall, my cheek landing with a painful thud as it connected. He pulled down my shorts and panties, and then he was on me. His chest against my back. One hand grabbing my breast and the other between my legs.

This wasn't about me or my pleasure. This wasn't sex. This was a motherfucking exorcism. But the second his finger swiped over my folds I became wet. So wet, I knew Preppy's fingers had to be soaked. He growled, thrusting his cock against my lower back.

Kicking my legs apart he lined up his shaft with my pussy. He grabbed a fistful of my hair and yanked so hard I felt some hairs tear from my scalp. Wrapping his other hand around my throat he surged inside me, pushing into me like he was pushing into his salvation, forcing himself past my tightness, groaning and growling until he was seated inside of me as far as my body would let him. He squeezed my throat, and although I could still breathe, I started to see stars as he began to pull out of me slowly, pushing back into me like he was punishing me.

There was no foreplay. No sweetness. There was nothing but us in that room. Preppy was haunted and I was willing to let him fuck me to death, if it meant he'd be free from the demon within.

It hurt. But with the pain came a pleasure I never expected, a jarring bolt of lightning that had my pussy squeezing his cock tighter and tighter as he fucked me harder and harder. Furiously, he pounded into me, slamming my head against the wall, squeezing my throat tighter. My pleasure escalated as he slammed into me one final time and I came and came and came as Preppy pulled out. And as he released, he screamed and cried, "Fuck him. Fuck all of them Fuuuuuuucccckkkk!" He spread my ass cheeks apart, shooting hot spurts all over my freshly fucked pussy while he continued to squeeze my windpipe tighter, until everything started to fade.

"Doc?" Preppy's voice sounded a million miles away. "Doc!" he shouted, and suddenly the blackness faded away and the blue wall again came into focus. He spun me around and grabbed me by the shoulders. He stared down at me as if he were just realizing I was there. His pupils were still dilated, a shit ton of coke will do that to a person, but now they were focused. Intense even. "Doc?" he asked again, lifting me into his arms. He carried me over to his bed and laid me down, climbing onto the mattress beside me and pulling me against his chest.

"Are you okay?" he asked.

"Yes," I said, still catching my breath.

He lowered himself down onto the mattress, resting his cheek against my stomach, smearing the blood on his eyebrow onto my skin. "Are you?"

She shook his head against me. "I don't think I've ever been okay," he admitted. His shoulders rose and fell. His inhales were erratic, and that's when I realized he was quietly sobbing against me. He wrapped his hands tightly around my thighs as if he were holding on for dear life. "He made me this monster. I'm sick and I'm twisted, and it's because he couldn't keep his fucking hands to himself!"

"He's gone now, he's dead," I reassured him, smoothing back his hair from his face.

"He's dead, but he's not gone," he pointed to his head. "In here, that fucker is very much alive."

I pressed my hand over his heart which was beating a thousand miles a minute. "He's not here, though, and that's a start."

Preppy slowly looked up with red rimmed eyes, white powder caked in his nostrils. "No room for him in there," he said, resting his chin on my stomach. "Because you're in there, and for a tiny thing you take up a fuck of a lot of space."

My heart warmed at his admission, but it could have been his pain talking. Either way, it gave me a flash of hope that he could climb out from the depths and overcome his demons.

"I need to take care of that," I pointed to his forehead, where the blood had stopped oozing from the wound but still needed to be cleaned and covered. I made a move to get up to go get a washcloth and a bandaid, but he stopped me.

"No, don't go," he pleaded, grabbing my hand and pressing my palm to his cheek. He then pressed his own palm to the center of my chest between my breasts. "Am I here?" he asked.

There was no denying that Preppy was there. Not anymore. Not after this. "You are."

"I'm sorry," he said, and coming from the man who didn't

apologize, it meant everything.

"There isn't anything to apologize for," I said, because there wasn't. "I wanted you, too," I admitted.

Preppy looked up at me with glistening eyes, his pupils the size of the moon. "I know what will make me feel even better," he said, releasing me. He climbed over my body, his face hovering just over mine.

This time is was him taking my head in his hands as he looked down at me, his thumbs tracing lightly over my lips and my cheeks, his fingers threading in my hair.

"What?" I asked.

He lowered himself on top of me, the bridge of his nose brushing mine. "This," he said, pressing his lips against my lips in the softest, most demanding kiss that ever existed. He opened his mouth and I followed, moaning into him when our tongues finally touched. The softness quickly turned to furious passion when he molded his lips to mine, and I know he was giving me everything he had in that kiss because I felt it all. His frustration, his sadness, his hurt, his desire, his anger, his confusion, but there was something else there.

Something stronger. More powerful. More *everything*.

Above all else, I felt his love.

He'd said he couldn't keep me.

That didn't mean I wouldn't always be his.

CHAPTER THIRTY-ONE

PREPPY

EVEN WHEN DRE was at her worst, a strung out junkie on the verge of suicide, she was still a better person than I'd ever be. I knew that now, more than ever before. She didn't need to come to my rescue, but she did. She rescued me from myself and sacrificed her own safety and happiness for mine.

I also knew now, more than ever, that I wanted to keep her. Unfortunately, I also knew now, more than ever, that I couldn't.

I don't know exactly how long we stayed there in my bed, locked away up in my room. For days we got up only to eat or shower. We fucked, watched movies, and we fucked some more. I couldn't get enough of Dre or her tight as fuck pussy. I spent my time coming in and on every part of her body.

We left the house once for me to take her over to Mirna's so she could grab some of Dre's things and then visit Mirna, who was still in stable condition. After, we'd come right back to my place where she taught me how to make pancakes properly, using one of Mirna's recipes while wearing this lacy red apron... and nothing else. I'm not a religious man, but I saw Jesus when I tasted those pancakes and almost cried when the fluffy deliciousness touched my lips. I vowed to her right then and there that I'd never make pancakes from a box ever again.

And then I bent her over the counter and fucked my gratitude into her.

There was no way I could ever repay her for what she did for me, no way to tell her "thank you" in a way that would accurately convey how much I appreciated her dragging me back from the depths my mother's visit had sent me down into. So instead of using my words, I dragged her back to my bed and used my cock. My fingers. My mouth. My tongue. I made her come with everything I had, until my dick was a deep shade of purple and about to burst with need, before I would even think about tickling her woman cave with my man meat.

We did something else I liked.

We talked.

We talked about almost everything. Her family. Her school. Books. Movies. I found out she played the violin in the sixth grade and she had to talk me out of going to the 24 hour pawn in the middle of the night to buy her one, because the image of her playing for me naked wasn't an easy one to shake.

Seeing her face light up as she was quoting *Anchorman* was an entirely new level of weird turn on for me.

I knew I needed to come clean with her. Things had changed. Shifted. The feelings I had for her were more than friends and more than just friends who fucked. They were just…more.

She deserved to know the truth about her dad and I planned on telling her.

Later.

She also needed rehab. Proper rehab.

But instead of bringing up what would inevitably break us, I did what I'd always done. I was selfish. I'm savoring every moment with Dre, although I knew we were fucking on borrowed time.

There was no better reminder of how short that time was when reality pulled up, in the form of roaring bike engines rattling the walls like deep thunder.

I knew we didn't have long.

What I didn't know was that time was already up.

CHAPTER THIRTY-TWO

DRE

PREPPY TOOK OFF downstairs when he heard the bikes and told me to stay put, and so I did. But when I got out of the shower and realized that an hour passed and he still hadn't come back up, I threw on some clothes and went down to find him.

I padded down the stairs in my bare feet. My hair slicked back, still wet from my shower, soaking my tight, white tank top and making my red bra visible underneath. When I pushed open the back door the music hit me first, and I realized that the bikers hadn't wasted any time. A party was already in full swing. Leather clad men were everywhere. Topless women strewn about their laps. Laughter and dancing surrounded the raging bonfire in the pit in the center of the yard.

A giant of a man with blond hair stepped in front of me, obscuring my view of the party down below. He looked very much like a tattooed viking. His blue eyes were the brightest I'd ever seen. "Hey, beautiful," he said, with a slow southern accent. He glanced up at the house and then back to me. "Any special reason why you think you're allowed in there? House is off limits. The party's out back." He gestured with his thumb over his shoulder to the people down below.

"I was changing my clothes," I explained, taken momentarily

off guard why this stranger was questioning why I was there. Why was he there?

"In the house?" he asked, as if he still couldn't believe it.

"Uh...I mean...yeah," I said, unsure why he was so confused. That's when the recognition hit me. I'd never seen him before, but there was no mistaking who he was from Preppy's description. But before the words "You must be Bear" could slip from my mouth, Bear's hands were on me, patting me down.

"You steal anything from in there?" he asked, running his hands over my skirt and up the sides of my tank top. He didn't stop when he came to my breasts, squeezing them roughly.

"No!" I said, stepping away and smacking his hand. "I was invited by Preppy, asshole. Before you so rudely frisked me, I was about to tell you that I know who you are. You're Bear, Preppy's friend, right?"

Bear nodded and was silent for a moment. He looked me up and down, his gaze lingering on the scars on my arms. "Sorry, beautiful," he finally said, extending his hand. I took it and he pulled me up against his massive wall of a body. "I know who you are, too." Suddenly, his frown turned into a smile. He draped his arm over my shoulder like we were old friends.

"You do?" *Preppy had told him about me?* "Well, it's great to finally meet you, Bear," I said, craning my neck.

"Likewise," he said. I beamed like a school girl. My face turned red and my heart fluttered. I felt practically giddy.

"Yeah, Prep said you'd fit in real nicely with the Bastards. Don't worry about a damn thing. We treat all our girls real good. You'll love club life. Parties, fuckin', blow, more fuckin'. Ain't nothing better than life with the club."

What in the hell?

"I know the brothers will like you because I'm liking you." He leaned close and whispered in my ear, "Tonight we can even have a party of our own before you get to know my boys. Get acquainted."

"Wait," I said, taking a step back and remembering his earlier comment. "Preppy said that I..." I started, as it all started to sink in.

Bear interrupted, like he knew what I was going to say. He didn't. "Preppy can watch. It's kind of his thing." He leaned down and brushed his nose against my ear. I was too full of rage to pull away, but at the same time had the urge to knee Bear in the balls. Thankfully, someone called his name from the fire pit. "I'll be right back," he said and with a smack on my ass, he stepped down off the back deck and took off across the yard toward the fire.

I was a stupid stupid girl.

Preppy had told me time and time again that he couldn't keep me.

He never said anything about throwing me away.

★ ★ ★

PREPPY

"THANKS FOR RECOMMENDING the talent," Bear said, coming up next to me and lighting a cigarette. "She's hot, like a weird cute kind of hot. Bet her pussy's cute, too. Told her you liked to watch and she seemed into it."

"Wait, who the fuck are you talking about?" I asked. I'd come downstairs to tell Bear to fuck off and get his biker bitches out of there when I'd gotten a call from the Georgia State prison. It was King and the news wasn't good. His two to five year sentence had jumped to three to six. All I wanted after ending that call was to go back to bed and back to Dre.

"I'm talking about her," Bear said, pointing across the yard.

To Dre.

FUCK. That's when I remembered our conversation and instantly regretted ever opening my fucking mouth. This night was too much. I had to get her the fuck away from these bikers. "Don't you have your own club to party at?"

"Gets old," was all the explanation Bear gave for the sudden intrusion, although it wasn't his first. "Besides, my place here is better." Which was true. His apartment he'd built in the garage was ten times the size of his room at the club.

"So you gotta bring everyone?"

"Fuck, don't get your panties in a twist. Thought you'd be liking us around after being alone with your crazy thoughts and porn for so long."

"King's got another year. Some sort of fight," I said on an exhale.

"Fuck, man." He stubbed out his cigarette and glanced across the yard to Dre, watching her every move. Suddenly, I had the desire to push my thumbs into his eye sockets.

Dre's black hair was still wet and slicked back off her forehead. A wet spot formed in the middle of the back of her white shirt, exposing the strap of her red bra. She took a sip from a red cup while she chatted and smiled with one of the Bastard prospects. Some young kid that was about to meet a quick and hasty end if he even so much as touched my girl.

MY girl?

Where the fuck did that come from?

As if she felt us staring at her, she looked over her shoulder and I was met with a very familiar pair of dark-brown eyes.

Correction. Dark-brown, ANGRY-AS-FUCK, eyes.

Well, she wasn't the only one who was fucking angry.

"Ain't shit we can do about it, man," Bear said. "Although, I'm thinking she can make me feel a fuck of a lot better."

I popped my jaw when the prospect leaned over to whisper something in Dre's ear. Maybe when she let me fuck my craziness away I somehow managed to fuck her common sense out of her, because when she leaned back and laughed at whatever the motherfucker said to her, I saw red. I popped my jaw from side to side, again.

I was going to fuck the sense back into her.

Bear was about to wonder why I was dragging his new BBB off by her hair into the house, when Wolf came over and whispered in his ear. "Duty fucking calls, man," Bear said, pointing again to Dre. "I see the way you're looking at her. Don't start without me. I want in on this one." Bear swallowed the contents of the shot Wolf just passed him. With a slap on my back he disappeared with Wolf into the shadows of the car port, where three other of his brothers were waiting for them.

I wasted no time making a beeline toward Dre and when she saw me coming, her eyes widened and her mouth fell open. When she realized her mistake in showing her emotions she slapped a mask over her face, but it was too late. I'd already seen her fear and my cock was already hard because of it.

I couldn't blame her.

She should've been afraid.

VERY fucking afraid.

CHAPTER THIRTY-THREE

DRE

"**W**HAT THE FUCK?" I shrieked, as I was lifted up by the waist and hoisted over Preppy's shoulder. He stomped off into the shadows, away from the house. He carried me into the garage, passed tarp covered vehicles, then through another door in the very back, which led to a small cluttered apartment of sorts. I pounded my fists onto his back and screamed at him to put me down.

Preppy kicked the door shut and bent at the waist, tossing me off of his shoulder, my back slamming against the door as I stumbled on my feet. Preppy loosened his bow tie then closed the distance between us. His body pressed up against mine. His knee between my legs didn't afford me much room to escape. I hated that my body didn't understand its reaction to him, my dampened panties weren't welcome. It didn't get that I was angry. All it understood was that Preppy was near and because of that, my clit thrummed with excitement when what I really wanted to do was pummel him.

"What the fuck do you think you're doing out there with that kid?" Preppy snarled.

"Wait? You're pissed...at ME?" I asked in disbelief. "You aren't allowed to be pissed. I'm the one that's fucking pissed!" I hissed, trying to rise off the door, but Preppy placed his hands on both sides of my head and pushed his hard body against mine. His cool breath on my face. His angry eyes looking down into mine.

I laughed. I laughed because the entire situation was so ridiculous that it was funny. I stopped laughing when Preppy pinned me with his hips against the door. "What's so fucking funny?" he growled.

I was so tired of being the stupid girl who made nothing but stupid decisions. "I know you think differently than most people, Preppy, and honestly it's one of the things I love about you. But I never thought that after everything, you'd think it was a good idea to pimp me out to Bear and his club."

Preppy gnashed his teeth together, his face reddened with his rage.

"Let me refresh your memory. I'm a addict. A junkie. I'm not a fucking whore. Yours or anyone else's," I said.

"That's where you're wrong," Preppy reached between my legs, stroking my clit over my panties. "Because you could be a million miles away," he moved down to my pussy, stroking it with two fingers, "and this pussy will still be mine. And apparently, you thought it was a good fucking idea because Bear wants to fuck you tonight. Invited me to watch him audition you for the club." The tendons in his neck tightened. He pushed forward with his hips to emphasize his point, pressing his massive erection right against my clit. My hips bucked involuntarily and I closed my eyes, briefly, to try and compose myself, calling on my anger while my traitorous body wanted nothing more than for him to strip me naked and fuck me so hard neither one of us could remember why we were mad. But I knew why because there was no mistaking the look on Preppy's face. The look that told me everything I needed to know and although the reasons *why* weren't clear, the message was.

This was the end.

Recognizing that feeling only enraged me more. "It makes sense, though, since Mirna will be moving to Sarasota soon. Maybe I'll sell the house and move to the club with Bear. See what being a club slut's all about, since you think I'd be so good at it." I bucked my hips against him and he hissed through his teeth. "After all, it's not like you can keep me." It felt good to throw his words in his face.

"You're right," he growled. "I *can't* keep you." He reached behind me and grabbed a handful of my ass cheek. "But that doesn't mean I can't fuck you." He covered his lips with mine in a rough kiss that was anything but apologetic. That kiss was downright hateful.

I was so furious I could hear my own teeth grinding in my head, but as much as I didn't want to kiss him I couldn't NOT kiss him. And when he parted his lips, I couldn't NOT bite down hard. He reared back and smiled down at me. He slowly licked the drop of blood from the corner of his mouth in a seduction of my senses. He smeared red on his cheek then wiped his thumb over my mouth, gathering another drop of his blood.

I don't know what came over me, but I opened my mouth and licked the blood from his finger. He groaned and kissed me again, this time harder with more passion, more hatred.

Just MORE.

Teeth clacked against teeth, lips connecting with chins and cheeks and necks, hands roamed over each others bodies like we couldn't get enough.

We nipped and sucked and licked and kissed, until nothing existed but the two of us and the hum of want hanging in the air.

A feeling between us buzzing louder than the bug zapper outside the garage window. Preppy walked backward to the bed, pulling me off the wall and dragging me with him. He fell onto the mattress with me in his arms and I had no choice but to straddle him, my short skirt riding up my thighs exposing my panties. Feeling his giant erection pulse against me sent a jolt of pleasure shot directly through my core and tightened my thighs around his torso, feeling the ridges of his abs against my hands as I dragged my fingers down until they were untucking his shirt. I moaned, loud, uncaring of who might be right outside the door. If this was our last time together, I wasn't going to hold anything back. My nipples tightened to the point of pain. My panties were drenched, my thighs were shaking with anticipation. I was breathing hard, higher on his unique scent, woodsy soap and pot smoke, than I'd ever been on H.

For a while he just stared at me, his own breathing labored, with a look so intense I bit my lip and had to look away. He pulled me back to face him. "Look at me, Dre. There's something I have to tell you. Something I've been wanting to say since the night we met." I held my breath, hoping he could fix whatever it was between us before it was too late. Brushing my hair behind my ear, he breathed, "You have epic fucking tits." I fought the urge to giggle when I realized that he'd changed his mind and decided against telling me whatever it was that was on his mind. His brows were drawn together in the middle of his forehead as he continued to stare into me. He moved his hand from my ear to behind my neck and pulled me down closer, inspecting my face like he was searching me, but I realized that was wrong. He wasn't searching me. He was memorizing me. My heart sank. I felt naked and exposed, although I was fully clothed. I tried to look away, but he held me firmly in place, his thumb tracing the line of my jaw. Instinctively, I leaned into his touch. "You really are fucking beautiful, Doc." He tightened his grip on my neck and pulled me down, lifting his head up off the mattress, meeting me halfway and crushing our lips together.

Preppy was funny, outrageous, ridiculous. Before that very kiss, the last way I'd ever have described him was "soft." Yet, when he molded his lips to mine and his tongue found its way into my mouth and he groaned when it connected and tangled with mine, it's the first word that came to mine. Soft, yet firm. He knew what he wanted from our kiss and he took it, just like he'd wanted me and he took me. His fingers tangled in my hair as he pulled me fully down on top of him, my breasts pressed firmly against his hard chest.

He was relentless in his pursuit of my mouth, his facial hair brushing against my face in another sensation that had me writhing on his lap, needing more of him than just his hands and mouth. He held my waist with one hand and lifted his hips, pressing his very hard and very large cock against my exposed panties, causing my entire body to shake with need.

I clenched my thighs around his waist to hold him closer, holding him against the spot I wanted him most, my core tightening suddenly and unexpectedly. I yelped into his mouth, but he didn't stop for a second, didn't pause, didn't ease up on me.

I didn't know if he was trying to fuck me or trying to kill me but, either way, I knew after that night a part of me would be broken.

Preppy was very much like heroin. Being with him sent me into a state of euphoria, free from the trap of my own thoughts, my past, free from anything and everything on the outside of that little room. Outside of us and our tangle of limbs.

He was an addiction. I craved him, and I wanted more.

But just like heroin, the high was all a fucking lie. I believed he was good for me when in fact, he was worse than any drug.

The door opened and Bear stepped in, setting down a half empty bottle of whiskey on the nightstand. He reached for his belt buckle. "Prep, you watching?" he asked, with a big smile that reached his sparkling blue eyes which were half lidded with both liquor and lust. I was still straddling Preppy as his eyes roamed over my body. "Or you want me to show you how it's done?"

CHAPTER THIRTY-FOUR

PREPPY

MY COCK WAS rock fucking hard. So hard that I was in physical pain. A beautiful kind of torture I never wanted to end.

Bear's words snapped me out of my Dre induced fog. What the fuck was I doing? I brought her in here to tell her everything and walk away from her so she could live a normal life. This was supposed to be done. Over. So why was there this annoying narration in the back of my mind telling me it was only just the beginning?

Dre was looking from Bear to me, still straddling my lap, her perfect tits heaving up and down, pressing her fingers against her swollen bottom lip, and I knew she was waiting for me to tell him to get the fuck out but that would just prolong the inevitable. This needed to be over and it needed to be over now.

"You first," I said to Bear. Dre's head snapped to me but I looked away, not wanting to see the look of surprise and disappointment on her face, or maybe because I didn't want her to see my heart fucking breaking, which I was sure was written all over my fucking face.

I lifted her off my lap and my poor hard cock practically weeped over the loss of feeling her warm cotton covered pussy through my pants. As I got up and leaned against the wall, I ignored my rapidly beating heart and tight chest, chalking it up to all the dry humping we'd just done.

I chanced a glance over at Dre, who was leaning forward with her hands against the mattress. The look of disappointment and surprise I expected was definitely there, along with something else. Dre was looking at me with her head tilted to the side, squinting like I was very small or very far away.

That look could've meant she was thinking about knitting or aerospace engineering, for all I fucking knew. All I knew for sure was that she'd be running out that door in the next few seconds, pissed to all hell and cursing me to the devil, and that would be the end of that.

The end of us.

She'd hate me, but that's something I would just have to fucking deal with. It's not like she'd be the first chick I'd pissed the fuck off. I'd rather her hate me for this than the truth.

My stomach flipped.

I leaned against the wall, suddenly ornery as fuck, crossing my arms over my chest. Bear slid his thick leather belt from the loops, dropping it to the floor with a clank. He approached the bed, shoving out of his boots as he pushed his jeans down by the waistband, stepping out of them when they reached the floor, shaking them off his foot, kicking them over to the side.

Why was she still there? Why the fuck wasn't she already turning tail and running for dear life?

I stared down at the floor and waited for Dre to run by, cursing up a storm inside my mind. But still, she remained. When I heard the mattress dip and the springs squeak, my eyes shot to the bed where Bear had positioned himself on his knees behind my girl, running his fingertips down her shoulders and arms. He moved her hair to the side and pressed his lips to her skin and STILL she didn't run.

When our gazes met, I knew that there was no misreading what she was saying with her gleaming black eyes. The bitch was calling my bluff. Her lips quirked up on the side, challenging me as she leaned back into Bear's touch, her eyes never leaving mine.

What in the holy-ever-loving-fuck.

This bitch wants a challenge, fine, she's got it.

For the most part I was awesome at life, but what Dre didn't know was that I was even better at games, and she just called me out to play a game of sexual chicken I had no intentions of losing.

She reached up and wrapped her arms around Bear's neck, encouraging him to explore more of her skin with his mouth. He dipped lower, running his lips across her collarbone.

I made my move, one I was hoping would win me the game right out of the gate. I tipped my chin to her and winked, hoping to piss her off and send her running once and for all, but no. Instead, she returned my wink with a smile. She sucked in her bottom lip and let out an exaggerated moan when Bear's hand grazed the bottom of her tit through her shirt. She took one arm down from around his neck and when Bear wasn't paying attention, because he was too busy running his hands all over my girl, she lifted her hand against her stomach where he couldn't see and she flashed me a finger.

Her middle finger.

Fuck.

Game fucking on.

★　★　★

DRE

FLIPPING HIM OFF may have gone a step too far, but I was already a step too far and it was only because Preppy was who pushed me there.

My heart lurched in my chest.

If this was how he chose to push me away then he was going to have to suffer the consequences of his decision. He'd made his bed, he could lie in it. Or better yet, watch ME lie in it.

With Bear.

I'd have to be blind not to notice that Bear was beyond attractive. Those bright-blue eyes and all that mess of blond hair, tattoos, and muscles, would make any girl twitchy for a touch. Bear did it for me, but that was just basic biology. It was NOTHING compared to the way that just one look from Preppy made my toes curl and left my body aching and tingling for his touch. That's when I realized that Preppy wasn't like heroin at all, he was like speed. Making my heart race, my muscles feel restless, and causing my brain to come alive with a million and one different thoughts about him, all at the same time, most of those about him touching me. Tasting me. Wanting me.

Needing me.

Bear was walking sex, but he was no Samuel Clearwater. Who I craved in my very soul. I didn't even know desire until Preppy pushed his way into my life, and the man who made me feel again was now standing next to the bed with his back against the wall, staring at the floor with his hands in his pockets. His hair mussed from our kissing session. I licked my lower lip in an attempt to taste his kiss again.

Preppy looked up suddenly, almost like he could hear what I was thinking. When he saw me staring, he plastered a fake smirk on his gorgeous face that no matter how hurt or pissed off I was or how fake his smile, it still made my belly flip and my nipples tighten.

He may be able to fool Bear, but there was no fucking way he was fooling me.

I wanted Preppy to send Bear away, strip me naked, and fuck me sideways. I wanted him to tell me I was his. Not just my pussy. ALL OF ME.

I wanted him to keep me.

But just then, I saw the mask click in place. The one he put on when he wanted to shut out the world, and I knew there was no coming back from where we'd just crossed over.

A part of me wanted nothing more than to hold him and tell him it was okay, and a part of me hated him and wanted him to hurt as badly as he'd made me hurt.

Bear's warm chest pressed against my back, his lips trailed over every inch of skin on my shoulders and neck, but it wasn't his touch making the hairs on my arms stand on end or drenching my panties. It was the look on Preppy's face. The cocky smirk was gone, replaced briefly with a flash of hurt that I would have missed if I'd blinked a second earlier.

Preppy cleared his throat and straightened his posture, putting his mask back in place and returning my hand gesture with a middle finger of his own, pressed against his closed lips.

Challenge accepted.

We were over well before we had a chance to get started, but we were about to go out with a bang.

CHAPTER THIRTY-FIVE

DRE

B EAR PULLED MY tank top off of my head and dropped it to the floor. He pushed down my bra, exposing my breasts to Preppy, whose gaze dropped from my eyes to my chest. Bear twisted and pulled at my nipples, rolling them between his fingers. Preppy watched with his mouth partially open as my nipples peaked and stood firmly at attention, pointing accusingly toward him. His jaw tightened, and a twisted part of me reveled in the fact that he was jealous and pissed off, even if it was his own fucking fault.

"Let's get rid of this," Bear said, pushing my skirt down. He pressed down between my shoulder blades, shoving my chest onto the mattress, my butt high up in the air. He slapped each ass cheek once, before hooking his thumbs into my panties and pulling them off.

Preppy's eyes went from my ass to my face, and that's when I realized that I was losing the challenge after all, a part of him was loving what he was seeing when I was hoping it would enrage him and make him feel guilty for what he'd done. I was still pissed, but witnessing Preppy turned on was enough to make me wet all over again. "Fuck you have a nice pussy," Bear said from behind me. He leaned over me, pushing me down further into the mattress. That's when I felt his hard cock, large and hot, throbbing against my lower back. He reached between my legs and circled the wetness at my opening. "Fuck, your so fucking wet and ready," he growled. He smelled like whiskey, cologne, and motor oil. A sexy combination of smells that had me arching into him when he touched me, my eyes never leaving Preppy's, who swallowed hard.

He pushed off the wall and, for a moment, I thought it was over. That I'd pushed him far enough and had won our little game. He stalked over to the bed. "Lift her up," he said to Bear, pulling down his pants and kicking off his boxers. His enormous cock bobbed up and down as it was freed from its confines. The tip swollen and purple, dripping.

I licked my lips and groaned at the sight.

Bear kept his body pressed against mine, he lifted me up by my shoulders until we were both back on our knees. His breath against my neck, one hand on my breast the other between my legs, his thumb strumming against my clit like he was playing the guitar. Preppy, now completely naked, the chords of muscles in his neck tight, the lines of muscle leading down to all his glory contracted as he laid down on the bed with his head on the pillow. "Come here," he said, his voice strained. Bear released his hold on me and I crawled slowly up Preppy's beautiful body until we were face to face, and I was hovering just inches over his lips. He reached down between us, his hand finding my wetness.

He grabbed my hips and ground me against his shaft. Desire coursed through my veins, along with the deep need to have him inside me, to fill me.

Preppy reached up, grabbing onto the headboard, his biceps flexing. I reached down and stroked him from root to tip and he hissed between his teeth. Another hand reached under me from behind, again circling my opening, gathering my wetness on his fingertips. The additional set of hands, the scent of two men, the heat of having them both surrounding me, took my body to the very height of sensation.

Preppy looked around my shoulder at Bear, whose hand was suddenly gone. Preppy pulled me down by my neck, bringing me down to him again. With his other hand he grabbed his shaft and rubbed it around in my folds, gathering my wetness on the tip. Just as he started pushing inside, I felt another type of pressure against my ass and that's when Preppy surged inside of me, kissing me like the crazed and crazy man he was.

Around my back entrance was a feeling very much like when your foot falls asleep and then comes back to life. A tingling. The pins and needles type of sensation that had me anticipating Bear's penetration. There was a pinch of pain that had me clinging to Preppy, who stilled inside me, my pussy tightening around his cock, as if even it, was holding on to him for dear life. Preppy swallowed my cries into his mouth and groaned. His kiss unrelenting as Bear fully seated himself inside of me. I felt full. So fucking full.

And, even though I wasn't supposed to.

I loved it.

Love wasn't the only unexpected feeling I had.

There was also POWER.

I was the one in control. Helpless between these two men, but in charge of their pleasure, and by giving them the power it was me who had the real power. Bear's hands again covered my breasts as I my face hovered just inches above Preppy's. Bear reared back and thrust forward into me, and I cried out. I expected it to hurt, but it didn't. It felt good. So fucking good, because when he pushed inside me again, I wanted to feel even more. I rocked on top of Preppy and it was like every part of my body was being touched, stroked, seduced. I was teetering on the edge of orgasm the second that Preppy began to fuck up into me.

I was dripping down Preppy's cock. He lifted me up, just so he could push me back down again, thrusting up into me and pushing me back onto Bear, who matched Preppy's rhythm which was quick and brutal, he fucked me like he was deranged. Bear's hips slammed roughly against my ass. He growled a deep angry growl every time he was fully inside of me and moaned when he pulled back out, his fingers digging into my shoulders as he held on to me like he was riding me. Preppy's hands trailed down the valley of my breasts and the flat of my stomach, until he was between my legs, stroking my clit yet again, playing it like an instrument he was well acquainted with. "You like that?" Bear muttered against my ear, as Preppy's leisurely stroking of my clit became a furious motion. Bear thrusted harder inside of me, his balls smacking against my ass.

I opened my eyes and locked on to Preppy's gaze to find him already watching me. It was the quietest he'd ever been since I met him. Especially during sex. He looked as if he were barely holding on. His forehead lined. His chest rising and falling quickly as he panted through his pleasure. The way he tipped his chin up and his cock throbbed inside my pussy, along with one long deep surge of Bear, was sending me closer and closer toward a thunderous release. "Yes, yes!" I cried, as my insides pulsed and contracted, drawing both men deeper inside of me.

This wasn't just sex.

It was beautiful torture.

Beads of sweat gathered on Preppy's forehead, his jaw clenched hard as he furiously fucked me, thrusting wildly into me from underneath, his grip on my hips so tight it was painful. The muscles of his thighs tensed as I rode him. Bear grunted, low and sexy, the sound vibrating through me with each stroke. "I'm gonna..." I started, but I couldn't even get it out because the sensation that had been building in my lower stomach, a slow burn, had turned into an all out raging wildfire, spreading from my core to the rest of my body and back, pulsing with each wave of pleasure that continued on and on and on. Preppy craned his neck, "Fuck," he groaned, his lips found mine once again and he absorbed my cries into his mouth as I screamed out my orgasm. He roared into me as I felt his cock grow impossibly hard before shooting his hot release deep inside of me. I crashed down from my out of this world orgasm so hard I could barley stay upright, falling forward onto Preppy with him still deep inside my pussy. Bear quickening his pace in and out of my ass, causing the dying sensations inside of me to start to grow all over again. I clenched around Preppy's softening cock which twitched in response.

"God damn, it felt so fucking good when you came around my cock," muttered Bear, who pulled out of me on the strangled cry of his own release.

Still drunk from my orgasm, I didn't move from Preppy's chest as Bear rolled off of me and onto his back at the end of the bed. "Holy shit," he said. I glanced over my shoulder to see him disposing of a condom I didn't know he had on, but was suddenly really grateful for.

Preppy finally spoke, "I'm glad it was good for you, Care Bear, now get the fuck out."

Bear looked to us with a questioning look in his his eyes. "You kids gonna be okay unsupervised?" he asked sarcastically, dressing quickly and grabbing his whiskey on the way out.

"Fuck you. We'll manage," Preppy responded, his cock again twitching inside of me. I wiggled my hips, needing more, but he grabbed my ass and held me still.

"Okay, just know that I plan on getting good and drunk tonight and don't feel like cleaning up blood, so don't take shit too fucking far." He took a long pull from his bottle and just like that he was gone, the sound of the party outside blasting through the partially opened door, then disappearing again with Bear.

All that was left in that room was me, Preppy, and the consequences of our little game.

A game neither of us had won.

CHAPTER THIRTY-SIX

DRE

W HEN THE DOOR clicked shut Preppy sat up and flipped me over onto my back, pinning my wrists above my head against the headboard. "Don't think that this is over just because he left," he said.

"Isn't that what it is, though? Over?" I asked, remembering my anger and trying to get up. Preppy held me firmly and all I could do was wriggle around, the muscles of his forearms barely straining under my struggling. "This game. Us. It's all over."

Preppy reached under my chin and turned my face toward him. He kissed the corner of my eye, absorbing the tear that had threatened to spill down my face. He pulled back and slammed into me. "No, baby, that's where you're wrong. This game isn't over. It's only just begun," he said, delivering another punishing thrust of his thick cock. "Except now, the game is whoever comes first, loses." He grinned down at me, his smile real, his hair falling into his eyes. "You wanna play with me?"

I arched my back suddenly and his cock slipped out of me. I jumped off the bed. He reached for me and I jerked my arm away. "I can take a lot of things," I said. "I've had my weak moments, but I know who I am and I'm strong as fucking steel when it counts. But what I can't take is this. Whatever you're playing at. Whatever reason you told Bear that I could be a club slut. Because we obviously see things differently, so let me explain this to you," I said, grabbing my clothes and pulling them on. "This isn't a fucking game." I pointed between us. "We're not a fucking game!" I choked out.

"I'm glad that you see it that way. Maybe having two cocks inside you at once fucked some sense into you after all," Preppy said calmly, standing up and pulling on his jeans.

"What?" I asked, frozen with my hand on the door. I turned around slowly. "What the fuck did you say?"

Preppy ran his hand over his beard and looked to the floor, like he was trying to make a decision. When he looked up at me and his eyes met mine, I knew it had been made. "I've been telling you that I can't keep you, Dre. Why the fuck do you think I was saying that?"

"I don't know. Because of your past and because of what happened to you and what you do…"

"Maybe that's part of it. But the other part is the lies I've been telling you to get what I want."

"What lies?" I said, taking a step back, afraid of what he might say.

"Where should I start," he asked, slowly walking toward me. "Do you want to know what I did to you? That night I brought you to Mirna's? Do you want to hear how I took off your clothes and I ran my mouth down your body while you were unconscious? Do you want to know that I spread your legs and licked your bruised pussy because I wanted to taste you, your weakness. I wanted to swallow you and devour you, so I shoved my tongue inside of you because I fucking could."

"No, no you didn't. You wouldn't," I stammered.

He huffed. "Now, I know you don't believe that," Preppy said, buttoning his shirt as if it was just another day. His cool emotionless expression plastered back on his face, while I was in a state of shock I didn't know if I'd ever be able to come back out of.

He shrugged. "I thought about fucking you too, but I settled for jerking off on you instead. I came all over your stomach."

"Fuck you," I said, only able to muster up enough of my voice to whisper the insult at him.

"I may have pulled you from that tower, Doc. I may have rescued you from that motel room, but I never saved you. You were never safe." His phone vibrated and the screen lit up, he looked down and tossed it on the bed that acted as a barrier between us, a bumper for the truth. "Go ahead. Answer it. It's your dad," he said, not giving me time to process the new information.

"How?" I asked as the phone stopped vibrating before starting back up again.

"He's been calling for weeks. He wrote you a letter, too. It's on top of Mirna's fridge. Blue photo album. He wants you to come home," he said.

"When?" I asked.

"Since the very beginning."

"But why?" I asked, but I didn't know what I was asking. Why he lied? Why he bothered with me?

Why I let him into my heart?

Every word he spoke was another bullet being fired at me, but he couldn't hit every target. His eyelids were red and heavy. His voice was raspy, "Why? Because I needed you to make those documents for me." He paused. "Or maybe just because I like unconscious pussy."

I leapt onto the bed. "You son of a fucking bitch!"

Preppy moved to the door. "Go the fuck home, Doc. You don't belong here. You never did." He didn't look up when he left, closing the door with such force the cheap plastic blinds fell from the window to the floor.

He'd slammed the door shut on the room.

On us.

On everything.

CHAPTER THIRTY-SEVEN

PREPPY

"**W**HERE YOU STOMPING off to?" Bear asked, catching up to me as I was doing just that, angrily stomping down the shell driveway. He slapped me on the back of my shoulder. "Everything okay back there?" he asked, lighting a cigarette and jerking his chin back toward the garage.

I was about to snap something back at him, my emotions all bubbling at the surface, a place I hated them to be. My mouth hung open, ready to fire off some sarcastic retort that would have Bear seeing right through me, but I stopped myself and shut my mouth when I saw the concern written all over Bear's burly face. Or maybe it was pity. Fuck, I'd already caused so much hurt for one lifetime, I could't stand to see him look that way. So I made a decision right then and there. My shit would be exactly that. My shit. I knew Bear and Grace well enough to know that if they knew how deep things ran with Dre, then they would take it on as their own problem. And for fucks sake, our little family had enough fucking problems to add my shit to the fucking pile.

I slapped a smile on my face and reached into Bear's cut, plucking his cigarettes from his pocket and tossing him back the pack after I'd slid one from the pack and lit it. "All is good, man. Just got a call from Patty who runs the GG operation off Sunset

Vista," I lied. "The mister in the grow-room is leaking. Gotta go dry out her hallway runner and fix the leak before her fucking pacemaker stops. Gotta keep the GG's happy. Keep growing that money."

"You sure that's it?" Bear asked, scratching his head. "I thought that maybe that girl…"

I cut him off. "That was fucking epic, right? Although, I'm not gonna lie, at one point I think I felt your balls on my fucking leg, dude."

"Preppy…" Bear said, still attempting to carry on some sort of serious conversation about my behavior. Wasn't gonna happen.

Not then.

Not fucking ever.

"At least now I know what to get you for Christmas. A good ball trimmer. Or maybe a wax if you're into the pain. On second thought, maybe I'll get waxed, might be something I'd dig." Bear's face began to lighten as he shifted his focus from Dre to my ridiculousness. The corners of his mouth turned upward into his signature cocky smile.

"That's where you're really fucked up. You had your fucking cock deep inside a hot chick and you were thinking about my balls? Sounds like that's your problem, not mine, motherfucker," Bear teased, punching me playfully in the shoulder. "But hey, any girl who likes to be double stuffed will make a great BBB. She'll fit in just fine with the brothers."

The rumble of an engine started and we both turned to where Wolf was mounting his bike. He rolled up slowly, and it wasn't until he stopped right next to where we were standing that I realized Dre was on the back. I almost dropped my cigarette, sending bits of red ash flitting around in the darkness when I caught it before it could hit the ground.

"You move quickly," Bear said to Dre with a knowing smile.

"Just getting a lift," Dre clipped. "I wanted to thank you for my AUDITION," she said, stressing the word, "to be one of your club girls, but something came up and I decided to go another route."

"Okay to give her a ride?" Wolf asked Bear.

"Shame, beautiful. Could have had a lot more fun," Bear said. He nodded to Wolf, who revved his engine in response. The look on Dre's face said everything and made me feel small.

I'd broken everything into so many pieces there was no way in fuck it would ever be able to be put back together again. So I guess you could say my plan worked.

But that didn't mean it wasn't tearing my fucking gut in two.

I stayed the course, shifting on my Preppy mask for Bear. I took a deep drag of my cigarette, casually blowing smoke rings into the air. "Real shame," I drawled. I grabbed my dick through my jeans. "Guess all this man meat scared her off." Bear laughed and turned back toward the house.

I felt Dre's eyes on me until the bike was well out of sight, the engine nothing but an echo through the trees.

And then she was gone.

For good.

Of course, fate is a nasty evil bitch, because it was in that moment, one of the shittiest of my life, after a confusing, yet fucking hot, unexpected threesome with one of my best friends, that I realized that the girl driving away wasn't just some girl I was saving from my twisted ass.

She was the girl I was in love with.
The girl I would always be in love with.
Until my very last breath.

CHAPTER THIRTY-EIGHT

DRE

HATRED IS EASY.

It's love that's hard.

It wasn't the betrayal that hurt the most. It wasn't the lies or the deceit. It wasn't even the way he'd made me feel more used than Conner or Eric ever had.

The way I felt had nothing to do with the bitterness that settled in my throat, so thick I was practically gagging on it.

No.

The thing that hurt the most wasn't the way things ended at all.

It was the way it all began.

It was the love.

I didn't want it anymore. It shouldn't of even been there anymore so I wished it away with everything I had, but no matter how much wishing and praying or meditating I did, nothing worked. Even though betrayal had moved in, love refused to pack its bags and get out.

Fucking squatter.

I wanted so badly for anger and rage to be my primary emotions and so I focused on his bitter words that ended us. The way he looked at me with no remorse in his eyes. The way the door echoed as he slammed it shut. But I couldn't stay in the darkness too long, the light always finding its way inside my thoughts, and soon I was remembering the warmth of his skin against mine the first time he touched me, the way he looked at me before he finally kissed me, the way he made me laugh in a time in my life when not a god damn thing in the world was funny to me anymore. No, love didn't magically turn into hate just because we want it to, because it's easier.

I learned very quickly that it turns into something else. Something much much worse.

A broken heart.

Little did I know that the real breaking was yet to come and the greatest lesson of all about love, I would be learning all too soon.

Love never dies.

CHAPTER THIRTY-NINE

PREPPY

M IRNA'S HOUSE HAD been sitting vacant since that night it all went to shit. I'd still come by from time to time, although I hadn't used it as a GG since Dre left. All of the furniture was gone. All of the pictures. It had been over a year since Dre set foot in the place, yet I swore I could still smell her there.

She was happy. She had to be. That's what I told myself anyway, in order to go through the motions and pretend like nothing was wrong. Her happiness was what kept one foot in front of the other, and the sometimes-fake smile plastered on my face.

Real smiles came in the form of King getting out of prison and him actually getting a girl. Or stole a girl. However you wanted to look at it. Doe was her name. She didn't have a memory but she had a great set of tits and an attitude to boot, and I think that she was my friendship-soulmate in a way, although I never told her about Dre. I never told anyone. I told myself I was fine and the plan was to try to believe my own lie until it became true.

After Dre left town I'd come for my plants. There on the counter was my folder. She'd done it. She'd forged every single document I needed, but it was all for nothing. The judge assigned to the case denied my petition before a hearing was even called. Before I could utter a single fucking word. When the lawyer I was using told me the judge's name who wouldn't even grant me a hearing, it all became clear. I actually knew him. Well, I knew his sister. All I did was fuck her in a pool. A public one. With people around, but apparently word had gotten back to him and the cock sucker must not like voyeurism because the gavel crashed down on my case, crushing any hope I had left of saving Max from the system.

I was high as a kite when I got in my car, and filed the fake docs with the clerk's office. It wasn't necessary. It wouldn't change a damn thing. But I did it, anyway. Maybe because it made her work not for nothing. Maybe because filing the documents made her more than just a memory, it made her real because her time with me seemed more and more like a fading dream.

But it was all too late.

In the movies the end of a person's life is slow moving, each fraction of a second drawn out, seeming more like hours as they take their last breaths and watch the highlight reel of their lives play out before their eyes while some kind of Titanic-esque violin music plays in the background.

It's all bullshit.

Death is quick.

Too fucking quick.

I remember walking with my friends to go into the meet with Isaac. On the way I saw this dark haired girl with innocent cheeks, and for a second I thought she was Dre. She was staring at me too, but when Dre's face faded it was replaced by the wide eyed look of another girl. One I was pretty sure had been on the sharp end of a Preppy/Bear fuck session a time or two.

The reality of my own death was a searing pain ripping through my gut, followed by a sense of doom as I bled out onto the concrete.

I didn't fade away, I dropped out of consciousness with lightening speed. I barely had time to register the horror on my friends' faces, who all seemed to be floating around above me like they were above the surface, while I was being dragged down to the dark depths below.

I reached out, wanting to grab them, wanting to hold on to this life.

But it was too fucking late.

For most people death was the end.

For me, it was only the beginning.

CHAPTER FORTY

DRE

*T*AP TAP TAP *tap tap tap tap*...
Mindlessly, I bounced my pen on top of my open text book in such quick succession the pages vibrated, lifting at the corners. I shuffled my feet, crossing and uncrossing my ankles, wishing away the constant feeling of restlessness that only seemed to intensify with each passing day.

My desk was pushed up sideways against the only window in the classroom, although there was no view to speak of. Nothing but a brick wall. The small space between buildings was just large enough to allow in the rain that had just started to fall, beading up and sliding down the thick glass. The clouds overhead shifted, casting the already muted light of the room in a wash of gray. With the new lighting the image in the window shifted, and suddenly I was no longer staring at the brick wall but at the reflection of a girl.

A girl whose hair had begun to shine again, although her ponytail could've used a smoothing, the humidity of the day sending every little hair not long enough to be tied in the elastic standing on their tiny curly ends. She wore glasses, simple dark-blue frames. Her complexion was pale, but not sallow. Her eyes tired, but not lost.

I knew the girl was me, but beyond the clean clothes and classroom setting I saw another girl, just beyond her shoulders. One who was slumped against a wall with a needle in her arm and cum in her hair.

A girl who was trapped both physically and mentally.

I shook my head, willing away the image of someone I never wanted to see again. I closed my eyes tightly and when I opened them again, both girls were gone. The clouds cleared and soon my reflection was gone as well, and I was again staring at nothing but an empty brick wall.

Without thinking, I raised my hand to scratch at an itch that didn't really exist, with fingernails that weren't long enough yet to actually do any real scratching. The scabs and pock marks were all gone, but in their place were the raised red scars just starting to take on their shapes, some of them were already turning their permanent shade of white, others lingering at bright red.

The teacher was a man in his sixties. He stood with his back straight and his head down at the podium. His voice was monotone, with zero inflection, as he read off his lesson plan.

I took a deep breath and tried paying attention but everything he was covering, about the founding of our country and the Declaration of Independence, I'd learned in the fifth grade. Leaning back in the chair I cross my arms over my chest and since my feet didn't touch the floor I swung my legs back and forth, accidentally kicking the chair of the boy in front of me.

"I'm…" I started, but then the kid turned around and the wind was knocked out of my chest when my eyes landed on the familiar, beautiful big smile and the tattoos covering his neck. I gasped, covering my mouth with my hand.

Impossible.

"Hey, watch it," he said, his unfamiliar high-pitched voice bringing me back to reality, where he was just a dark-haired boy with olive skin who didn't look anything at all like the man I mistook him for.

"Sorry," I whispered. The boy turned back around to face the teacher who'd turned off the lights so we could follow his slides on the overhead projector, which was blurry at best. The Sons of Liberty's heads were all large and skewed, distorted pictures of a probably already distorted tale of American history.

It wasn't the first time his face appeared on someone else's, just like it wasn't the first time my stomach dropped with my disappointment when I realized it wasn't him.

It would never be him.

Later on that day, I sat in the small cramped office space of Edna Elinberry, my counselor who my dad insisted I see three times a week. One of the many terms of my return home, and one I didn't really mind all that much. Edna was quirky and kind of funny. Being a recovering addict herself, she could relate to me in a way not a lot of other mental heath professionals could.

"I saw him again today," I told her, staring at the books and other knick-knacks on the overstuffed bookcase in the corner. *Lord of the Flies* was on the top shelf dangling over the edge, one heavy footed passer-by could send it crashing to the floor.

"Brandon?"

"No," I said, shaking my head. Brandon was someone who'd recently started working with my dad. He'd asked me out a few times and, even though he was good looking and seemed nice enough, I just wasn't ready to complicate my life in a way it didn't need to be complicated. "Not Brandon. HIM," I said, still finding it hard to utter his name without feeling a sense of sickness wash over me.

"That happens when we lose somebody we cared about," Edna said, watering each of the thirty some odd plants in her little windowsill. She wore loose, light-faded jeans with a long, white, ribbed sweater. Her bright red hair was something from the eighties, permed in tight curls and cut longer in the back and short on the top. She had pink lipstick on her teeth at all times. "Especially, one who'd had such a huge impact on your life. It will fade with time."

"But…but what if I don't want it to fade?" I asked, realizing by asking the question it meant that I wasn't entirely sure that moving on was what I really wanted.

Edna put down her watering can on the floor and side stepped one of the seven coffee tables in the cramped space, plopping down on the denim sofa and motioning for me to do the same on the one across from her. We both kicked off our shoes and sat Indian style across. She closed her eyes and took a deep breath, and I copied. When she opened her eyes she asked, "You cared for him a great deal, right?"

I nodded. "I…he saved my life." Immediately the words felt wrong. "I think I…no, I KNOW that I LOVED him," I corrected. "And I just don't see him when I sleep. I hear him, too. In my head, chatting away and making jokes and being ridiculous…" I trailed off, biting back tears.

Edna smiled and reached across the coffee table to give me a reassuring pat on my knee. I watched her hand but didn't jump away, her smile grew brighter. "Dre, when you love someone it's very common to carry that person around with you until you're ready to let go. You hear their voice, you think you see them on the street, you dream about them at night. It's all very normal and a very healthy part of grief. It will fade with time. But only when you're ready."

I bit my lip. "I don't want him to leave," I said, surprising myself when the tears welled up in my eyes. Edna side stepped the coffee table and sat down next to me, pulling me in and holding me tight against her ample breasts. Everything about her was comforting, and in a way she reminded me of a younger version of Mirna.

"He saved your life. It's natural that you feel something toward him, along with a sense of guilt because you lived and he didn't." Edna paused, gathering her thoughts before she continued. "You know, kid, it sounds to me like you still need that closure we've been talking about."

"Closure?" I squeaked. The idea of it sounded ridiculous. "I'm not sure about that. How can you close something that never really opened?" I felt myself starting to tear up and immediately felt embarrassed.

Awe shucks, Doc.

She nodded and handed me a tissue. "From what you've told me, you've never gotten a chance to really grieve, to close that chapter in your life and move on."

"But I don't know how to get it." Or if I even wanted it. I'll never forget the day my dad and I went down to Sarasota together to help transport Mirna to a facility closer to our house. I was debating taking a solo ride down to Logan's Beach when one of the nurse's mentioned his name and wondering why he stopped visiting. The other explained to her why he couldn't visit. He was dead.

Right then and there I couldn't breath. My heart stopped. A piece of me died right there along with him.

Edna held me tighter and rocked me back and forth like Mirna used to. She pulled me back and looked down to my hands where I was now staring. She snapped her fingers and smiled brightly. "When you're ready, and ONLY when you're ready, I think you should seek out those who cared about him. His friends, family. Have a conversation. Talk about his life. I truly think it will help you find what you need."

"I'll think about it," I said, and I did. The only "interaction" I ever had with his friends was that one encounter from Bear.

"At least read the letter," Edna suggested. "Maybe that will help you decide." She pulled out the envelope that had arrived a few months earlier with no return address, just a stamp from the Logan's Beach Post Office. "It's time," she said, handing it to me.

"Can you open it?" I asked. Edna shook her head.

"No, that's for you to do, but I'll give you a minute alone," Edna said, patting me on the shoulder and stepping out of the room.

I tore open the envelope quickly, thinking that if I did it fast like a Band-Aid it wouldn't hurt as much.

I was wrong.

Doc,

There's this place where light and dark meet in the sky when the sun's setting where it's not quite day and not quite night. A grayish mist among the black and yellow.

I like to think of it as a place where right and wrong, black and white, life and death aren't finite.

I call that place 'the in-between' and to me that's where you and I will always exist.

Together.

It's where we can't be hurt. Where our pasts don't haunt our present. Where there's no such thing as lies. Where pain isn't even a thing.

We couldn't be together in this life. Maybe not even in the next. Who knows. My luck is pretty shit these days. But now when I think of you, which is still every fucking day, and when I can't catch my breath wondering what could've been, I drag my ass outside, I sit in the yard, and I wait for it. That brief glimpse of the changing of the guard in the sky. And every day, even though the pain cuts just as deep as the day you left, even though I know the truth is that I'll never see you again, I smile.

Because you and I are there.

And we'll always have the in-between.

LOVE,

Samuel Clearwater

Preppy, BAD-ASS MOFO

PS – If you are receiving this I'm dead so I think it's safe to tell you that you are by far my biggest regret. The light amongst all my dark.

I'm so sorry.

CHAPTER FORTY-ONE

DRE

SEVERAL MONTHS LATER

W ITH BRANDON SITTING by my side on the plane to Florida, I was finally ready to go and seek the closure that my dad, counselor, and my sponsor were always so adamant about.

As we flew over the still waters of the Caloosahatchee River, I tightened my grip on Brandon's hand. He offered me a reassuring smile and gave me a thumbs up, covering my hand with his own. He probably thought it was the flight that had me freaking out. And although flying wasn't my favorite activity in the world, it wasn't the fear of plummeting to the ground below that had my windpipe tightening like a guitar string as the plane descended. No. It was the water tower. The one that stuck out on the flatland, towering above the earth like a redneck statue of liberty, reaching up toward the plane. Its huge black spray painted dick was in full frontal view as the landing gear clattered and screeched, locking into place.

I wanted to both laugh and cry at the sight of it.

Suddenly, it was all too real.

I was going back. Back to where it all started. Back to where it all ended.

Back to where it would only just begin.

CHAPTER FORTY-TWO

DRE

I RAISED MY trembling hand to the door and knocked. The sound of squealing children playing in the back yard echoing over the house.

I was about to change my mind and turn around when a blond girl with the lightest-blue eyes I'd ever seen opened the door. "Can I help you?" she asked with a small but friendly smile.

"Um…Hi, I'm Andrea Capulet, but I go by Dre," I said, holding out my hand. She shook it tentatively. "I'm a friend or, I was a friend of Samuel's. Preppy's." My chest tightened as his name crossed my lips. It had been years, and although I expected that feeling to die off, it never had. If anything, it had only gotten worse.

The girl remained silent, looking me over several times like she was trying to place me. "I'm Ray," she finally offered. "What can I do for you?"

"Ray, Hi. I just wondered," I trailed off, looking down to my feet.

"Do I know you?"

"She was going to be a BBB once," Bear said, coming to stand behind her. "You ain't here to drop off any kids with uncanny resemblance to people who may or may not be here, are you?" he asked, and I couldn't quite tell if it was a joke. Shit, I was surprised he remembered me, but obviously he didn't remember everything because last time I checked you couldn't get pregnant through anal. My cheeks grew red at my own thoughts.

I shook my head. "Hi, Bear," I said with a small nervous wave. I pushed my glasses up my nose. Bear looked me over and as if he'd decided I wasn't a threat, he'd turned around and went back inside the house.

Ray seemed to agree. "Well come on in," she said, stepping aside.

Another large and equally beautiful man was sitting in the living room. He lifted his head and glanced at me briefly before Bear sat back down and they both leaned over the coffee table, speaking softly, instantly deep in what seemed like an important conversation.

Ray waved in their direction. "Don't mind King and Bear, they've been a little crazy this past week with all that's gone down," she told me, as she led me through a neat and newly updated living space that smelled of fresh paint and cleaning products, down a narrow hallway. My heels clacked against the shining hardwood. She stopped in front of a closed door.

Preppy's door.

Or, what used to be Preppy's door.

My heart stilled.

I was suddenly mad at everyone who insisted that I come here and get closure by talking to his friends. It was too much. I wasn't ready. I couldn't breathe. My memories flooded with his face. His sent.

HIM.

"No, I mean, I don't need to go in there…" I started backing away from the door.

Ray sighed, "I know what you mean. It's hard to see at first. The prognoses shifts around a bit from doctor to doctor, but he's a fighter. We have hope and we have time."

"Huh?" I asked, confused as to what she was talking about when she pushed open the door and stepped aside. Tentatively, I entered the room, taking a deep sigh of relief when I noticed the room wasn't at all like it used to be. Preppy's things were no longer there. The relief was followed by deep disappointment and a sick feeling. A longing for what once was.

For who once was.

The walls, once a deep blue, were now a bubble gum pink with stenciled daisies and clouds surrounding the window. A Cinderella lamp sat upon a small white nightstand next to the bed.

Of course his things weren't there you idiot, because he's…

I paused. My ears picked up a steady beeping sound, my eyes followed the sound across the room to the IV stand in the corner, set up next to a rollaway hospital bed. Lines raced across the screen that was mounted below the IV, little green mountains peaked and fell, followed by a chirp of the machine in even two second increments.

"I don't understand," I said, not allowing my eyes to travel to the bed. I wasn't sure if I was afraid of what I would see or what I wouldn't see. WHO I wouldn't see. I turned back around to face Ray. "Who…who is that?" I asked, dread and hope fighting a battle in the pit of my stomach…and my heart. I pointed to the mound of blankets rising and falling in rhythm.

"Wait, you don't know do you?" Ray breathed, "I thought everyone in Logan's Beach knew by now."

I shook my head. "I'm not from here." Not able to take another minute of my rapidly beating heart fighting its way out of my chest, I spun around and small step by small step I made my way over to the bed where a shell of a man lay unconscious with tubes running through his nose and mouth. His eyes and cheeks sunken in. His hands resting above the clean navy comforter. I didn't even need to see the tattoos running across his knuckles to know it was him, but there they were, in all their familiar glory.

I let out a strangled cry, that startled even myself, as hot tears fell down my face. Elation and an overwhelming feeling of confusion smashed into me, like I was finally run over by that train. I leaned over him, careful not to disturb any of the tubes, I pressed the side of my face against his chest, I needed to hear it for myself and sure enough, it was there. The thump thump. The most beautiful sound in the world. His heart.

Beating.

Heavy footsteps entered the room. King, Bear, and a girl with pinkish-red hair stood around the doorway, gaping at me as if I were the one risen from the dead. "How?" I asked, without moving my head from his chest. My hand covered one of his own and squeezed as I breathed deeply, inhaling this new life, inhaling him.

"You really didn't know?" King asked skeptically, pulling Ray into his chest. "Thought everyone knew."

"No," I said, although no sound came out so I just mouthed the word. "I didn't know anything."

"What's going on?" the pink haired girl asked. Bear wrapped

his arms protectively over her waist, which was when I noticed her rounded belly. Bear leaned down and whispered in her ear. She nodded in some sort of understanding, but continued to stare me down like she was unsure of me at best.

But that didn't matter. SHE didn't matter.

Nothing mattered.

Overwhelming joy consumed my entire being. How he was alive didn't matter just then, all that mattered was that he was alive.

My Preppy.

My Samuel.

"Who exactly are you, again?" Ray asked, staring at me as I practically laid across Preppy's body.

Reluctantly, I lifted my head from his chest, although I kept my hand over his. I sniffled and wiped the tears streaming down my face. I took a deep breath to steady myself and when I spoke, I made sure I was looking at each and every one of Preppy's friends. I was about to speak when I was interrupted by a scratchy voice. I spun around and was met with bloodshot amber eyes that were locked on to mine when he spoke.

"She's my wife."

The End (for now)

Other Books by T.M. Frazier

KING SERIES:
KING
TYRANT
LAWLESS
SOULLESS
PREPPY, PART ONE
PREPPY, PART TWO (COMING SOON)

STANDALONES:
THE DARK LIGHT OF DAY, A KING SERIES PREQUEL
ALL THE RAGE, A KING SERIES SPIN OFF

About the Author

T.M. Frazier is a *USA TODAY* BESTSELLING AUTHOR best known for her *KING SERIES*. She was born on Long Island, NY. When she was eight years old she moved with her mom, dad, and older sister to sunny Southwest Florida where she still lives today with her husband and daughter.

When she was in middle school she was in a club called AUTHORS CLUB with a group of other young girls interested in creative writing. Little did she know that years later life would come full circle.

After graduating high school, she attended Florida Gulf Coast University and had every intention of becoming a news reporter when she got sucked into real estate where she worked in sales for over ten years.

Throughout the years T.M. never gave up the dream of writing and with her husband's encouragement, and a lot of sleepless nights, she realized her dream and released her first novel, The Dark Light of Day, in 2013.

She's never looked back.

For more information on books and appearances please visit her website:

www.tmfrazierbooks.com

FOLLOW T.M. FRAZIER ON SOCIAL MEDIA

FACEBOOK:

facebook.com/tmfrazierbooks

INSTAGRAM:

instagram.com/t.m.frazier

TWITTER:

twitter.com/tm_frazier

For business inquiries please contact Kimberly Brower of Brower Literary & Management:

www.browerliterary.com

CPSIA information can be obtained
at www.ICGtesting.com
Printed in the USA
LVOW11s1242190117
521521LV00001B/94/P